OLD VINES

OLD VINES

MICHAEL HARTWIG

Herring Cove Press

Contents

First Printing, 2021

Cover Photo
kirkandmimi - Pixabay

I

Chapter One

Patrick pressed his face to the window as the plane made its descent into Naples. It hugged the coastline just north of the city, a beautiful stretch of rugged hills covered with gnarly pines and dotted with villas overlooking the blue sea.

As the plane got closer to the ground, he noticed more details. He felt as if he was approaching a world where time had stood still, where one's sense of self and place were grounded in simple but satisfying routines and relationships. He noticed ancient umbrellas pines lining timeless Roman roads, small coves filled with colorful fishing boats, workers tending terraces of vegetables, laundry drying in the sun, and people gathering at markets. The coastline was unchanged, weathered but still as it was hundreds of years ago – rocky bluffs covered with wild vegetation dotted here and there with wind-swept pines that shaded narrow paths.

The plane flew over the city of Naples, which stretched out below the intense morning sun. Dense apartment buildings lined crowded boulevards running to the boat-filled harbor. Haze rose from the traffic-clogged streets and the busy waterfront where cargo vessels, cruise ships, and ferries were being serviced by an army of dock hands. The plane banked to the left over an industrial area and made its final approach and landing.

At the gate, Patrick waited patiently for other passengers to file out ahead of him. It had been a long overnight, with a flight from Boston and another from London. He felt clammy as they cut the air conditioning and hot, humid air filled the space. The terminal offered no respite, a chaotic and intense mélange of tourists, business executives, and families meeting relatives. The contrast between Boston and Naples was overwhelming - the earthy smell of bodies weathered in the salty sea air, the expressive exchange of lovers with arms slung over each other, and the jarring local dialect projected loudly by taxi drivers, porters, and hoteliers offering services.

He breathed a sigh of relief as he walked outside, felt fresh air and sun on his face, and walked across the causeway to the car rental area. For the most part, Patrick could pass as a local. His olive skin was darkened with a summer tan, he had a large Italian nose, and the stubble circling his mouth and lining his chin was dark and heavy. An agent, sweating profusely, greeted him in Italian.

Patrick answered, "*Buon giorno, sono Patrick Benevento.*"

"Welcome to Italy, Mr. Benevento," the agent replied, shifting to English after noting Patrick's American accent. "I see you have a 2-week rental. Do you drive standard transmission?"

"Yes. What kind of cars do you have?"

"Let me see," the man said, looking at his computer and then pulling a set of keys out of a drawer in his desk. "I have a six speed Alfa Romeo. How does that sound?"

"Incredible!" Patrick said excitedly. He lived in the city and looked forward to driving, getting on the road, and exploring the coast. He hoped to shake the frustration and stress of the summer, the passing of both his parents, and the recent discovery that his husband of 10 years was having an affair.

"Do you need insurance?" the agent inquired.

"In Italy – on the Amalfi coast – I think so."

The man chuckled, completed the paperwork, and handed him the keys. Patrick rolled his bags behind him to the garage and followed signs to the spot for his car. It was a dark red Alfa Romeo mini-SUV. He placed bags in the rear, his shoulder bag on the front seat, and took a seat behind the wheel, adjusting the settings.

The sun was blinding as he left the garage. He slipped on a pair of dark glasses and followed signs to the Amalfi coast and Pompeii, following a highway that hugged the shoreline and the slopes of Mt. Vesuvius, an area of rich farmland and vineyards. A few wispy clouds clung to the edge of the volcanic crater above. He had been here only once, as a little boy. His parents had talked often about returning, but between his grandparents' deaths, his years in college, and his marriage, the trip never happened. He felt his parents and grandparents were sitting with him in the car, Roberto and Chiara chatting in the back seat, pointing out landmarks and settling into their native language. Patrick turned on the radio and listened attentively to the melodic sounds of the announcer introducing popular hits and promoting businesses in local dialect.

He practiced phrases - "*Buon giorno. Sono Patrizio. Grazie. Per piacere. No grazie. Mi scusi* and the ever important – *dove ci sono le toilette*?" The exit for Sorrento and Amalfi came sooner than he expected. He downshifted and took the exit. The smaller road hugged a scramble of poor fishing villages before more luxurious villas, hotels, and beaches finally came into view, with Sorrento off in the distance.

He took another roadway that dumped him onto the famous coastal route heading to Positano and Amalfi. The first kilometer was jarring – the road narrowed, just barely wide enough for two cars to pass. On the left, sharp irregular granite rock rose from the pavement up the mountainous slopes; on the right, a low cement curb delineated the road from perilous cliffs that dropped to the sparkling blue sea below. Motor scooters whizzed by, weaving in between cars, buses, and trucks. Most cars remained in queue but, from time to time, a daring driver raced his engine and passed others who had to brake quickly to let him in.

Patrick got into a rhythm – downshifting on curves and speeding up on hills. As he got more comfortable, he looked out at the landscape - luscious green mountains cascading to the sea, small, nearly hidden, inlets filled with fishing boats, terraced groves of lemon trees, and a ribbon of roadway winding around the ridges connecting small villages clinging tenaciously to steep inclines.

His grandparents came from a small town in the hills above Praiano – a little distance beyond Positano. Praiano still served as an authentic fishing village, the town beach littered with wooden boats filled with nets thrown into the waters each morning to haul in local fish and squid. All along the coast, winding roads connected towns like Praiano with terraced farmland high in the hills, where peasants continued to tend rich volcanic soil lined with grapevines, lemon trees, and vegetables.

Positano was the queen of Amalfi towns, a colorful sprawling enclave of terraced villas and hotels overlooking a large beach. A mosaic-domed cathedral anchored the main square around which boutiques, bars, and restaurants served wide-eyed tourists sipping limoncello and watching fishing boats and ferries tie up to the town pier. Patrick made a few sharp turns, and the pastel terraced buildings of Positano came into view, an immense city carved out of a steep mountain with a few large rock formations that formed bookends to a broad beach lined with colorful umbrellas and beach chairs. He stopped at a small café perched on the edge of a 1000-foot cliff. He squeezed his car into one of a few small parking spaces and took a table on the terrace, shaded by a large, orange-colored umbrella.

The café was dusty, weathered, and unremarkable except for the views which extended for miles up the coast. There was a breeze - the air warm, soothing, and slightly salty. A waitress came out from the café. The lines on her weathered face made her look older that she undoubtedly was. She offered him something to drink using as few words as possible, conserving energy for the long, hot day ahead. She dropped a menu on the table and pointed to a stapled piece of paper enumerating the day's specials.

Patrick ordered some wine and a plate of spaghetti with tomato and basil. When it arrived, he efficiently twirled the noodles on his fork and, as it touched his tongue, the flavors exploded in his mouth. Even *nonna* Chiara's sauce couldn't compete with basil and tomatoes that had been picked that very morning, crushed, and then simmered in sea salt. He took a long sip of the wine that had come from the nearby hills and savored the subtle hints of mineral and citrus.

He glanced down at his phone and noticed a few unread texts. One had come in from Girard: "Patrick, I feel terrible. Call me when you get to Italy."

At the end of the summer, after his parents' death, Patrick discovered his husband had been having an affair. Girard blamed it on Patrick's parents, who were conservative and unwelcoming, but Patrick sensed there was more to it. Girard always had a roving eye, and Patrick wasn't convinced he was invested in the relationship to the extent Patrick was. Girard was surprised when Patrick moved out of their city condo and took off for Italy. Girard continued to send pleading texts and emails about wanting to reconcile.

Patrick thought about how to respond and was tempted to write, *vaffanculo* – Italian for go fuck yourself – but saved that for a more dramatic occasion. He wrote: "We can talk when I get back."

He finished his lunch, paid his bill, and jumped back into his

Alfa Romeo for the last leg of his journey. His cousin Alberto had instructed him to go to Praiano then, just past the harbor, take the mountain road to the small village and go directly to the family restaurant run by Alberto's sister, Laura, and Paolo, her husband. As the road ascended the steep mountain, the turns became sharper and more tortuous as it passed narrowly between farm buildings and around boulders broken loose from the mountain.

The town, Cava dei Lupi, was a small compact village, a collection of buildings lining a curve in the road and nestled in a natural indentation that, according to legend, was the home of wolves. As Patrick got closer to the village, his GPS dropped off, and he followed written instructions Alberto had sent. The pavement widened around a dry fountain, and Laura's and Paolo's restaurant stood at the far end of the square, a few blue and red umbrellas still open over tables, now cleared of lunch.

Patrick parked the car and walked through a curtain of beaded strings separating the terrace from the inside of the restaurant. It was siesta time, and only a stray dog seemed awake - picking at bits of food dropped around the tables. Inside the restaurant, a barista was wiping glasses dry and looked up as Patrick entered.

"*Giorno*," the man mumbled grudgingly, not wanting another customer late in the afternoon.

"*Buon giorno*," Patrick began hesitatingly, adjusting to the darkness of the room and glancing around at the empty tables. "*Sono Patrizio*?" he stated as a question, hoping someone was expecting him.

"Ahh! Patrizio! Welcome," the man said enthusiastically, coming out from behind the counter to give Patrick a big hug. "*Sono Paolo*, your cousin. I'll call Laura."

He stuck his head into a doorway leading up to the apartment above the restaurant, "*Laura, Laura – è arrivato Patrizio.*"

Patrick could hear steps hurrying down the stairway and then Laura poked her head into the bar area and yelled, "*Patrizo, Patrizio*

– *che meraviglia!*" She gave him two warm kisses on his cheeks and held him firmly in her hands.

"My English is not too good, but welcome."

"*Il mio italiano non è molto bene.*"

"We'll each practice – you Italian and me English."

Paolo stood nearby, smiling profusely at his wife and Patrick. "*Lasciami chiarmare Alberto.*"

He dialed a number on the phone on the counter and spoke in local dialect, presumably with Alberto. He then put down the receiver and turned to Patrick. "Alberto will be here in a few minutes. Do you want some coffee, something to eat?"

"*Un caffè – per piacere.*"

"*Subito.*"

Paolo pulled a leaver, releasing aromatic ground coffee into an espresso pod, inserted it into the large stainless-steel machine, and pushed a green button. A deep hum began, and dark brown coffee began dripping into a small white cup. He placed it on the bar in front of Patrick who, in one gulp, swallowed the rich frothy espresso. "Hm," he said. "*Molto buono!*"

A few moments later, Alberto pushed through the beaded curtain. He could have been Patrick's grandfather's twin – the same robust upper torso, dark complexion, and warm, expressive face. "Patrizio – it's so good to see you. Welcome. You look just like the pictures your father sent us a few years ago."

"And you look just like Roberto!" Patrick said in reply.

"People tell me that all the time. How was your trip? *Molto traffico?*"

"No – the traffic was fine – and everything smooth."

"You must be exhausted. Let me take you to the farm and to the house we have ready for you. Why don't you follow me in your car?"

Patrick said *ciao* to his other cousins and went out into the square where he got into his car and followed Alberto out of the town higher into the hills. The roads were gravel and clay and, in the late summer heat, dry and parched. A cloud of dust followed Alberto's truck, and Patrick squinted to keep on the road. They passed several nicely maintained farmhouses and then turned onto a smaller road, passing terraced rows of vines heavy with ripening grapes.

At the top of a ridge, they turned left and, on the right, was a small cottage. Alberto pulled over and waived Patrick to park behind him. He got out, and with a sweep of his hand, exclaimed, "Your palace awaits!"

It was a low-to-the-ground white stucco structure with a terra cotta tile roof, surrounded by a small clearing of parched land. To the left of the front door and along the road, there was a narrow patio paved with irregular pieces of ceramic and terracotta on which stood a small table and a couple of chairs. Alberto pushed open the red wooden door and welcomed Patrick into the dark, cool room. He opened a few shutters, and the bright mid-day light flooded the space.

"It's simple – probably built in the 1700s - but has modern conveniences. Here's a little refrigerator." He opened the door. "We got you a few things – some fruit, cheese, salami, and wine."

Patrick nodded gratefully.

"There's a stove on which you can make coffee or other things. Here are some cabinets," he pointed above the sink, "where you can keep dry goods. The higher the better – to prevent any animals from getting them first."

Patrick raised his eyebrows.

Here's a dining table, a few comfortable chairs, a fireplace – although you won't be needing that now. And back here is the bedroom and bath." He walked around the corner to a room with a full-size bed, a small table and lamp, and a door leading to a simple but clean bathroom – toilette, sink, and shower. "The bed is comfortable and has clean sheets. The towels are clean, too. Just let us know when you need them laundered."

"This all looks perfect. You're so generous letting me use this."

"Oh, it's not so altruistic. We expect you to work," Alberto said with a grin. "The grape harvest – the *vendemmia* - will begin in a few days and we'll get our money's worth," he added with a wink. "The only thing you don't have here is internet or telephone. You'll have to go to town for that – to Laura's place."

Patrick felt a flutter in his stomach at the thought of being so unplugged. Alberto led him back onto the front patio and pointed, "If you need something, our house is up the road." Alberto pointed around a section of the vineyard where a road led up the hillside. "And Pepe, our groundskeeper, lives in that house over there," Alberto said, pointing down the hill to another house. It stood in the shadow of a steep ridge covered in shrubs and knotty pines. "I'll introduce you to him later. He's a bit shy but a hard worker and friendly."

Patrick looked out over the vineyard, rows of yellowish green vines stretching down the slope between two ridges with unobstructed views of the Mediterranean in the distance.

"This is so breathtaking. How do you not just want to sit here, breathe in the sea air, and contemplate the view?"

Alberto took a deep breath. "Yes – it's quite nice and pleasant here. I think that's where our family name comes from – Benevento – good breeze. Even in the hot summer, the shadows of the mountains behind us and the sea breezes coming up the hills make for a nice cooling effect. The grapes love it – taking slightly longer to ripen, gathering more minerals and sugar for an exceptional wine."

"I can't wait to try it."

"Why don't you come to our house tonight for dinner if you're not too tired. I'll introduce you to Maria and our children."

"That would be great. What time?"

"Let's say 7 PM?"

"Perfect. I'll take a little siesta and get unpacked."

Alberto shook Patrick's hand and got into his truck, driving up the hill towards his home. Patrick stood on the patio, looking out over the vineyard and sea, took out his phone and took some pictures. He grabbed his bags from the car, carried them into the house, and unpacked in the bedroom.

The tile floor felt cool to the touch, and the room had a pleasant earthy smell to it. He sat on the bed and laid back on the mattress – it felt comfortable. It surprised him. The white stucco walls were plain, broken up only by the deeply set windows surrounded by bleached wooden sills. As Alberto's truck receded further in the distance, a deafening stillness descended, pierced only by the rhythmic sound of cicadas.

He sat at the dining table, unpacking his shoulder bag filled with documents and photos he brought of Roberto and Chiara – including the one that inspired his journey – of Roberto and Stefano. A week earlier, cleaning out his parents' house, he had opened a brown shoe box filled with loose photos, a few in color, most in sepia or black and white. A few photos slipped out of the stack, his cousins lined up in front of a Christmas tree, his dad and one of his brothers sitting on new bikes Santa had brought them, and neighbors building a snow man during a heavy winter storm.

Patrick had reached to the bottom of the box, pulling out a few old envelopes with Italian scribbled on the front. He had studied the language in school but had never had much of a chance to use it, his grandparents passing when he was ten. His father spoke a little Italian, mostly profanities picked up during family arguments.

His grandparents married just before they left Italy in 1950. There was a beautiful photo of their wedding day, Roberto dressed in a classic dark suit, Chiara in a traditional white wedding dress and long veil flowing from a glittery tiara – both surrounded by a large extended family. His grandfather was a short, robust man, having worked most of his life on the family vineyard. He was dark, tanned from the central Italian sun. Chiara was slightly shorter and had a luminous complexion, even apparent in the black-and-white photo.

Chiara used to tell Patrick stories when he was a little boy, stories of her parents' café on the town square, a gathering place for old men playing cards, young couples having a drink on Saturday night, and housewives sharing gossip over a quick shot of grappa on their way home from the market. Patrick imagined an idyllic hillside village, surrounded by vineyards, overlooking the deep blue sea. He wondered why they left, leaving behind extended family, friends, and traditions.

Roberto and Chiara met during the war. Rations were scarce and, until the Americans had secured the area and brought in supplies, villagers partnered with farmers to till small patches of ground. Chiara's family took over a small section of Roberto's family's vineyard, and the rest was history. Chiara recounted the searing heat in the summer, bent over withering vegetables in the morning and climbing fruit trees in the afternoon. Roberto was the youngest of three, and arguably the most congenial of the bunch. He had an unbending energy, doing chores in the morning and helping villagers in the afternoon. Chiara always looked forward to his gentle smile and eagerness to help carry water or gather ripe tomatoes and fruit.

A sepia print had slipped out of a handful of photos Patrick had pulled from one of the envelopes. It was slightly faded, the protective sheen worn from the surface, as if someone had handled it often. He instantly recognized a younger version of his grandfather, his robust build, affable smile, dark tan skin, and hairy chest. He had his arm slung around the shoulders of another young man - tall, lean, light complexion, with a thin covering of dark hair that ran from his broad chest down his abdomen. Their shirtless torsos gleamed in the sun, sweat dripping down to their waists, pants hanging loosely on their hips. They were at the edge of a vineyard, baskets of grapes on the ground. They stared at each other affectionately.

Patrick lingered dumbfounded over the image - one he had never seen before. He turned it over: "Roberto e Stefano, 1948." His grandfather and Stefano were gazing into each other's eyes and, even by Italian standards, their affection seemed out of the ordinary, as if ravenous, ready to consume each other.

Patrick grabbed the rest of the photos in the box and spread them out on the kitchen counter, searching for other images of the enigmatic Stefano. All he saw were more pictures of Roberto's and Chiara's wedding, a reception on a terrace overlooking the sea, and groups of friends and family posed for portraits. Not one image of Stefano, not even in the background.

As a 10-year-old when his grandparents died, Patrick would never have had vocabulary to think about Roberto as anything other than his grandfather, his grandmother's husband, and father of his own father and uncles. The word gay wasn't in his vocabulary, much less the idea that someone might be other than the roles they lived. His grandfather was a warm, friendly, and affectionate man. He was curious, always asking his grandchildren about school, sports, and hobbies. He was the life of a party, the glue that brought people together, the person sought for advice, and the one who intervened when there were problems.

Chiara and he played off each other nicely – affectionate, complementary, respectful. He never saw them fight or exchange harsh words. Chiara had her friends, but he remembered she and Roberto going out to dinner, to the movies, on vacation. They loved each other – at least it seemed.

Could his grandfather have harbored a secret love all his life, something simmering under the surface, a regret for a lost opportunity. Was he forced to leave Italy – fleeing a scandal or perhaps putting distance between himself and Stefano – between someone he could not resist and who couldn't return his love?

Patrick held the photo in his hand, a tattered and fragile link to his own ancestry. He closed his eyes and imagined his grandfather sitting down with him, face to face, a bottle of red wine between them. He loved his grandfather's deep-set eyes surrounded by alluring dark lashes, his large sensual nose, the dark stubble around his mouth and chin, the security he felt when his grandfather would embrace him with his strong arms and broad chest, and the lingering subtle scent of patchouli oil.

How would his grandfather describe Stefano - a friend, a confidant, or perhaps a cousin or distant relative? Was he something more – someone with whom he had shared dreams, a hoped-for future, an understanding? What had they done after the photo was taken? Who took the photo? What did the photographer know?

The only links to his grandfather were two surviving uncles, neither of whom were gay friendly. He imagined they would scoff at the idea that their father harbored a secret lost love. He wondered if his dad and uncles had developed an aversion and antipathy to gay people out of a suspicion about their father – perhaps an unspoken sense that something was amiss.

Over the years, his parents had been hostile to his being gay, realizing at some point that their son's orientation was not a phase. When he and Girard married, his parents refused to attend the ceremony, creating a rift between Patrick and Girard. It was only in the last year, as his father succumbed to cancer and his mother to a broken heart, that they softened and were more welcoming.

The stories his grandparents told of Italy and his mother's family's colorful legends about homesteads in Ireland and run-ins with the law had inspired Patrick to study his ancestry. He had mapped out several generations of a family tree and had taken a DNA test that showed genetic links to central Italy and western Ireland. Some hints and information popped up from time to time about cousins he didn't even know he had.

As he sat in the hillside cottage, sorting through the photos he had brought from Boston, he clicked on the ancestry app and an extensive family tree populated the screen. He followed the Italian line from his father to his grandfather and then to his great grandfather. On his grandfather's tree, there were three siblings each with large families – all his father's first cousins. They, in turn, had children – some showing up on the tree – leaving Patrick with countless second and third cousins, but no Stefano.

Patrick had planned a trip to Italy when he found out that his grandfather, Roberto, had left his father, Bruno, the deed to a portion of the family vineyard, and he, in turn, had left it to Patrick. He took a family bereavement leave from his teaching job so that he could travel for a couple of weeks to find out more about the property and sign papers. But it was the discovery of the photo of his grandfather and Stefano, only a week ago, that now fueled his imagination and inspired his journey.

Now in a little cottage on the edge of his family's vineyard, he realized that the photos before him had been taken from the place 70 years ago and were making their way home. He felt as if they were alive, that they had a kind of force or energy in them. Maybe Chiara and Roberto never wanted to leave and, over the years, had left traces of their regret each time they handled the photographs, a charge that eventually rubbed off on Patrick and compelled him to return, to bring the circle to a close.

He opened one of the bottles of wine on the counter, poured some into a glass, and swirled the red liquid around the interior of the goblet. He breathed in the mineral scent mixed with the aroma of plum and cherry. He took a small sip – the dry smooth wine trickling down his throat. He had never tasted anything like it before – a wine that evoked the toasted earth of late summer, that was smooth as the gentle breeze blowing up the hillside and finished with rich flavors – enough sweetness to soften the minerals but dry enough to sip slowly and hold in one's mouth.

Patrick continued to feel the presence of Roberto and Chiara – no longer chatting in the back of the car but now standing on the front porch, pointing out landmarks, talking about friends, and hugging each other in delight at returning home. He took out a couple of larger prints of them and placed them on the mantle over the fireplace.

After taking a shower and changing clothes, Patrick took a walk along the road, picking a few grapes off the vines and gazing out over the seascape below. He realized he was walking in the very footsteps of his grandparents. The soil, the vines, the trees, and the surrounding mountains were their world, and he now stood immersed in it, caressed by the same breeze and sunshine as they had enjoyed years before.

He wandered up toward Alberto's house and knocked on the door. The estate had been in the Benevento family for generations, perhaps dating back to the 1600s. It was the last farm on the roadway, with a steep crest rising behind the rambling two-story stone house. Behind the house was a tall stone wall surrounding a vegetable and herb garden. To the left of the house there was a barn, now used for storage of equipment. Across the roadway was a modern cement and glass building where the Benevento wine was made, aged, and bottled.

"*Ciao, Patrizio,*" Alberto greeted him at the door. Maria stood behind him, beaming. "*Patrizio, Patrizio, vieni qua.*" She reached for him and gave him an affectionate kiss and hug. She was shorter than Alberto and thin. She had a regal countenance, as if she had been raised with privilege. Two children – a boy and girl – clung to her dress.

"This is Ricardo, and this is Gabriela." *Ricardo and Gabi – questo è vostro cugino – Patrizio – dall'America.*"

They nodded shyly, extended their hands, and shook Patrick's. "*Piacere*," he said warmly.

"Come in," Alberto continued. "I hope everything is good at the house."

"It's marvelous. Thanks for welcoming me and having me here."

"Thanks for coming. We're going to put you to work!"

"Alberto, don't scare him like that," Maria noted. "We're happy you have come for a visit. I'm sure it has been a difficult time since your parents passed away. We are sorry and hope this can be a little vacation for you."

"*Molto gentile*," Patrick thanked her.

Alberto invited Patrick into the large, spacious living area. Turkish carpets covered the dark red tile floors. There was a historic stone fireplace around which a sofa and several large chairs were grouped.

"This is spectacular," Patrick began, pivoting in a circle. "I don't remember this when I was here as a boy."

"We've made some improvements, although the basic floor plan is the same."

"You've done a great job."

"Thanks," Alberto replied.

"So, was all of this here when Roberto and Giancarlo were boys in this house?"

"My father, Alberto, enlarged the kitchen and added some utility rooms in the back, but he inherited it more or less as it is."

"They must have had quite a life," Patrick said with enthusiasm.

"Yes, but it wasn't always easy, and it was isolated from the amenities of more urban areas."

Patrick nodded and continued to look around the room, noticing the artwork hanging on the light-yellow plaster walls. He walked up to one – the portrait of a farmer. "This painting is incredible. It looks like something you would see in a museum."

"My father loved to paint. It's his."

"Wow! He was very talented."

"Yes, he was. We miss him terribly."

Maria came in from the kitchen with a platter of antipasti – red and orange peppers, salami, cheese, nuts, and bruschetta. She laid it on the table.

"Some wine?" Alberto offered. "A nice vintage."

"I tried some of the wine at the cottage. It's superb – and has a distinctive texture and flavor."

"We have a nice following. The soil gives the wine a nice mineral taste and the slow ripening of the grapes adds sweetness. We age it in oak barrels, giving it a velvety texture."

Alberto poured some into Patrick's glass. He twirled it and then raised it to his nose, breathing in the subtle aroma. "Hm," he said. He took a sip. "Incredible."

Alberto smiled proudly. "You'll have to take some home with you."

"That would be great. Do you sell to anyone in the States?"

"We have enough demand here in Europe that we don't need to. But we can always ship some to you."

Patrick smiled and took another sip.

They sat down and picked at the antipasti.

"So, you are Giancarlo's grandson? When did he die?"

"About 10 years ago – and his wife, Francesca, a year later."

"And your father, Alberto, had three children – you, Nunzia, and Laura, right?"

"Yes. You met Laura at the restaurant. You'll have to visit Nunzia in Priaiano. She owns a small pensione on the beach."

"So, you're the oldest. How was that growing up?"

"Everyone expects the oldest son to take over the vineyard.

There's really no choice. Fortunately, I enjoyed the work and the business. My sisters did well for themselves – Nunzia marrying Davide who had a family hotel in Praiano and Laura, the youngest, who married Paolo who had a restaurant in town."

"Where did you two meet?" Patrick asked of Alberto and Maria.

"Maria grew up in another vineyard down the coast. We met at a wine fair where local vintners unveil new releases." He looked over proudly at Maria. "She captured my heart."

Maria blushed.

I look forward to meeting everyone. Roberto died when I was young, so I missed hearing about his youth and his family. It has been part of my quest to reconstruct the family tree.

"Well, you have to meet Nunzia. She's been doing a lot of research on the family heritage and has a lot of documents and notes."

They finished the antipasti. Maria had returned to the kitchen, making final preparations for the dinner. She called everyone to the table in a long, formal dining room.

Patrick walked into the room, and his eyes lit up. "Wow!"

Maria smiled. She had just finished arranging several platters of food on a long solid oak antique table. A low hanging chandelier cast a soft yellow glow around the room filled with antique sideboards and chests. Gabi and Ricardo sat on one side, and Maria invited Patrick to sit across from them. She and Alberto sat at the ends of the table.

Alberto poured wine and Maria began passing the platters filled with ravioli, roasted vegetables, and chicken.

"This looks amazing," Patrick noted, placing several of the ravioli on his plate and covering them with the mushroom sausage sauce.

"It's not every day that we have our cousin from America visit us," Alberto said, raising his glass in a toast, "*Benvenuto a la casa di Benevento*!"

"That has a nice ring to it," Patrick said after taking a sip of the wine.

Ricardo blurted out in Italian, "The chicken is from the garden."

Patrick made out enough of what Ricardo had said and asked in English, "And who caught it?"

Maria translated and Ricardo grinned, "*Io* – I did."

"Ahh," Patrick said, "*Bravo. È molto buono*! – it's very good."

Patrick cut a slice of chicken and placed it in his mouth. He paused and began to identify flavors – salt, pepper, garlic, rosemary, and lemon. "Everything is so fresh here," he added, smiling warmly at Maria.

"Yes, we take it for granted. When tourists come to the area, they always remark how the food tastes different," Alberto noted. "There's been an effort to support local farmers and bring more produce to local restaurants and markets. It's helped our business immensely."

"Congratulations!" Patrick said, raising the glass of wine in a toast.

People ate their dinner in earnest. Maria broke the silence asking, "Patrick - you're an only child, right?"

"Yes. My parents wanted a larger family, but it didn't happen."

"And you, are you interested in starting a family," she inquired timidly, glancing at his ringless hand.

Patrick pondered his response. He knew Italians were more traditional, and he didn't want to begin his visit with any awkwardness around his being gay. He stated without emotion, "I'm in between relationships. It has been a tough couple of years since my father's illness. When I get back, I will begin dating again."

"Maybe we can find you a nice girl here in Italy!"

Patrick nodded, smiled, and then reached for a ravioli. To shift subjects, he asked, "So, when does the *vendemmia* begin?"

"It depends on the grapes and the weather, but we think in a couple of days."

"What happens?"

"Well, each farm in the area establishes a schedule, and every able-bodied person in the village helps with the harvest. It's quite a spectacle."

"I can't wait. In the meantime, I'd love to see more of the village and the surrounding areas. Do you have any suggestions?"

"Paolo and Laura can show you around. Since you have a car, you might visit Praiano and some of the little villages on the coast. The weather is still warm – and if you want to swim – it's very nice. There are fewer people now that August is over. As I mentioned, Nunzia has a pensione there, and she can help you with the ancestry work. She knows everyone."

"I might go introduce myself tomorrow, if you think that's okay?"

"I'll call her and let her know you're coming. I'm sure she'd be delighted to meet you. You and I will also need to talk at some point. I'm sure you would like to know more about the inheritance from your grandfather – his part of the estate."

Without wanting to sound too eager, Patrick began calmly, "Yes, whenever it is convenient for you, I would like to find out what that entails."

"We'll make an appointment later – perhaps just after the *vendemmia*."

"That sounds perfect. No hurry."

Patrick, Alberto, and Maria continued getting to know each other, sipping grappa after the dinner, and making plans for the upcoming week. Patrick felt jet lagged and excused himself for the evening.

He walked down the road. It was pitch dark and the absence of ambient light made the stars in the sky brilliant. Several shooting stars raced across the sky as he walked down the hill toward his cottage. He considered it a good omen and made a wish for a successful visit.

Once inside the cottage, he closed the windows and went into the bedroom, where he stripped off his shorts, hung his pullover on the back of a chair, and slipped under the cool covers. He remarked to himself how amazing it was to have left Boston the night before and now to be laying in a bed on the farm where his grandfather had grown up. The ease of travel and the dramatic change of place were exciting and jarring at the same time.

As he laid in bed, he remarked how different things smelled from home – the unique scent of the starched sheets, the earthy aromas of the tile floor, the ripe fruit in the kitchen, and the end-of-summer sweetness of grapes and vines just outside the window.

Although he was tired from the long journey, the deafening silence kept him awake. There were no firetrucks, sirens, or horns to muffle the thoughts racing through his brain. He tossed and turned in anticipation of the coming day, tugging the soft pillows close to him, hoping they would calm his mind. He slipped a pillow between his legs and found a comfortable position and finally dozed off to a deep sleep.

2

Chapter Two

The sun rose early over the sea, light beaming through a window Patrick forgot to close. He slipped on some shorts, went into the kitchen, and made a pot of thick expresso on the stove. He sliced some bread, cheese, and salami and brought everything out to the little patio overlooking the vineyard and the sea. He let the syrupy coffee slide down his throat, its toasty aromas lingering in his nose.

The dew on the grass began to vaporize in the sun and, as the temperature rose, Patrick returned to the shade of the kitchen. He pulled out some folders with family trees, reviewing them for his meeting with Nunzia. There was his own line – Giancarlo, his great grandfather, Roberto and Chiara, his grandparents, and Bruno and Catherine, his parents. Roberto had two siblings, Anna and Giancarlo. Giancarlo's son, Alberto, had three children – Alberto, Laura, and Nunzia. Anna married Franco, a man from Naples, and they had several children who settled in Rome. While he was interested in learning more about the origins of the Benevento line, he continued to be fascinated with identifying Stefano. Who was the man looking into his grandfather's eyes? Where did he come from, where did he go, did he marry, have children?

He slipped some photos of Roberto and Maria's wedding in the folder so that he could ask about the people in the picture. He also included the photo of Roberto and Stefano to see if Nunzia might know who he was.

A shadow passed by the window. Patrick got up and looked out, noticing a man with clippers and a pole walking down the road. He wore hiking boots, shorts, and a tee-shirt hanging from one of his belt loops. He stopped at the edge of a row and examined the vines and grapes. As he turned, Patrick got a fuller view of the man. He was young – maybe in his mid-twenties. He had a thick muscular torso and sweat trickled down his dark hairy chest, soaking the upper part of his shorts, hanging loosely on his hips. Patrick gulped as his eyes traced the man's strong, muscular shoulders gleaming in the sunlight.

He assumed it was Pepe, the groundskeeper. He casually walked out the front door and leaned against the house with a cup of espresso in hand. Pepe looked over and nodded.

Patrick walked a few meters down the road and began, "*Sono Patrizio, cugino di Alberto.*"

"Pepe," he replied without elaboration, barely looking at Patrick, continuing his work.

At a loss for what to say next, Patrick asked, "*Cosa fa*– what are you doing?"

"*Esamino le grappole d'uva per determinare il momento giusto per la vendemmia.*" Pepe replied, Patrick catching a few words about whether the grapes were ready for the *vendemmia* or not. He nodded. Pepe nodded back and returned to his work; his thick, powerful arms raised toward the top of the vines. He glanced furtively at Patrick with a look of curiosity mixed with indifference.

"*Allora – buon lavoro,*" Patrick wished him a good workday. Pepe nodded and turned calmly to the vines.

Patrick walked back to the cottage and, once on the patio, continued to look out over the vines, watching Pepe work, ready to pivot quickly should he look his way. He took a generous sip of espresso and ducked inside the door, positioning a chair near the window. Pepe didn't seem in a hurry to move onto other rows, and Patrick enjoyed studying his features, dark tousled hair laying on a thick neck, a curved back, and thick muscular legs covered in soft dark hair.

He wondered if his grandfather had met Stefano in the same way – a farmhand who caught his eye, who worked close by – perhaps lingering at the edge of the vines. Had they worked side by side - examining grapes, repairing stakes, maintaining equipment, and taking breaks in the nearby shade where they drank wine and dreamed of their future?

Although Patrick enjoyed watching Pepe and the pastoral scene before him, he was eager to get the day started. He wanted to visit Nunzia and explore some of the coastline. He got up, took a quick shower, and then pulled on some light cotton shorts and a blue pullover. He gathered the photos and notes in a folder and headed out the door.

The drive down the mountain was breathtaking as views of the sea opened at every bend in the road. As he got closer to the water, he could smell the salt air. In Praiano, he took the main road and, just past the harbor, found the sign for Nunzia's inn – the Belvedere. It was a small pink pensione overlooking the coast – a dozen rooms with balconies overlooking a large terrace where guests took their meals. Below was a platform for sunning on the edge of a rocky ledge and a staircase to the water.

Nunzia stood at the entrance, waiting for Patrick. She was a short, stocky woman – dressed in a dark blue dress and comfortable work shoes. The Benevento genes were kind to the men in the family, but not so much to the women. Nevertheless, Nunzia had a warm, affable smile and dark, expressive eyes. "Patrizio, Patrizio," she began as he stepped out of the car. "*Benvenuto*!"

"*Nunzia – piacere*," he replied, kissing her warmly on her cheeks and giving her fresh flowers he had picked up en route.

"Come in – welcome!"

"This is so beautiful – what a place you have," Patrick said as he pivoted in the entrance and looked around the bright lobby decorated tastefully with colorful ceramics. A large window looked out over the terrace and the sea beyond.

"It's okay – not like the big hotels in Positano, but we have a nice loyal clientele and a good life here."

"It looks like it!"

"I can't believe you are here," she continued. "I'm sorry to hear your parents have passed."

"Thank you. I feel like I'm making a voyage they wanted to make."

"It's been many years since they and Roberto and Chiara were here – *tanti anni fa*."

"I know. I was just a little boy then."

"And I, a little girl."

Nunzia took Patrick out to the terrace, shaded by a large, single palm tree. It overlooked the harbor – fishing boats bobbing in the waves and a few larger pleasure boats anchored off-shore.

"Some coffee?"

"Sounds great. Thanks," Patrick replied.

She came back with a double espresso and some mineral water and invited him to sit at a table in the shade. "So, Alberto says you are interested in learning more about our family tree, right?"

"Yes. I have done some research, but there are so many gaps in my work."

"I may be able to help." Nunzia pulled out a folder, thicker than

Patrick's, and flipped through the pages, documents, and photos. Patrick's eyes widened as he realized how much information Nunzia had amassed. She smelled of lemon and rosemary and took an occasional sip of a small cup of coffee she had poured for herself. "I have enjoyed tracing our roots and documenting them. For years there were stories and legends but, through this research, I have been able to find out so much more. I've been using Ancestry."

"Me, too," Patrick said. "I imagine we have a lot of overlapping branches to share."

"Did you know we have roots going back to Spanish royalty?" Nunzia noted excitedly.

"I found something about that in my research. I assume it comes from the time when this area was part of the Kingdom of Naples that belonged to Aragon and the Spanish kings and queens."

"Yes, that's right. And from what I can gather, several generals were granted land – our land. Since this is all heavily documented, it's relatively easy to trace the tree back to the 1300s."

"So, when did the family become Benevento? That doesn't sound Spanish."

"It was in the 1500s. The Spanish family line, De Pedroia, faded out. From what I gather, they needed money and married one of their daughters to the Beneventos, a successful maritime merchant family in the area. The name Benevento does not come from the gentle breezes here on the hillsides, as some allege, but from the wind that filled the sails of the Benevento boats. The daughter had the rights to the farm but took the name of her husband and, thereafter, the vineyard was known as Benevento."

"That's fascinating, and it confirms some of what I had found before."

"So, the farm can be traced back at least to the 1500s with the Beneventos?"

"Yes, and that is why there is so much pride in our family regarding the vineyard and our traditions."

"I can imagine."

"In part, that's why your grandparents' departure for America was so shocking. Here are some pictures I have of their visit and a photograph of their wedding."

"I have the same picture but am not sure who all the people are."

Nunzia laid the photo on the small table and pointed to various members of Roberto's large family – people Patrick already had included in his family tree. He could now put a face to the names. Patrick asked if anyone was missing. Nunzia nodded no. "*C'erano tutti*. Everyone wanted to be there – to see them off to America, too."

"They left just after the wedding?" Patrick asked.

"Yes. It was their honeymoon and departure for America at the same time."

"People must have been sad and happy all at once."

"Yes, my grandfather told stories of that day – a momentous one. People had left Italy earlier in the century but, in the 1950s, things had changed, and people could find work, start businesses, support their families. He pleaded with Roberto to stay, but he had made up his mind."

"Why do you think he wanted to leave?"

"I don't know. Sometimes people find it very confining here – the family, traditions, and expectations are difficult to manage."

"Your father and mother – and your brother and sister all remained."

"Yes, we have a close family, and everyone has a nice business."

Patrick could see the pride in Nunzia's eyes as she looked around the pensione, nodding at guests and workers, and looking out over the sea.

Patrick pulled out the image of Roberto and Stefano and asked,

"By any chance, do you know who this person is," he turned over the picture, "a Stefano?"

Nunzia scrutinized the image, rubbing the surface with her finger as if to detect some hidden script or message. "This is clearly Roberto – his eyes, his build, his smile – but I don't know who this man is. I'm not aware of anyone by the name of Stefano in our family tree, either. I'm not sure – maybe he was a schoolmate, someone from the military, or perhaps a neighbor."

"I just discovered the photo last week. I had never seen it before, and Roberto never mentioned him. It seems odd."

"*Veramente*," Nunzia nodded, clearly intrigued by the couple. She set the photo down on the table but couldn't take her eyes off it.

"Do you think there's any connection between this photo and Roberto's leaving?" Patrick pressed.

"I don't know what that could be." Nunzia pretended to be baffled by the question, but Patrick noticed a slight hesitation in her voice.

"Maybe there was a misunderstanding, an expectation unfulfilled, an indiscretion kept quiet?"

Nunzia shook her head no. "My father or grandfather never mentioned anything – only that everyone was surprised and sad at your grandfather's departure. He was much loved and respected."

Patrick smiled. Nunzia's comments confirmed what he knew of his grandfather – a man of integrity, compassion, affection, and devotion.

Nunzia handed Patrick the folder and said, "Why don't you keep this during your stay and do some research, fill in some blanks and then, when you're ready to go back, return it to me."

"That's very kind of you. It will help a lot, and I'll take care of it."

Nunzia took a sip of coffee, looked down pensively at the papers and, in a complete change of subject, asked, "So, did Alberto rope you into helping with the *vendemmia* – if so - *attenzione*!"

"*Attenzione* – why?"

"*È molto lavoro – è molto duro.*"

"How could cutting grapes be that difficult?"

"You'll see. Most of the workers we get from the city don't last more than a day or two." She winked.

"What are your plans for the rest of the day? If you have your swimsuit, you can sit on the sun terrace, have some lunch, swim – rest up for the coming work."

In reality, Patrick didn't have plans, and the idea of sitting by the water sounded wonderful. "Are you sure it won't be a problem?"

"We're in the shoulder season – the hotel is not full – and we can make space for you." She pointed to a chaise lounge and a small table toward the side of the terrace. "*Ecco – il tuo letto.*"

She stood up, went into the office, and brought back a beach towel and some Italian magazines. "*Per leggere.*"

"*Grazie – molto gentile.*"

Patrick went back to the car to retrieve a bathing suit he had packed just for such an opportunity. He changed in the lobby bathroom and set up camp on the lounge chair at the edge of the terrace, filled with people lying in the sun or reading under shade umbrellas. He opened his umbrella and extended his lower torso out into the sun to pick up some color. The gentle lapping of the waves under the terrace and the warm breeze were intoxicating. He could feel the tension in his shoulders relax and the knot in his stomach loosen. He picked up one of the Nunzia's magazines and thumbed through the photos – provocative shots of celebrities spotted on yachts offshore, pictures of soccer stars with thick muscular legs protruding through thin shorts, and images of politicians angrily debating new taxes. He loved Italian tabloids – mindless tidbits of news that allowed him to pick up useful Italian phrases and words.

He dozed off. Later, Nunzia awakened him. "Patrizio, Patrizio. It's time for *pranzo.*"

Patrick leaned forward, got his bearings, put on a shirt over his swimsuit, and rose to walk toward the higher terrace for lunch. A group of mostly English tourists sat at various tables, swirling strands of spaghetti and tomatoes in their forks. At each table, Nunzia had placed a generous salad with mozzarella, tomatoes, and arugula. Wine was being poured liberally.

He noticed he had reception on his phone and a text from his real-estate agent: "The house is ready to be listed. We hired a crew to do a deep cleaning. When you give me the green light, it will be active."

Patrick picked at the salad and took a large sip of wine. The idea of selling his parents' home, the one that Roberto and Chiara had purchased when they first came to the States, had been appealing earlier in the summer before he and Girard had broken up. They were going to use the proceeds to purchase a larger condo in the city. Now that plan didn't seem such a good idea, and he wasn't sure he wanted to part with a home that had been full of so many memories.

Patrick took a forkful of spaghetti and savored the thick sauce clinging to the firm noodles. He glanced out over the blue water, sparkling in the midday sun. A soft breeze blew across the terrace. The fragrance of rosemary and basil in the nearby garden evoked powerful memories. He still remembered his grandfather walking him through the garden as a little boy, picking herbs for his grandmother's sauce. He remembered her meatballs, her ricotta pies cooling near the window, and the laughter of his cousins gathered for a traditional Sunday dinner.

He texted back to his agent: "Bill, can you hold off for a couple of weeks? I'm in Italy, and when I get back, I want to review several things, including whether to sell the house."

Bill texted back: "Sure. We'll hold off. But the market is good, and you will get a good price for it if you move quickly."

"Thanks. I'm just not sure," he texted back.

Nunzia wandered amongst the guests, chatting with each as she checked on their tables. She looked like a mother hen watching over her chicks. He imagined they felt her affection and was the reason they were so loyal, returning each year to be pampered. She glanced over at him and winked, a gesture of familiarity and warmth.

After lunch, he spent another couple of hours reading and dozing on and off in the sun. The other guests on the deck were elderly, English, and pale. But just off the deck, local fishermen were stripping down to their shorts, diving into the clear blue water to freshen up after a long day of work. Several pulled themselves up on a rocky ledge and leaned back to let the late afternoon sun dry them.

Patrick was overwhelmed by the sensuality of the setting, the orange sunlight reflecting off the cliffs, the blue hazy horizon in the distance, ethereal sailboats gliding past the shore and the raw, masculine beauty of the men drying on the rocks. He remarked how different the setting was from his neighborhood in Boston and how being away for just a couple of days could change one's mood so quickly.

He realized he needed to head back to the cottage before dark. He thanked Nunzia for her hospitality and the clues for his family tree. He packed his day bag in the car and took off, taking the mountain road up toward the Benevento vineyards. He pulled into the space in front of the cottage, pushed open the door, and turned on a small lamp, finding a note on the dining table: "*Caro cugino – la vendemmia* will begin tomorrow. If you want to help, we will begin at the lower part of the vineyard at 7 AM. Get a good night's rest – you will need it."

Patrick sliced a few tomatoes and some mozzarella and poured a glass of wine. He sat in one of the comfortable chairs in front of the fireplace and opened a book on his iPad – a novel he had been wanting to read. He glanced out the window and could see the light in Pepe's house down the hill.

He wondered if he was alone and, if so, was it by choice? Was he a solitary person or just shy, awkward? His eyes were haunting, and he had an intriguing self-composure – quiet but intense. He heard a woman's laugh in the clear silent air - then *fermi* - stop - repeated playfully. He went to the window, peered through the vines, but could see nothing.

"*Peccato*," he said in disappointment, now convinced his rustic farmhand was straight. He felt a stirring, a lingering arousal that had begun early in the day and had continued at the coast, watching local fishermen strip down to swim in the sea. The air had been warm and aromatic, filled with the scent of the sea. He felt overwhelmed by the raw beauty that surrounded him – the luscious landscape and blue sea and the uncanny number of people who could be models for fashion magazines – male and female. The Italians were endowed with beautiful silky skin, dark hair, and deep, sexy eyes. The temperate climate encouraged people to wear shorts and loose-fitting swim trunks and shirts and blouses open generously at the top. People took pride in looking good, striking languorous poses in picturesque cafes or along piers with waves lapping up against large boulders catching the late afternoon sun. Everyone seemed to be flirtatious and indiscriminately so – men flirting with women and men; and women flirting with men and women.

People took the time to savor life, the sunshine, and simple but flavorful food. No one was in a hurry. People stopped, shared gossip, lingered, embraced, and kissed. Patrick felt the caress of the soft air, the flood of fragrances floating through the air – the sweet minerally earth, the late summer geraniums, and the mix of rosemary, basil and thyme lining the perimeter of the small plot of land around his cottage. He felt aroused – but not in the usual sexual sense – a more diffused arousal, a sense of intimacy with the air, the earth, the sun, the wind – an almost primordial sense of timelessness and presence.

Patrick breathed deeply, rubbed his hands over his abdomen,

and felt a deep sense of calm, serenity, and joy. Oddly, he felt the strong and warm embrace of his grandfather, the hint of patchouli oil on his skin, and a few words whispered in his ear – "I'm glad you're here. I'm glad you've brought me back."

Patrick wasn't particularly psychic or inclined to give credence to psychics or paranormal phenomena, but he definitely smelled his grandfather's scent, felt his warm presence, and sensed the words he pronounced in his head. It was comforting rather than disturbing, a sense that his presence here at the ancestral vineyard was propitious, meaningful, and would bring something full circle – he could feel it deep within himself.

The photo of Roberto and Stefano laid on the small table near his glass of wine – an image of male companionship, one that felt so natural to him. He felt as if there was a new bond between him and his grandfather – an experience that solidified their connection – a connection that went deeper than blood, one resting on an understanding and appreciation of love, friendship, intimacy. He sensed that he had come here to close a circle, to secure something that had been elusive for so long. He hoped he could make peace with his own father and put to rest the demons that haunted his own self-esteem.

He laid down his iPad, turned off the light, and walked into the bedroom. He undressed in the dark, slipped under the covers, and stared out the window at the moon – a bright half-moon. It was odd to think that for centuries the same moon had shone brightly on this cottage - that countless ancestors before him had felt its forces, witnessed its cycles, and had felt their own emotions rise and fall. He closed his eyes and fell into a deep sleep.

3

Chapter Three

Patrick awoke to the sound of tractors passing outside his cottage. He looked out the window and saw a cloud of dust trailing several trucks and trailers coming up the hill with workers sitting in the back. The sky was clear and the air already warm. He splashed some water on his face, made a quick cup of espresso, and sliced some juicy peaches that he ate with a little goat cheese.

He put on a heavy pair of socks and shoes, shorts, and a loose-fitting tee shirt. He tossed a baseball cap on his head and put on a pair of dark sunglasses. He headed out the door where people were spaced out in the rows of vines, cutting bunches of grapes, and tossing them into large straw baskets.

"Patrizo," Alberto yelled from a truck. "Are you ready for the *vendemmia*?"

"Absolutely. Show me what to do."

Alberto jumped out of the truck and handed Patrizio a pair of clippers and a large basket. They walked down to one row and Paolo said, "You can do this row here – cut the bunches like this and toss them into the basket. Pepe and his assistants will pick up the baskets when they are full."

"That looks easy enough."

Alberto chuckled. "We'll see in a few hours."

Patrick took up position in the row and he began to cut the grapes. They were ripe, full, and juicy. The first bunches came off easily. He nibbled a few grapes as he tossed them into the basket. They were sweet. As the hour progressed, Patrick felt the muscles on the back of his arms burn. He tried changing the angle of his stance and the extension of his arms, but there wasn't a comfortable position. The juice from the grapes trickled down his arms and onto his chest and small, pesky fruit flies hovered close to his face. Paolo walked up behind him – "Not bad for a beginner! Here's some water – make sure you drink enough in this heat."

Patrick lifted the container and gulped in the cool mineral water, letting some of the water rinse his arms and hands.

"We'll work until about 2 or 3," he said, "and then we will stop for a nice late lunch or early dinner. Laura will bring food from our restaurant later."

Patrick nodded and Paolo proceeded onto the next row, chatting with workers, and making sure they didn't overlook bunches of grapes.

The work was solitary – each person with their own row. Occasionally, Patrick would catch up to someone on the other side of his row, and they would nod and introduce themselves. Most were local villagers and spoke a thick dialect. They could understand Patrick's basic Italian, but he found it difficult to make sense of what they said.

A few rows up the hill, Patrick noticed Pepe. He supervised the gathering of the baskets into the trailer, spreading the grapes evenly in the truck's bed and returning baskets to each row. When he came to Patrick's row, he lingered, staring at Patrick's work. Patrick felt self-conscious, nodded, and waited for Pepe to move on. He didn't and walked toward Patrick. He took the clippers from Patrick's hand and, holding his arms, showed him how to reduce the strain. "*È meglio così.*"

"*Ah, grazie,*" Patrick responded nervously to his suggestions, Pepe still holding his arm and the clippers, his sweaty chest pressed up against Patrick's shoulder. Patrick felt himself get hard.

"*Niente,*" Pepe added, lingering a bit. He smiled warmly but spoke little. He walked back down the row, his moist muscular back glistening in the intense mid-morning sun.

As Pepe turned the corner, Patrick took a deep breath and returned to his work, invigorated by a shot of adrenaline. His stamina amazed him. It didn't hurt that young Italian men – all shirtless – were working nearby. Their statuesque figures, dark tan skin, and affable smiles energized him. Some sang local songs, and a few of the women joined in chorus.

Patrick felt transported by a kind of proximity or union with nature. He felt the rich soil beneath his feet and patches of dry flattened grass laying between the rows, gnarly dark trunks clinging to wooden posts, branches of greenish-yellow vines spread along steel wires. He was immersed in a vineyard, not driving by. He noticed an ant running along the post, a gnat circling his face, a cobweb shimmering in the light, and the translucent color of grape skins – ruby red with a sheen of light gray. The air was warm but softened by the salty, moist sea breeze gently flowing up the hill. The repetitive cutting of the grapes was meditative, Patrick drifting off to a form of mindfulness. At the same time, he felt fully immersed in his body – aware of the sweat on his skin, the strain in his muscles, the strength in his legs and the expansion in his chest as he breathed in the earth's smell, the grapes, and the bodies around him.

Around 2, a bell rung, jolting Patrick out of his altered state of consciousness. People finished their rows and carried baskets of grapes to the road in preparation for *pranzo*. A cloud of dust trailed a van coming up the hill. A few bursts of a horn signaled the much-anticipated feast. In the shade of old oak trees at the edge of the vineyard, Paolo had set up several long tables, and Laura set out platters of food.

The workers rinsed their faces, arms, and hands, pulled on fresh shirts, and gathered along the tables. Nunzia was there with her husband, Davide. Alberto stood at the head and made sure everyone had enough to eat and knew how much he appreciated their work. Laura helped pass the plates and kept pouring wine. Maria watched her two children and chatted with several women who had come to help.

Patrick sat a place at the center of one table near Nunzia and Davide. Nunzia was busy chatting with a young woman Patrick recognized from the *vendemmia*, someone who had been a few rows away from him. He recalled her having glanced his way several times. They had nodded but hadn't spoken. She wore a sleeveless beige cotton shirt over a pair of dark red shorts. She had long, thick brown hair pulled together in a band, which she playfully pulled over her shoulder toward her front. She had deep dark brown eyes, full lips, and high cheekbones. Her bright teeth gleamed as she laughed. Nunzia brought her over to Patrick.

"Patrick, I want to introduce you to Sylvia. Sylvia, this is Patrick, one of our cousins from America."

"*Piacere*," she said warmly.

Patrick replied similarly, "*Piacere*."

"Sylvia is a teacher in Rome. She comes each year to help with the *vendemmia*," Nunzia added. "She speaks perfect English."

"Oh," Patrick said in surprise, "I'm sorry my Italian is rather primitive."

"*Fa niente*," she said with a smile.

She sat across from Patrick and began filling her plate with pieces of grilled meat, pasta, and salad. Patrick glanced down the long line of tables, people passing platters of food and lifting glasses of wine. She passed Patrick the platter of meat, a mix of chicken, pork, and beef – all grilled to a beautiful golden-brown color garnished with sprigs of rosemary and slices of lemon. Patrick filled his plate and passed the platter along to Nunzia, who handed him, in exchange, a plate of pasta – rigatoni covered in grilled eggplant, roasted tomatoes, olives, and leaves of basil.

Nunzia served herself some salad and then reached for the bottle of wine on their table. She refilled her glass and lifted it in a toast. "*Salute*!" she said.

"*Salute*," Patrick, Nunzia, and Davide all said in unison.

"So, what do you teach in Rome?" Patrick asked Sylvia.

"*Letteratura* – to 12-year-olds."

"That must be a challenge," Patrick noted.

"It is, but I enjoy it. And you – I understand you teach, too. What subjects?"

"History, politics, social studies – also to roughly the same age group."

"Wow. That sounds exciting!" Sylvia said, placing a fork full of pasta in her mouth.

Nunzia continued to eat but kept her eyes on Sylvia and Patrick, following their conversation carefully.

"Yes. I enjoy it a lot. And, these days, with American politics so contentious, it is important to help young people understand the political process and the history of our democracy."

"Yes, we are all preoccupied with America. It always used to be the model of democracy, but when it shows signs of corruption and weakening, we all get nervous," Sylvia explained. Nunzia nodded in affirmation as well.

"We are preoccupied, too – at least a certain percentage of us are.

We hope the new president will help guide us to a more civil form of government."

"Us, too. By the way, why are you here. Isn't this the school year?"

"Yes. I have a short leave. My parents passed away this summer. My grandfather is a Benevento – so I've come to do some research on my family tree and take care of some business."

"I'm sorry to hear about your parents," Sylvia said warmly.

Nunzia leaned in and explained, "Sylvia is Davide's niece. His brother married a woman from Rome and has lived and worked there since he finished college."

Patrick nodded as he chewed some of the grilled chicken. Sylvia took a drink of wine and leaned her head back in a subtle but provocative way. Patrick noticed she didn't have a wedding ring and presumed Nunzia and Davide were trying to work their magic. Patrick was still reticent to come out to his cousins, wanting to keep a low profile – at least for the time being.

"Have you been to Rome?" Sylvia inquired.

"Only briefly when I was younger. I came her with my grandparents and parents."

"If you are free after the *vendemmia*, I would be happy to show you around," Sylvia offered with a warm smile, Nunzia smiling as well from the side.

"That would be very gracious of you. I'll see how my schedule unfolds here."

Sylvia nodded and glanced over at Nunzia, who winked. Patrick pretended not to notice, but Davide caught him glancing at Nunzia and nodded knowingly to Patrick.

At the end of the table, Pepe leaned over and caught Patrick's eye. He nodded. He sat next to a young lady, leaning against his shoulder, laughing from time to time as he spoke. She had caramel skin, brown curly hair, and wore a low-cut blouse that opened to her well-developed breasts that bounced as she laughed. She had long lashes and deep, alluring eyes. Her body was facing Pepe but, from time to time, after taking a sip of wine, she would turn her head provocatively toward others. She caught Patrick's eyes and lingered. He was unsure if she was flirting or staring him down – a message not to challenge her relationship with Pepe.

Patrick felt women had exceptional abilities in the area of gaydar, the ability to identify someone of questionable sexual orientation, particularly someone who they considered competition. Patrick assumed they could see written on his forehead – queer – and much as he tried to conceal his proclivities, they always seemed to sniff him out.

He glanced over at Sylvia, hoping she hadn't noticed the woman's scrutinizing look. She hadn't – and she returned his glance with a warm, affectionate smile.

"So, how long will you be in Italy, Patrick?" she inquired.

"A couple of weeks – at most. I have to get back to work sooner than later."

"*Peccato* – you need more time in Italy." She added.

Patrick assumed she really meant she would need more time to court him. "I know. It's a quick trip. But I'll be back."

"Well, my offer stands. Call me, and I can show you around Rome." She handed him a slip of paper with her cell phone number.

"It's been a pleasure," Patrick said warmly, shaking her hand as she excused herself and headed to her car.

"Sylvia's such a wonderful young lady," Nunzia noted to Davide. Davide nodded and glanced at Patrick. They picked up plates as people got up and excuse themselves.

Patrick helped clear the table. Pepe approached him with the woman he had been sitting with.

"Patrizio – I would like to introduce you to Angela. *Angela – questo è Patrizio – cugino di Alberto.*"

"*Piacere,*" Patrick said to her as he extended his hand.

Angela replied, "*Piacere*," and then rested her hand on Pepe's shoulder. She stared defiantly at Patrick. He couldn't think of anything to say to her, so he simply stated, "*È una bella giornata* – it's a beautiful day."

She replied, "*Sì*." She looked bored, turned to Pepe and said, "*Andiamo, caro*."

Pepe had been talking to another worker, turned toward Angela and Patrick and said with his eyes, "Sorry, we have to go."

Patrick nodded as if to confirm Pepe's dilemma – the desire to stay and make conversation and Angela's haste to return home. Pepe and Angela began walking away.

Patrick felt the soreness in his back and arms. He thought to himself that a nice plunge in the ocean would be soothing. Nunzia was walking nearby, and he yelled at her, "Nunzia, do you think I could come down and take a swim at the hotel? It would feel good after a long day of work."

"Yes – certainly. Make yourself at home. I'll be there later."

Patrick walked inside his cottage, changed into a pair of swim trunks and a pullover shirt, slipped on some flip-flops, hopped into the car, and drove to the shore. When he arrived, he parked the car and walked down to the sun terrace. He pulled off his shirt and climbed down the ladder to the sea.

He leaped off into the clear blue water. The soft briny liquid felt like a gentle massage, the soreness of the day floating off with each stroke he took away from the shore. A few meters away, several young men were jumping off their fishing boats, jostling with each other playfully in the water. They glanced his way, and he nodded to them. One of them smiled at Patrick as he pulled himself onto his boat, his swimsuit sliding partway off his buttocks as he straddled the side of the vessel. Patrick nodded back, but he decided not to join them, just treading water back and forth nearby. He listened attentively to their bantering, trying to catch a word or phrase here and there.

He swam out beyond the breakwater and looked back at the shoreline, a beautiful mix of rocks, sand, and terraced buildings with green mountains and vineyards in the far-off distance. The water had grown placid, the fishermen no longer swimming. They were exchanging cigarettes and slipping sweatshirts on over their weathered torsos, ready to return home after a long day of work. Patrick swam back, climbed up the ladder to the terrace, and reached for the towel he had left on a vacant chair. Nunzia waved from the upper deck. He wondered if she had noticed him observing the others swimming nearby.

He pulled on his shirt and slipped into his flip-flops and walked up to Nunzia.

"That felt so good. Thanks!"

"I know. The water here is heavenly, and after a long day of work, it feels even better."

"*Vuoi un caffè?*"

"That would be nice, but I don't want to keep you from anything."

"I'm through for the day. It will be nice to join you."

Nunzia went inside, prepared two espressos, and brough them out onto the deck. They sat facing the water and the fishermen on the beach nearby.

Nunzia observed them, and Patrick inquired, "Are they locals – do you know them?"

"Yes. They are neighbors, and they provide me with seafood for the *pensione*. That's Enrico," she pointed to one tying up the boats, "and that's Pietro over there," the one who had nodded to Patrick earlier. "Pino and Gabi are the ones folding the nets by the turquoise boat over there," she added.

"You must know everyone." Patrick noted.

"Yes, afraid so. Sometimes it's comforting - and other times it's a little too suffocating. Everyone knows everyone and everyone knows everyone's business."

"It seems idyllic to me." Patrick said smiling.

"So, what did you think of Sylvia? She would love for you to visit in Rome."

"She's very nice. We obviously have a lot in common. I'll have to see how my schedule goes."

"Hm," she mumbled as she glanced off in the distance at the young men, as if a light had gone off. Patrick wasn't sure if Nunzia had come up with another plan for a meeting with Sylvia or if she was sniffing out Patrick's secret. She looked at Pino and Gabi and gave them a wave. It was at that point he suspected she was onto him and wanted to signal that she was open minded.

"Well, Nunzia, I had better get back home and get some sleep before tomorrow."

"Yes, it will be another long and hot day. Feel free to come down here at the end of it and take a swim!"

"You're very gracious. *Grazie*!"

The next morning Patrick woke suddenly to the morning light and realized he had fallen asleep early only to face another day of manual labor – tractors pulling into place, workers streaming in from various directions, and Alberto yelling instructions to Paolo and Pepe. Patrick made some espresso and downed a quick slice of bread and cheese. He slipped on a pair of shorts and hiking boots and tied a pullover around his waist. He walked out into the morning sun, grabbed a pair of clippers, and selected a free row down the road.

He paced himself and alternated between cutting higher bunches and lower ones – giving his arms and back a break. People were quieter – tired from the previous day's work. Pepe continued to move up and down the road dumping full baskets into the back of the trailer where they would be hauled to the presses near Alberto's house. Pepe nodded to Patrick.

Pranzo was another big spread but less festive, people tiring from the two days of work and looking forward to the end of the *vendemmia* – at least at the Benevento vineyard. Patrick asked Alberto, "How much more work is there?"

"Looks like we have another half day. We'll finish tomorrow. Are you tired?"

"I can't believe how tired – it's a lot different from teaching."

"It's hard for all of us. We're not used to it either."

"That's reassuring. Everyone looks so strong."

"They are – but it's the kind of work that takes it out of you. Next week we begin the more technical work – pressing the grapes, measuring sugar content, and getting the conditions ripe for fermentation."

"I'd love to see how that's done."

"We'll show you."

"I sure appreciate your hospitality."

"We're happy you're here. There's going to be a celebratory party early next week at Laura's and Paolo's restaurant. Make sure you put it on your calendar – it's the people here you've seen and some others from the village – other vintners and prominent members of the community. People will be eager to meet our cousin from America."

Patrick excused himself after lunch and walked back to the cottage, sitting on the front porch with a glass of cool wine. He looked out over the rows of vines and the sparkling blue sea in the distance. The cool breeze felt good on his skin, and he closed his eyes to savor the subtle smells. Except for the rustling of leaves, it was quiet, the farm situated far from the highway and town and nestled high within the mountain ridges.

As he scanned the horizon, he noticed Pepe just outside his house – stripping off his clothes, ready to hose himself off. He was facing away from Patrick, his full, round buttocks and muscular upper legs gleaming in the last rays of light streaming over the crest above. Just as Pepe began hosing himself, Angela popped out of the back door wearing a bikini. She walked up to him, put her hand on his shoulder. He turned around and pulled the strap of her top off, her breasts falling out of the loose fabric. Pepe took hold of them, firm and full, and massaged them.

He then pressed himself against her and ran his hands over her back, pulling off her bottom and running his fingers deep between the folds of her buttocks. She leaned her head back, and he kissed her neck and then her breasts. She rubbed her hands over his broad muscular hairy chest, slick from the hosing.

Pepe picked her up, put her on the edge of a table and pressed himself up next to her – his large thick cock bouncing hungrily over her abdomen. She smiled, grazed the top of his erection playfully with her hand, and opened her legs slightly. He then pressed himself inside of her, squeezing his buttocks with each thrust, Angela moaning with delight. It didn't take long for Pepe to come. He writhed in spasms of release as Angela screamed loudly in cadence with him. Pepe pulled himself out and reached for the hose, rinsing them both off.

When finished, he threw her a towel. She dried herself while Pepe wrapped another towel around his waist. He went inside and brought out some wine and a plate of cheese that they nibbled on while drying in the sun. At one point, Pepe leaned back, took a sip from his glass, and glanced up the hill at Patrick's cottage. Patrick lowered his head, pretending to be engrossed in a book. He was certain Pepe caught him looking.

Patrick was both embarrassed and aroused. He avoided looking at Angela, women's breasts always disturbed him and concentrated on Pepe who conveniently leaned back on a chair, his legs sprawled in the sun and the hair of his chest running down his abdomen into the dark folds of the towel. Patrick imagined his cock, erect and engorged. Patrick rubbed his hands down under the top of his shorts and felt his own hardness. The image of Pepe thrusting himself into Angela was etched in his mind. He closed his eyes and imagined himself in her place, sprawled on the table and being taken by Pepe, Pepe's mouth licking his chest and his hands stroking his erection. His hand and Pepe's became one. He felt his pulse race, his skin tighten, and heat rise from deep within him, exploding in spasms of pleasure.

He opened his eyes and looked down the hill. Pepe and Angela had gone inside. He went back inside, too, dried himself, poured another glass of wine, and sat in one of the easy chairs of the living area.

The photo of Roberto and Stefano laid on the table just next to his glass of wine. He looked at their young, dark bodies glistening in the hot sun and pondered the familiarity with which they looked at each other. Did they know each other's bodies as he fantasized knowing Pepe's? The picture had been taken at the *vendemmia*. He wondered if they had hosed each other off after a hard day of work. Had they sat together afterwards, eating some cheese, drinking some wine?

As easy as it was for him to imagine having sex with Pepe, he struggled to imagine his grandfather having sex with Stefano – as affectionate as they were in the picture. Roberto loved Chiara. He had obviously made love to her, shared their home, had children. He took their wedding picture out – their joy apparent in their smiles, in their look of contentment, delight, excitement.

He wondered – is sexuality more fluid than we think? While he had never been attracted to women, and had never made love to a woman, maybe there were people who really felt passion and desire for both genders. How does that work, he asked himself? How does one decide who to pursue and what to do with the other side of one's feelings? What would it be like to be with someone who loved you for who you were, not necessarily because of your gender?

He tired. He knew there would be one more day of the *vendemmia* – and he had better get some rest. He turned off the light, stripped, and slid under the cool sheets of the bed, falling quickly asleep.

4

Chapter Four

Patrick rose early. He felt restless. He made a cup of coffee and sliced some bread and cheese for breakfast. The sun was just beginning to rise above the horizon, a few lights coming on here and there along the road coming up from the village.

Pepe's lights were on, and he heard Angela's voice in the cool, still air. She seemed agitated, shouting in local dialect. He heard the motor of Pepe's small truck crank on and, shortly thereafter, the sound of it passing swiftly over the gravel road towards town.

Around 7, vehicles gathered at the top of the vineyard, ready to begin work on the last rows of grapes. Pepe's truck barreled up the hill and stopped with a skid near the others – Angela not with him. He walked briskly toward Alberto, gesticulating wildly with his hands, and began to organize workers.

Patrick walked up the hill and took a row, familiar now with the routine and pace. As the sun rose higher, the heat increased, and he began to sweat. By now he had grown accustomed to the juice running down his arms, the gnats buzzing his ears, and the burn in his upper arms and back.

He looked forward to a few days after the *vendemmia* to relax, go to the beach, maybe visit Pompeii or other sites in the area. He needed to visit Nunzia again and follow up on some leads she had texted him regarding their ancestry. She had identified some more cousins with DNA matches on remote branches of the tree.

Pepe paced up and down the rows, supervising the work and gathering baskets as they filled. He stood at the end of Patrick's row, lingering. He nodded to Patrick and smiled. Patrick pointed to his basket full of grapes.

Pepe walked toward him, looked inside the basket, and nodded. He lifted his arms and pulled off his sweaty shirt, tying it to his belt loop. Patrick stood facing him, mouth agape, frozen in place. He tried to put on his best poker face but assumed it was all too obvious that he was mesmerized by Pepe's muscular, hairy, sweaty chest only inches in front of him. He looked toward the ground, only to find himself faced with the image of Pepe's thighs pressing firmly against the openings of his shorts. To make matters worse, Pepe stretched in front of him, raising his arms high above his head and then lunged back and forth on his legs before lifting the heavy basket of grapes, carrying it to the road, and dumping it into the truck. He walked back toward Patrick, dropped the basket, and smiled provocatively.

Patrick was perplexed. Pepe was ordinarily obtuse, walking around with an air of indifference. Now he seemed to flirt with him. He was more friendly toward others as well, helping them, encouraging them. Despite two grueling days of work, he was light-footed, full of energy, enthusiastic. Even Alberto scratched his head as he watched Pepe toss heavy baskets of grapes into the truck with ease.

As predicted, they finished around noon. Paolo explained to Patrick that there would be no *pranzo* – that people would be paid and were usually eager to take off, spend their money, celebrate with friends and family in their own homes or along the coast with a swim in the sea.

Patrick walked back to his cottage and rinsed the dust and juice off his arms and legs with the garden hose. Pepe walked past - toward his house. He nodded and kept going. Patrick laid down the hose and yelled, "*Ciao, Pepe. Che fai*?"

"*Torno a casa – a mangiare*."

Patrick interjected, in Italian, "You want to join me for lunch? I have some bread, salami, cheese, wine."

Pepe hesitated and turned around. He bent his leg slightly, shifting most of his weight to one side. In one hand, he held his sweaty moist tee-shirt and placed the other hand on his hip. It was a defiant pose, and he stared at Patrick. After a long pause, he replied, "Why not?"

Patrick waved him in. Pepe laid his tee-shirt on a chair outside and walked inside. He looked around the room. He had undoubtedly been there before, perhaps had even prepared it for his arrival. He seemed curious, as if to uncover clues – some items whereby he could figure Patrick out – make some kind of connection. He noticed the photos on the dining table. He looked inquisitively at Patrick, who nodded, "Take a look." And then, "Some wine?"

Pepe nodded.

Patrick opened a bottle and poured them both a glass. "*Salute*."

"*Salute*." Pepe replied, flipping through the pages of Patrick's notebook.

"*Ma – cosa sono queste*? What are these things?"

"They're photos of my grandfather and his wife and my family."

"*Sei di qua*? – you're from here?"

"Yes - well, at least my family is," Patrick said with his forehead creased – as if Pepe should have known he was part of the family. "Alberto's grandfather and my grandfather were brothers."

"This is him, right?" Pepe inquired as he pointed to Roberto and Chiara in their wedding photo.

"Yes."

Pepe seemed genuinely curious, examining the photos carefully and running his hands over the outlines of the family trees sketched in note form.

"Are you part of the family?" Patrick asked Pepe in return.

"*No – orfano.*"

"Oh," Patrick said with surprise and then quickly added, "I'm sure they must consider you family, nevertheless."

"Yes – but as an orphan I always feel like I don't belong."

"I'm sorry. I'm sure that's difficult."

"*Molto*," Pepe noted, emotionally. Then, seeing a few photos of Patrick and Girard, he looked at Patrick with an inquisitive face. "Who is he?"

Patrick cleared his throat nervously, "My husband – or perhaps I should say – my soon to be ex."

Pepe didn't look up. He said quietly, "Ah, I see."

Patrick was worried about Pepe's reaction, so he quickly interjected, "Can I offer you some salami, bread, cheese?"

Pepe nodded, still rummaging through the images, lingering over the one of Patrick and Girard.

Patrick prepared a platter of food and asked, "Shall we sit inside or out?"

"I like the fresh air – outside."

"Perfect," Patrick said. The angle of the afternoon light cast shade on the porch, so they pulled the chairs out of the sun, sat in them, and leaned back against the wall of the cottage.

"You know, you look like your grandfather – the same sexy eyes," Pepe noted as he lifted a slice of salami toward his mouth.

Patrick blushed, startled by Pepe's sudden forward compliment.

He looked down evasively at the platter of food and reached for a slice of cheese.

"*Veramente* - truly," Pepe said emphatically, making sure his earlier comment had not been overlooked.

Patrick now had to acknowledge the remark and looked over at Pepe, who was grinning like a little kid. He was a strong muscular man but had a playful, almost boyish face – round, with dimples, short-cropped hair, and a large but button-shaped nose. He hadn't shaved in a day or two, dark stubble lining his jaw and chin. In an ordinary situation, he would have been grateful for the compliment, but felt apprehensive. He wanted to conceal his own fascination with Pepe. "*Grazie*," was all he managed to get out as he took a sip of the wine.

Pepe turned toward Patrick, a furrow of curiosity on his forehead. "Why did you come here?" he asked.

Patrick thought it a loaded question, one rummaging for a deeper narrative, one Patrick wanted to conceal. "To visit my family," he answered.

"When do you go back?"

"Saturday."

Pepe was fidgety, finished his wine, and placed the glass on the nearby table as if ready to go. He looked around and then said stoically, "*Devo andare*."

"No," Patrick replied in alarm – then added more calmly, "I mean – there's no need to hurry. I'll make coffee."

Pepe nodded.

Patrick got up and welcomed Pepe inside. Pepe brought in the platter and placed it on the counter near the sink while Patrick prepared the coffee. Pepe remained uncomfortably close to Patrick, leaning against the counter, arms crossed over his bare chest. Patrick turned to fill the coffee machine with water, reaching around the side of Pepe. Pepe didn't move back and, when Patrick leaned back up, Pepe turned toward him and gave him a kiss.

"*Ma*," was all Patrick could get out – a timid "but."

"*Ma – cosa*?" Pepe replied, opening his mouth again and pulling Patrick's face up close to his, plunging his tongue deeply into Patrick's mouth.

Patrick pulled back slightly, concerned he might be intruding on another relationship. "*Ma – Angela*?"

"*È finita* – it's finished." Pepe said as he rubbed his hand over Patrick's shoulder, fingering the neck of the shirt and tugging on it gently.

Patrick wanted to rub his hands over Pepe's hairy muscular chest but held back, worried that he was being led into a trap. Pepe placed his hand under Patrick's tee-shirt and rubbed his chest, his warm fingers gliding across his moist skin. Patrick felt his pulse quicken and his heart pound. He felt the heat of Pepe's breath hovering over his neck. He felt himself become aroused and his self-control weakening.

He placed his hands on Pepe's pecs, fingered the soft dark hair, and squeezed the firm muscles playfully. Pepe then leaned into him, kissed his neck, moved his mouth up the side of his face, and then opened his mouth wide to take in Patrick's mouth, running his tongue around the inside of his lips.

Patrick replayed the scene of Pepe making love to Angela in his head, their wet bodies propped on the table and Pepe's buttocks - firm, round and tight – thrusting himself into her. As he imagined the scene, he realized Pepe hadn't kissed her. He had fucked her.

Pepe was making love to him, licking his face tenderly with his warm, wet tongue and rubbing his chest as he moaned. Patrick became harder, and noticed Pepe was too, his loosely hanging shorts bulging out. He hesitated, worried he would regret what he was about to do, and then reached down and unzipped Pepe's shorts, brushing the top of his hand over his tall, thick erection as the shorts fell to the floor.

Pepe smiled and sighed. He grabbed Patrick's hand and led him into the bedroom. He threw him down on the bed, pulled down his shorts, and sucked him. His lips were warm and moist, and Patrick could feel intense pulses race up and down his engorged shaft. Patrick looked down, rubbing his hands over Pepe's muscular shoulders. He thought to himself, "He seems awfully experienced to be straight."

Pepe rolled over on his back and stroked himself playfully, turning his head toward Patrick. Patrick pivoted and pulled himself up on Pepe's moist chest, taut with desire, and took Pepe's sex in his mouth. He bathed it in hot saliva; the liquid running down around Pepe's balls to his perineum. Pepe moaned and after a while whispered, "*Fermi* – stop." Patrick pulled away and but left his hand on Pepe's chest, stroking his pecs. He pressed his own hardness up against Pepe's thighs. Pepe looked at him intensely and said, "*Quanto sei bello* – you're so handsome."

He reached his arms over Patrick, rubbing a hand down his waist, and grazed the top of his erection. He looked into Patrick's eyes again, as if asking permission. Patrick leaned toward him and gave him a long, moist kiss. Pepe pulled himself on top of Patrick, nudging his erection into Patrick's, their warm, sweaty bodies gliding back and forth.

Patrick reached his arms around Pepe's back and ran his hands down his buttocks – firm and round. He ran his fingers deep within the crack. He pulled him close and, suddenly, felt Pepe erupt in spasms, his head arched back in pleasure. It only took a small jostle under Pepe's weight for him to feel himself come as well, the warm, slippery substance spreading between them.

To his surprise, Pepe didn't pull away. He remained on top of him, his nose nuzzled tenderly into his neck. Patrick rested his hands on Pepe's back and let his head fall back on the pillow, enjoying the momentary serenity of their bodies melded into one. Eventually, Pepe rolled off and lay on his back. Patrick chuckled.

"What's so funny?" Pepe inquired, grinning.

"This. I fantasized about this."

"So, you noticed me?"

"How could I not notice? *Guarda!*" he said, looking at Pepe's handsome body sprawled out next to him.

Pepe blushed. He looked intensely into Patrick's eyes and then said, "Why are you here?"

"I told you. I came to visit my family."

"But why, why now?"

"My parents died, and I needed a break."

"*Mi dispiace*," Pepe said tenderly, offering condolences.

"I wanted to reconnect with my grandparents."

"You're sentimental. I can see that in you."

Patrick was surprised at Pepe's observation. On the surface he seemed like a simple farm hand but, the more he spoke, the more he surprised him with a deep thoughtfulness.

"*Grazie*!" was all Patrick could say in reply, stroking the round of Pepe's shoulder. Patrick slid over to the edge of the bed, stood up, and went into the bathroom to wash. When he came back out into the room, Pepe was walking toward the living room, where he picked up his shorts and slid them on. He ran his fingers over some of the photos on the table, inspecting the wedding picture of Roberto and Chiara. He picked it up and said, "What a happy wedding – everyone is having fun."

"Yes, it must have been wonderful!"

Just as Pepe was about to lay the photo back down on the table, he noticed the photo of Roberto and Stefano partially concealed under a few pages of the family tree. "*Cosa è questa*? – what's this?"

"A photo of my grandfather with a friend."

"Hm," Pepe mumbled to himself. "*Forse di più* – maybe more."

"What do you think?" Patrick inquired of Pepe.

"*Sono innamorati – si vede* – they're in love – you can see it."

"They're just friends." Patrick said, testing how resolute Pepe might be with his hypothesis.

"*Non è possibile – c'è un desiderio intenso*!"

"I know – there's an intensity there – but my grandfather loved his wife Chiara and I saw nothing that would suggest anything else."

"*Sei venuto a trovarlo* – did you come to find him?"

Patrick nodded.

Pepe's brow furrowed and his body tensed. "*Questa è la tua fantasia* – this is your fantasy – to fuck the farm hand," he said with increasing consternation.

"No, no, no," Patrick pleaded, realizing Pepe was agitated.

"But you said you fantasized about me."

"Yes, you're very handsome – but it has nothing to do with this photograph."

"I'm just a fun *scopata* – a quick fuck – that's it."

"*Guarda*, Pepe, you came onto me!"

"I've seen you looking. Don't tell me you are so innocent."

"I admit that, but I would never use you."

"No, well what's next?"

"Well - what about you – are you interested in a relationship?" Patrick retorted, calling Pepe's bluff.

At first, Pepe remained quiet, staring at the floor. Then he looked up, red in the face, jaws clinched and let out an angry howl and stormed out the door. Patrick's hands trembled. He wasn't used to such an intense exchange. He sat down and took a long sip of wine from the glass that had been sitting on the dining table.

"What was that all about?" he murmured to himself. He had clearly touched a raw nerve. Had Pepe been abused? Was he still uncomfortable with his sexuality? Was he blaming Patrick for his own reluctance to come out, to form a long-term relationship with someone? Was there an unspoken code here to keep people in the closet that proved maddening for men like Pepe?

Patrick felt flush, a sense of shame coursing through his body. He rarely engaged in casual sex and felt bad that Pepe felt exploited. "What had he done?" he asked himself. "Was this just a quick fuck - was Pepe right – was he just using him?"

Against his first inclination to let it go and just stay put inside the cottage, he decided he should check in on Pepe. He didn't want there to be animosity between them or, worse, that Pepe would poison his relationship with his cousins. He put on a shirt and shoes and headed out the door and down the road to Pepe's.

He knocked on the door. Pepe responded, "Go away. I don't want to talk."

"I'm sorry. Clearly, I hurt you, and I didn't mean to."

"It's too late," Pepe replied.

"It's never too late to talk."

There was silence then footsteps coming to the door. Pepe pushed the door open and waved Patrick in.

"Have a seat," he offered to Patrick, pointing out a comfortable chair in the small loving room. Pepe pulled up a dining chair, turned its back toward Patrick, and sat on it, facing the back and Patrick. He looked at Patrick to begin.

"I'm sorry. Obviously, I hurt you in some way."

"It's been a bad day. Angela and I had a fight this morning and now this."

"What did you fight about?"

"She doesn't want to get married."

"Why?" Patrick pressed, thinking perhaps she had her suspicions.

"She doesn't think I have enough to offer."

"What do you mean?"

"She thinks this isn't enough – no job, family, future."

"But you have work, a home, and even if you are not officially a Benevento, I'm sure they consider you one of them."

"She wants me to move, to get a proper job, to live in the city," Pepe said with his eyes downcast.

"What do you want?"

"I like it here. I don't want to leave," he said emotionally.

"Then don't. Someone will appreciate what you have."

Pepe nodded.

Patrick then continued, "So why were you upset with me?"

"I think when I saw the picture of your grandfather and his friend, it reminded me of my relationship with the Beneventos. They've been very generous, taking me in, giving me work and a house. But it will never be enough for someone like Angela."

"But why be angry at me?"

"I'm just frustrated at being used by people who see me as expendable."

"But you kissed me. You came onto me."

Pepe grinned and blushed.

Patrick continued pressing Pepe, "Are you gay? Is that why Angela is hesitant?"

Pepe quickly responded, "I'm not gay. I don't use those labels."

"But," Patrick replied, leaving a long pause for Pepe to continue.

"You just have sexy eyes," Pepe said quietly.

"Okay, but I wasn't trying to use you. You're very handsome, but I had no intention of taking advantage of you. I like you."

Pepe looked off into the distance and then said, "I'm sorry. I overreacted."

"I can understand why. It must be difficult."

"It is."

"So, if Angela was to marry you, how would you deal with your feelings toward men?"

"I don't understand the problem," Pepe said, creasing his forehead in bewilderment.

"You seemed very comfortable making love to a man. You don't think that would cause trouble if you were married to a woman?"

"Not if I loved her."

Patrick rubbed his forehead in disbelief. He had a difficult time believing Pepe could sustain a faithful relationship with a woman given his clear attraction to men – although he had to admit Pepe didn't seem to have any trouble being passionate with Angela, either.

"So, what if you and a man fell in love? Would you get married?"

"It's not possible."

"What's not possible – falling in love with a man or marrying a man?" Patrick inquired further.

"Both. I can't fall in love with a man, and it's not possible to marry here."

Patrick wasn't convinced. He remembered the difference he noted between Pepe fucking Angela and making love to him. He was more convinced now that Pepe wasn't comfortable with his sexuality, that he probably got angry at male lovers not out of indignation around class but more as a way to shift blame onto others, to keep them at a distance. He also realized that, in fact, it was Pepe using him for sex, not the other way around.

"Well, I'm sorry if there was any misunderstanding. I hope we can be friends."

"Certainly."

"Will you keep your shirt on around me?" Patrick asked playfully.

Pepe blushed and nodded and then asked, "You want something to drink?"

Patrick nodded. Pepe got up and walked into the kitchen. His house was larger than the cottage, undoubtedly meant as a more permanent structure and residence. The living area included a fireplace surrounded by a sofa and some large stuffed chairs. There was a small dining area and then a door into an enclosed kitchen. Like the family estate house, the floors were made of dark red tiles and covered here and there with area rugs.

There was a small study off the living area. Patrick stood up and walked toward the dark space, curious about what was there. Pepe came back into the room with some wine and two glasses and noticed Patrick. "Go ahead, take a look."

Patrick walked inside the doorway and turned on the overhead light. It was a larger area than he had expected. Perhaps it had been a bedroom at one time. On the far side of the room, just under a window, there was a simple wooden desk with two drawers. There was a lamp on the desk, along with some papers and pens. On the right side of the room were a couple of bookcases filled with old leather-bound books. On the left, to Patrick's surprise, were some easels with several canvases.

"You paint?" Patrick inquired of Pepe, leaning on the doorjamb.

"I try."

"They're quite nice – are these some of yours?" Patrick pointed to several canvases leaning against the wall.

"Yes," Pepe acknowledged.

The scenes were of vineyards, small fishing villages, and other settings along the coast. Pepe had a way of capturing the light filtering through the vines or sparkling off the water and casting various hues on boats, wharfs, and shoreline. They were luminous, colorful, and evocative of the area.

"Did you study art or go to school for this?"

"No, I just picked it up – a hobby of sorts."

"You're very talented," Patrick continued, walking up close to one of the easels and looking closely at a sketch Pepe had started of a small cluster of boats.

"And these books – are they yours?"

"Some were here when I came but, over the years, I have purchased more."

Patrick walked to the bookcase and looked at the bindings – most of them history books.

Pepe smiled proudly as Patrick approached him. He offered him a glass and poured some wine into it, and they walked into the living area and sat down.

"So, you said you were an orphan. When did you come here?"

"When I was a teenager."

"Where were you before?"

"I was in an institute in Salerno."

"So, what happened that you came here?"

"Alberto visited the institute one day and had expressed interest in adopting. He and Maria had no children. They wanted someone younger, but no one was available. The director of the institute liked me and spoke highly of my abilities and Alberto must have realized he could groom me for the business."

"So, how old were you then?"

"Thirteen."

"You must have been cute!" Patrick said.

"I was past the cute stage. I was an awkward teenager," Pepe said pensively.

"And so, what happened?"

"Several years later, Maria got pregnant with Gabriella. A few years later, they had Ricardo. Alberto still felt affection toward me, but things changed. When I was 18, they moved me to the house here – on my own."

"That must have felt terrible."

"No, I actually liked it. It was freedom and independence."

"So, when you say Angela doesn't think you have anything to offer, what is she talking about? You have foster parents who are nobles, you are well-educated, and you can paint."

Pepe blushed, then continued, "She thinks I should move to Naples or Salerno and get a proper job – not something that depends on the generosity of the Beneventos. I don't have any savings or money of my own."

"But don't they pay you?"

"Well, it's complicated. I have a house and I have living expenses paid for, but if I want something more, I have to ask Alberto, and he's been so generous already."

"Hm," Patrick sighed. "I see."

"So, we have to find you a young lady who wants to be a farmer's wife."

"*Appunto* – and there aren't many who aspire to that."

"What about a farmer's husband?"

"*Stai scherzando* – you're joking, right?"

"*Non è fuori questione* – it's not out of the question."

"As I said, that's not possible." Pepe said emphatically.

"Ok – I understand – but keep your mind open," Patrick added with a wink.

Pepe nodded and took a sip of wine from his glass. Then he asked, "And you – what do you do?"

"I'm a schoolteacher for teenagers."

"That must be challenging."

"It is, but I love it. I feel like I'm making a difference."

"So, you go back to Boston on Saturday?"

"Unfortunately, yes. I've come to like it here."

"Stay!"

Patrick was thrown by Pepe's plea to remain in Italy. He paused and then said, "It's not possible."

"Your husband?" Pepe asked, guessing the root of the problem.

"No. That's finished, but my life in Boston isn't."

He then looked up at Pepe. He thought to himself that in another setting, time, and place, he would have considered Pepe a great prospect – handsome, smart, talented, and thoughtful. He could even imagine himself living on the edge of the vineyard, helping Pepe and Alberto with marketing in the US, and raising a couple of kids.

But Pepe seemed unassailable, just out of reach. He couldn't make sense of someone who clearly was comfortable making love to another man, but not able to even consider the possibility of a relationship. He wondered if he had inadvertently stumbled upon the missing piece of the Roberto-Stefano saga – a love that could never be solidified for reasons of deeply entrenched cultural biases. If he had to bet, he believed his grandfather probably couldn't take the step that perhaps Stefano could – or perhaps both couldn't take the step – a step that in the 1950s would have been even more unthinkable than it was today.

Patrick looked at his watch and said, "Well, Pepe. Thanks for the talk. I'm sorry for what happened today – and hope we can be friends."

"I'm sorry for overreacting, but I'm not sorry about what happened. You're very handsome!"

"And you're very difficult to make sense of."

Pepe smiled. They both stood and embraced. Patrick walked out the door into the cool night air and walked up the hill to the cottage. It had gotten dark, and far off in the distance, lights twinkled from a few yachts and cruise ships offshore. The stars were brilliant, and the moon had not yet risen over the horizon.

As he pushed open the door, the deafening silence made him feel lonely. He sat in one of the chairs in the living area and held the photo of Roberto and Stefano in his hand. He rubbed his fingers over the image of his grandfather and his friend. For the first time in his life, he felt utterly alone – no grandparents, no parents, and no companion – adrift and without mooring. He felt restless and wished he were back in Boston, where he could at least go out to a restaurant bar or a club and chat with people – maybe meet someone.

He turned out the light, walked into the bedroom, and slipped under the covers with his clothes on, hoping he would fall asleep quickly.

5

Chapter Five

A few days later, Paolo and Laura were hosting the celebration of the *vendemmia* at their restaurant in the village – a meal of appreciation for those who had helped and an annual gathering of the extended family. It was a more formal occasion. People dressed. Neighbors exchanged gifts. Announcements were made. It was at this same time that Roberto and Chiara had married and began their journey to America. The coincidence was not lost on Patrick, who felt like he had come full circle.

In the days following Patrick's afternoon with Pepe, Pepe was cordial, but distant. He was busy with Alberto at the farm, pressing the grapes, testing conditions for fermentation, and getting equipment ready for the months long process of producing the wine. He would walk past Patrick's cottage, yell hello from outside the building, and continue on his way.

Patrick wasn't particularly upset. It had been fun, and Pepe was certainly intriguing and exceptionally sexy, but the last thing he needed was to complicate things. Pepe's distance made it easier.

Patrick put on a pair of dark slacks, a light blue dress shirt, and a light cotton jacket. He spritzed some cologne on his neck, put a few errant locks of hair in place, and hopped into his Alfa Romeo for the drive to town. He parked the car, adjusted his belt and pants, and walked toward the crowd. Nothing had changed since Roberto's and Chiara's wedding, seventy years ago. The same large dusty oak tree shaded the square where tables spilled out onto the pavement. A stage was set up with a band, and lights strung between buildings gave everything a festive feel. People were milling about, drinking wine, and catching up on family news.

Patrick felt many eyes following him, a welcome novelty about which to talk, speculate, gossip. A single man drew much attention, and everyone was interested in introducing him to their daughters. Alberto walked up to Patrick. "Welcome, *cugino.* I want to introduce you to some other family members."

"You mean there are more?"

"Afraid so."

Alberto introduced him to his distant cousins. He could see the Benevento resemblance, particularly in the men who had broad torsos, dark complexion, and deep eyes set off by wispy and full eyelashes – responsible for their so-regarded "sexy eyes." He had brought the wedding picture and the picture of Roberto and Stefano, slipped in the chest pocket of his jacket. As he met people, he pointed to the wedding picture to identify their ancestors or, sometimes, them as little children.

Alberto rose to a small podium and began, "*Attenzione, attenzione prego.* I want to thank everyone for helping with the *vendemmia.* This should be an excellent year for the Benevento wine – the grapes were in perfect order and the weather has been cooperative. I welcome all our extended family. We are glad you are here. In particular, I want recognize our cousin Patrick from America – Patrick Benevento –

the grandson of Roberto and Chiara who married in this very spot seventy years ago."

Everyone applauded. Alberto pointed to Patrick, who waved and smiled to the large gathering.

Alberto called up the priest for a blessing and then invited the band to begin playing music and for people to take their seats and begin enjoying the antipasti.

Large white platters loaded with grilled zucchini, artichokes, prosciutto, salami, peppers, and cheese were spread out on the tables. In addition, there were bowls of shrimp and calamari. Large pitchers of wine – white and red – were placed amongst the guests. Loaves of rustic bread rested on cutting boards – sliced thickly with saucers of olive oil nearby.

The small orchestra played music, and a few couples jumped on the platform to dance. The afternoon shadows from the surrounding mountains cooled the air, and the salty breeze from the ocean blew up the hill, picking up scents of sweet grapes and ripening tomatoes from the terraced land. Patrick sipped the deep ruby red wine and picked at the antipasti, visiting with cousins, and chatting with workers he had met during the harvest.

His Italian was improving, and he felt increasingly at ease – almost as if he belonged, that he had always been a part of the community. He sensed the deep furrows that traditions and history carved in people's identity, in the land, in their souls, and he could see how someone like himself might even consider marrying – a woman – and starting a family. It was an unsettling thought, but one he had to admit made some sense. He glanced over at Sylvia chatting with one of their cousins and at Pepe not far from her. She made practical sense – someone who shared his professional interests and with whom he could have a family, raise children, and take part in this rich quilt of relationships. Pepe made his blood race, his loin stir, and his heart pound. He could imagine long nights wrapped in his arms and afternoons swimming in the sea and drying on the rocks with other local men.

It was all hypothetical, he reminded himself. In a few days he had to go back to Boston and face Girard and the complicated documents for an eventual divorce and division of property.

The title he had inherited from his father was minimal, more honorary and symbolic than lucrative. He could return to help with the harvest each year, enjoy his new family connections, but his life was in the States. He took a seat near Nunzia and Davide and their children. As he put a large slice of prosciutto in his mouth, Nunzia inquired, "So, how was the *vendemmia*?"

"A lot of work – as you told me. But it was fun, and it meant so much to connect with the land and do the work that Roberto and others had done for generations."

"It's magical, isn't it," Davide underscored. "My family has a vineyard in a few towns over. We will help them next week."

Nunzia leaned over to Patrick and, in a quiet voice, asked, "Any luck identifying Stefano?"

"Not yet. You?"

"Well, I have a potential lead – not too promising – but worth pursuing."

"Tell me," Patrick said enthusiastically, placing his hand playfully on Nunzia's.

"Well, I did a DNA test a few months ago. As you know, the website identifies people who share a part of your DNA that have also had tests done."

Patrick encouraged her to continue. She paused, looked at him, "I know, it's a little creepy."

Patrick chuckled, having taken the same test and having had many cousins from his mother's side send inquiring emails about his family.

"A couple of cousins were identified in a nearby town. I checked out their tree. Their parents are Nicola and Francesco. I haven't found anything more of Francesco, but Nicola's parents are Rita and Stefano."

Patrick gave her an encouraging smile.

"I know – it's one of the first Stefano's I have found."

"Is he our Stefano?"

"I don't know. I don't think so. There's nothing more in the tree about Stefano. Rita's surname was Marcello, and she has links further back. Her surname after marriage was Voluto. But, when I search Voluto for Stefano, I find nothing."

"Could he have been an orphan – this Stefano?"

"Hmm, an interesting idea. What brought that up?"

"Oh, nothing. It just dawned on me that it might explain the lack of any records that could complete the tree. Do you think it's a dead end, or something to pursue?"

"That depends on you. How eager are you to find this Stefano?"

"The more I'm here, the more intrigued I am. It's worth talking with these women to see if they know anything."

"That's what I thought. I did some research and have their contact information. They live near Positano – along the coast – not far from here."

Davide interrupted their conversation, passing Patrick a plate of calamari and shrimp and refilling his glass. Patrick glanced down the table. Pepe had taken a seat nearby and looked eager to join the conversation. He looked up and nodded, raising his glass in a toast. Patrick nodded back.

Later, plates of steaming pasta arrived on carts, servers placing them strategically between guests. Patrick took a large spoonful of the rigatoni covered in an eggplant-olive-tomato sauce and grated some fresh parmesan cheese on top. "Mmm," he said, the flavors of the fresh ingredients exploding in his mouth. He raised his glass to Laura, thanking her for the delicious food.

Patrick leaned against Nunzia who had just finished taking a sip of wine, "Who are all these people who are serving – Laura and Paolo can't have a staff this large."

"Some are mine; others are from Paolo's family's restaurant in Positano."

"Paolo is from Positano?"

"Nearby – yes. His family has run a restaurant there for years."

"Where did he and Laura meet?"

"I believe at an event like this. Paolo had friends in the village, and they invited him to the *vendemmia* and the feast."

"How romantic."

"Yes – as we say in Italy – it's love." "*È l'amore,*" Patrick thought to himself.

"When do you have to go back?" Nunzia inquired just before taking a large bite of the ravioli.

"I'm supposed to return on Saturday. I had a short leave for family reasons from work."

"Well, we'll have to work quickly."

Patrick looked perplexed. "What do you mean?"

"We have to find a way to get you to stay here. You belong here. It's your home."

Patrick frowned and said, "I know, I've become very attached to you all and to this place, but I belong in Boston – that's my home; that's where Roberto and Chiara raised a family and started a prosperous business. I want to carry on their legacy."

Nunzia looked sad. The main course arrived – a mixed plate of grilled meats and risotto. Nunzia excused herself and went to say hello to Paolo and Laura. She gave them a warm embrace and kisses on both cheeks. She whispered something in Paolo's ear. He looked in Patrick's direction.

The meal finished, people began to dance and, as the light receded over the mountain, the lights strung across the square cast an increasingly bright glow over the pavement and on the faces of the guests swirling now on the dance floor. Patrick was popular with the female cousins. He was the exotic American who had returned home. He enjoyed the attention but, as he glided across the platform in their arms, he felt restless and unsettled.

He took a break. Paolo approached him. "Patrizio – you're quite the dancer and charmer."

"It's the Benevento lure, no doubt."

Paolo chuckled. "Nunzia said you're leaving next Saturday. You haven't had much time to explore the area. Have you ever been to Positano?"

"Just passed through."

"I have business there on Wednesday. I need to see my family."

"Yes, Nunzia said you were from there."

"Would you like to come? We can have lunch. You can spend some time in town or on the beach while I'm working – and then we can come home."

"Sounds great. Actually, Nunzia has some ancestry leads on some distant cousins just outside of Positano. Maybe we can go to town, have lunch, you do your business, and I will follow up with these cousins."

"Perfect."

Two days later, Patrick dressed for his excursion to Positano. He put on a pair of tan shorts, a light blue pullover, and a baseball cap. He packed a few things in a bag in case an opportunity to swim or lay on the beach presented itself. He hopped into his car and drove to town. Paolo was sitting outside the restaurant, sipping some coffee, and reading the paper.

"*Buon giorno, Paolo,*" Patrick yelled from the car. "You ready?"

"*Sì – vuoi un caffè?*"

"No, I've had enough already. Let's go."

Paolo got into the passenger seat, and Patrick shifted the car into gear and headed down the curvy road to the shore. The rows of vines had yellowed a bit, and the sky was a hazy blue.

"When does autumn come?" Patrick inquired of Paolo.

"We don't really have an autumn here. Crops just get dry and yellow at the end of the season. The days get a little cooler and the sea less blue. Shops begin to close as the tourists leave, and locals either travel or begin repair projects on their properties. It's sad, but for those who have been busy since May, it is a much-needed respite."

Patrick nodded, shifting the car into a lower gear as the grade of the road steepened and several curves approached. As they got closer to the highway, farmers had set up stands selling tomatoes, lemons, grapes and all sorts of jams, spreads, and liquor.

They caught the coastal route near Praiano enjoying the vistas that opened at each bend – majestic mountains plunging into the sea, small villages clinging to hillsides, and picturesque coves filled with fishing boats. As they approached Positano, traffic increased, and the road widened slightly to accommodate sidewalks and shops.

"My cousin's restaurant is toward the bottom of the town, just overlooking the beach. We have a private parking garage here along the road. There – see that sign – that's it. Pull in."

A short older man guarding the small lot looked at them disdainfully until he recognized Paolo and grinned, many of his front teeth missing. "*Paolo, bentornato.*"

"Pino – good to see you again. *Possiamo?*" he asked, looking covetously at one remaining space.

"*Sì, certo.*" He waved them in.

Patrick squeezed the car into the narrow space, and they began the long descent to the restaurant. Paolo said there were 500 steps, he had counted them. He assured Patrick there was a less tortuous route back. The whitewashed stairway was squeezed between houses and villas, terraced on the steep hillside. From time to time, the angle of a wall or the slope of the walkway revealed the sparkling blue water below. Patrick felt the muscles on his legs quiver as they continued walking without stopping.

"Here we are," Paolo said with delight, standing in front of a large stone doorway. "My cousin's restaurant. It's been in the family for years."

The entrance opened to a glass enclosed room with unobstructed views of the sea. The windows were open, and a gentle breeze cooled the area, filling with tourists. "*Paolo, benvenuto*!" A tall, formally dressed maitre d' welcomed Paolo with a big hug and kisses on his cheeks.

"*Carlo, questo è Patrizio, un cugino dall'America.*"

"He must be from Laura's side – I see the Benevento influence."

"Yes, he's Laura's cousin, Roberto's grandson."

"Welcome," he said warmly. "Let me show you to your table."

They walked down a few steps to a shaded terrace right on the beach. Carlo put them at a table in the front row. "*Va bene così*?"

"Are you kidding? This is perfect, Carlo. Maybe we can get Patrizio to hang around a little longer."

Carlo grinned and returned to his station.

People were walking up from the beach for *pranzo*, some in robes loosely tied at their waists, others in swimsuits and sandals. It was a handsome crowd, mostly Italians, tan and trim. Some women were topless but had draped light linen jackets over their shoulders for lunch.

The staff was attentive, darting back and forth, taking orders, and delivering drinks and food. Many people leaned over between tables, gesturing with their hands, presumably to family and friends who had gathered for a late summer break.

"This is unbelievable," Patrick began. "We don't have anything like this in the States – maybe a snack bar with sandwiches and chips but never a place where you can have fresh pasta and wine steps from your beach umbrella."

"Yes, we are fortunate. We have to keep reminding ourselves of that when we complain about taxes or politics or other unpleasantries."

A young man came to their table and offered to get them a drink, "*Da bere*?"

Paolo ordered some local white wine and mineral water and then opened the menu. "I have this memorized, but it's a habit to open the menu and look. Everything is wonderful, fresh."

As the waiter was retreating up the steps to the kitchen, Patrick had a strange sensation, as if he had known him or seen him before. He shook his head slightly, as if to dislodge an errant thought, and Paolo looked up from the menu.

"You okay?"

"Yes, I just thought I recognized the waiter from somewhere. Must be my imagination."

"We all look alike – tall, dark, handsome, right?"

Patrick laughed. "*Giusto*!"

The waiter returned with their wine and water and stood attentively to take their order. He was lanky, tall, and broad-shouldered - handsome, but not in a take-your-breath-away sense. Pleasant, well proportioned, glowing complexion. He seemed jovial, affable, curious. He had a warm smile and seemed eager to make eye contact. He had an angular, handsome face, dark brown eyes, wispy lashes, and short, dark hair.

Patrick stared at him intensely as Paolo ordered. He thought to himself that he looked so familiar. He searched his memory of faces he had seen recently in the village and at the *vendemmia*, but nothing came to him. As the waiter looked at Patrick to take his order, it struck him. "Those eyes," he said to himself. "They are haunting, intense, and playful." Then he realized. He pulled the photo of his grandfather and Stefano out of a little leather folder, held it up, compared Stefano with the waiter and said, "That's it, he looks like Stefano – particularly his eyes," Patrick said to himself.

He put the photo back in his shirt pocket and ordered a salad and some ravioli. The waiter left and Paolo inquired, "Did you figure out that you know him?"

"He reminded me of someone – of a person in a photo with my grandfather." Patrick pulled out the photo and showed it to Paolo.

Paolo leaned over and stared at the photo. "Wow, that's a unique picture of your grandfather – undoubtedly of the *vendemmia* – but who is that with him?"

Patrick turned the photograph over and showed Paolo their names and date. "I've been trying to find out who this Stefano is. I asked Nunzia and others – but no one remembers a Stefano. That's why I'm meeting some of Nunzia's cousins this afternoon – to follow a lead."

Paolo took the photo and looked closely at it. "They seem very close - almost as if they were in love."

"I know. But Roberto was so in love with Chiara – it seems like they must have been just friends."

"Maybe, maybe not. Who knows?" He winked.

When the waiter returned with their food, Paolo looked at him closely and creased his forehead. The waiter looked nervously back, and Paolo smiled. "*Grazie*," he said as he left their food on the table.

"See?" Patrick said to Paolo.

"*Sì, lo vedo.* They really look alike. It's a common look to this area, but there is something in the eyes that is unique."

"I know. I thought the same thing," Patrick added.

Paolo's cousin Carlo came to their table to check on things. "*Tutto va bene*?"

"Sì, as always, delicious. Hey Carlo, who is our waiter?"

"Is there a problem?" He asked with concern.

"No. He just looks like someone."

"His name is Zeno. He's been working here since he was a teenager. His father works here, too – Giovanni – you've probably met him before. Nice family. Who do you think he looks like?"

Paolo looked over at Patrick, who pulled out the photo. Carlo leaned over. "Yes, I see the resemblance. Who are these people?"

"My grandfather and someone he knew here before he left for the States."

Zeno approached the table to check if everything was okay. Carlo leaned over Patrick and pointed to the photo, saying, "*Guarda*! Look at this photo."

Patrick extended his arm with the photo, and Zeno took a look. His face blanched, then turned red. "It's my grandfather."

Paolo and Patrick looked at each other in disbelief. Patrick began, "Your grandfather?"

"Yes, Stefano."

Patrick realized Zeno hadn't seen the names on the back, that he must have recognized the man as his grandfather. "I've been trying to figure out who he is."

"He's my grandfather – and this must be Roberto in the picture with him."

"You know my grandfather?"

"Not really, but I have heard stories of him – and met him once."

Zeno took hold of the photo in one hand and tapped it with the back of his other. "*Cazzo – che coincidenza.*"

"Yes – quite a coincidence," Patrick affirmed, looking intently at Zeno, his mouth wide open. "This is unbelievable. No one in my family knew who he was."

"That makes sense – there was a falling out," Zeno said.

Patrick gave Zeno an inquisitive look, and Carlo interjected, "Patrizio, Zeno finishes work in about two hours. Can you come back later and visit? Sounds like you have a lot to share." He looked over at Zeno, who looked back, nodding hesitantly.

Carlo looked over at Paolo for a reaction. "I have business here in town. Patrick was going to look up some cousins." Looking now at Patrick, Paolo said, "I imagine you don't want to follow up with these other cousins. Why don't you hang out here at the beach, chat with Zeno later, and we can drive back home before dinner."

Zeno and Patrick, looking at each other, nodded.

Zeno bowed, asked if they needed anything, and looked after some of his other tables.

Patrick watched him as he worked. Paolo was checking emails and texts on his phone. Occasionally, Zeno would glance over at Patrick. His warm, affable smile had cooled. He looked more alarmed and anxious.

Carlo finished taking care of their table and showed Patrick two beach lounge chairs near the restaurant. "This is our beach establishment. These were a couple of unused chairs. I'll send Zeno over when he's finished."

Patrick sat down, leaned back in the chair, and let the late afternoon sun warm his face. He loosened his shirt and checked emails. The effects of the wine and pasta hit, and Patrick dozed off. A little while later, he felt a hand on his shoulder and, "Patrizio, Patrizio."

He looked up and saw Zeno. Patrick rubbed his eyes, leaned the back of his chair forward, and said hello. "Do you speak English? I speak some Italian, but not much."

"Yes. We have a lot of American and British tourists."

Zeno sat in the chair next to Patrick's. Patrick leaned forward and sat on the edge, facing Zeno.

"So, you are Roberto's grandson?" Zeno began.

"And you, Stefano's. Amazing!"

"*Veramente.*"

"I just discovered the photo of them a couple of weeks ago, cleaning out my parent's home. My grandfather died when I was 10, so

I never heard him talk about Stefano. And I never heard my father mention him, either. What do you know?"

Zeno edged further on the side of the chair. He had taken off his jacket, unbuttoned the top of his white shirt and rolled up the sleeves. He was barefoot. He gave Patrick a scrutinizing look. He looked hesitant to begin. Patrick felt as if Zeno was taking his pulse, establishing what kind of camaraderie or antipathy might exist between them. Patrick tried to reassure him, raising an eyebrow playfully, almost flirtatiously.

"Stefano was my grandfather. He married Rita, who was part of the staff here at the restaurant. They had a son, Giovanni, who is my father."

Patrick nodded to continue.

"Stefano died 5 years ago. He lived a long life. We were close."

"I'm sorry to hear."

Zeno nodded solemnly. "He spoke of your grandfather often. I believe they saw each other once when your grandparents came here to visit."

"Did you meet them, my grandparents?"

"Yes, there was a reunion here."

"Did you go to the Benevento farm?"

"No, there was an understanding. We never went."

Patrick creased his forehead. "What kind of understanding?"

Zeno hesitated. "As I understand it, Stefano wanted to marry Roberto's sister, but his father wouldn't permit it."

"Why not?"

"He was an orphan. He was the caretaker of the vineyard – had been brought there when he was a teenager. He was treated like one of the family but, when he and Anna showed an interest in each other, Roberto's father put his foot down. Anna and he were upset and went behind Giancarlo's back. They continued to see each other until Giancarlo fired Stefano."

"And Anna was Roberto's sister, right?"

"Yes."

"That's harsh," Patrick said thoughtfully.

"Indeed. Since he had no lineage or inheritance, Giancarlo considered him unacceptable. To your grandfather's credit, he protested and tried to convince his father to change his mind, but he couldn't persuade him. That's why he left for America."

Patrick nodded, now finally connecting the dots. "They looked very close, Roberto and Stefano."

"Yes. It must have been hard for Roberto to leave. I know it was hard for my grandfather."

"So, there wasn't any other reason Roberto left for America," Patrick pressed, wondering if there had been some indiscretion or misunderstanding that Zeno might be able to reveal.

"I don't know what you mean. No, as far as my grandfather was concerned, Roberto left in protest over Stefano's not being able to marry Anna."

"Then Stefano married Rita here in Positano?"

"Yes. They seemed very happy, despite Stefano's sadness at having to leave the Benevento farm. They made a nice life here together – giving birth to my father, Giovanni, who then married my mother, Joanna."

"It seems like a pleasant life here." Patrick commented.

"Yes, it is. But it's also a very small town. Everyone knows everything about you, and there are few opportunities to do anything other than what your family has done for generations. My grandmother and grandfather were servers – my father is a waiter – and I am a waiter. Story over."

"But it's good, no?"

"*Beh!*" Zeno grunted, throwing his hands up as if saying, 'more or less.' "And you, what do you do?"

"I'm a teacher. In Boston."

"How is it that you're traveling during school time?"

"My parents died this summer, and I have a family leave. I'm trying to settle their estate."

"I'm sorry to hear," Zeno said warmly.

"Thanks. It's been difficult."

Zeno looked intensely at Patrick, a warm extended glance. Patrick sensed Zeno's compassion but wondered if there was something more in the look – a curiosity or interest. Patrick caught him looking at his hand, checking to see if he had a ring. Patrick pretended not to notice and glanced indiscreetly at Zeno's hand, which was ringless, too.

In Boston, Patrick could have easily discerned someone's orientation but, in Italy, it was more complicated. Italian men – even straight ones – dressed with more flare, showcasing their attributes. They used their eyes to communicate and weren't afraid to show emotions. As he looked at Zeno, he could imagine Roberto looking into Stefano's eyes – a look of friendship, camaraderie, and companionship, not sex. It was very Italian.

Zeno leaned back. "Tell me more about your grandfather. What was he like?"

"Ah," Patrick began, "he was such a warm soul, full of life, passion, and love. He was the glue of our family, someone who always brought people together, even during times of conflict."

"My grandfather was the same. Even after leaving the Benevento farm, I never detected resentment, anger, hostility. He was sad, and he missed the family that had taken him in, but he wasn't someone to dwell on misfortune. He was enthusiastic, optimistic, and resourceful."

"I would have liked to meet him," Patrick said, thinking to himself that, in some way, he was – in his grandson.

"So, did your grandfather preserve some of the Italian customs when he moved to Boston?"

"Yes – he and my grandmother, Chiara – who was from the same town, loved Italy and wanted us to be Italian. My father married an Irish woman, but she learned how to make Chiara's sauce and meatballs. My grandfather tried his luck making homemade wine. He said the grapes he could buy were shit, so the wine was pretty rough. Occasionally, his brothers would send him some of the Benevento wine. All of our family gatherings were lots of fun – lots of passion and noise and chaos – but full of love and affection."

"So, you speak a little Italian?"

"I learned it in school – but since my grandparents died young, I didn't have anyone to practice it with."

"What did you think of the Benevento vineyard?"

"It was amazing – and the *vendemmia* was a lot of fun – and work."

"What are your plans?" Zeno asked.

"I have to go back on Saturday – to work, unfortunately."

"I have to go back to work in a little while. Would you like to come back later in the week? I could show you around – take you for a boat ride?"

Patrick's eyes widened. The idea of a boat ride along the Amalfi coast was a dream – and he found it easy – in fact enjoyable – to talk with Zeno. "That would be great. When?"

"I'm free Friday. Why don't you come in the morning? We can hang here on the beach and then take a ride in the boat in the afternoon."

"Perfect!" Patrick replied enthusiastically.

Zeno grinned warmly but was at a loss for words. Hesitantly, he said, "*Allora* – well – I probably should head back to work."

"And I should go find Paolo and head back to the vineyard."

"It's been a pleasure," Zeno said enthusiastically.

"*Anch'io*," Patrick added in Italian.

They walked up the steps to the restaurant. Paolo was talking with Carlo and gave him a hug goodbye. He then turned to Patrick and asked, "Did you guys have a nice visit?"

Patrick nodded. Zeno looked at Carlo and nodded as well.

"You ready to head back to Cava dei Lupi?" Paolo inquired of Patrick.

He nodded yes. They again thanked Carlo and Zeno for their hospitality and began climbing the stairs to the car at the main road. They gave Pino a tip and retrieved the car, heading down the road toward Praiano.

"So, how was your visit with Zeno?"

"Yes, he's very nice. He had a lot of information about his grandfather – even stories about Roberto. It sounds like Stefano wanted to marry one of the Beneventos, and the patriarch was against it. That was the reason my grandfather left, in protest."

"I'm not surprised. Giancarlo senior was quite opinionated and wouldn't have let a farm hand marry his daughter."

"I still can't help wonder if there's more to the story."

"There probably is – it's Italy – there's always a back story." He winked.

"I'm going to meet Zeno on Friday to continue our discussion."

"Sounds like a great idea. He seems like a nice guy. I've always been fond of my cousin Carlo – and he seems to take care of his staff. If he's still working there, he's a good person."

Patrick dropped Paolo off in town and continued up the hill to his cottage. He went inside, poured some wine, cut a few pieces of cheese and prosciutto, and settled into the comfortable chair in the living area and pulled out the picture of Roberto and Stefano. "Amazing!" he murmured. "After all these years, this photo has brought me back to this place and to these people. It's almost as if the photo had a spell on it."

As he glanced at the two men arm and arm, he couldn't help but conjure up the image of Zeno. He had the same lanky body, the same alluring wispy dark eyes, and a similar smile – affable and playful. He sensed his own grandfather, Roberto, had a role to play in his returning to Cava dei Lupi, but he wondered if Stefano was at work, too, orchestrating a reunion that might heal the ruptured affections so many years ago. But even more interesting, Patrick thought to himself, were the parallels between Stefano and Pepe. Both were orphans brought by the head of the family to the vineyard to learn the business. He wondered what more he might uncover. He placed the photo on the table, went into the bedroom and undressed, sliding under the covers, and letting the thick down blanket and pillows surround him in a warm embrace.

6

Chapter Six

Two days later, Patrick rose, showered, and made a quick cup of espresso on the stove and sliced some peaches and cheese. He slipped on a pair of turquoise swim trunks, a long-sleeve gray tee-shirt, and flip-flops. He packed a change of clothes in a small bag and headed out the door.

As he drove the coastal route, he asked himself if he had made a mistake in agreeing to meet Zeno. Aside from finding out a few more details about Stefano and Roberto, he worried that an entire day together would be laborious, as he and Zeno had little in common. Maybe he should have agreed to a coffee and then driven to Pompeii or to one of the museums in Naples.

He pulled up to the garage. Pino recognized him and waved him into a space – just barely wide enough for him to inch the door open and squeeze gingerly between several cars. He began the lengthy trek to the bottom of town, his legs shaking as they had done a few days earlier.

Zeno was leaning against the wall at the entrance of the restaurant. When Patrick approached, he exclaimed enthusiastically, "*Ciao Patrizio!*"

"*Ciao Zeno*," Patrick replied, giving him a casual embrace and a kiss on one cheek.

Zeno was wearing a tight-fitting short black swimsuit and a gray linen long-sleeve shirt, open in the front. It was difficult for Patrick to avoid stealing a protracted look through the folds of the translucent fabric at his lean and beautiful chest, lightly covered in dark hair. He had on a pair of dark sunglasses and a Yankees baseball cap.

"So, you're an enemy?" Patrick said pointedly.

"What do you mean?" Zeno asked in alarm.

Patrick pointed to the baseball cap.

"Oh, *scusi.* I forgot you are from Boston."

"I'll let it slide for now."

"Follow me," Zeno waved him forward playfully. They walked down the steps to the beach, and Zeno pointed out their chairs in the third row. "It's better not to be in the front row. This way we can watch people as well as have a nice view of the water."

"Looks perfect to me." Patrick took one of the chairs and slid his bag under the seat. He adjusted the back, opened the umbrella, and took a seat.

Zeno took off his shirt and draped it on the back of the chair. He left the umbrella closed and laid down with the sun shining directly on him. "I don't get to the beach too often in the summer. I want to get a little sun."

"I have to be careful. With my Italian heritage I tan, but if I stay out too long, the Irish side of me burns."

"So, your mother was Irish?"

"Yes, from a long line of immigrants."

"We see them here – although most go to Ischia. They are usually bright red from the sun."

Patrick gave a forced smile, thinking the conversation was off to an awkward start – a few pleasantries and observations – but nothing of substance. He had enjoyed speaking with Zeno on Wednesday but wasn't sure what more they would have to say to each other.

He glanced nervously up and down the beach. The chairs were filling, and people strolled to the edge of the water to let the waves wash over their feet. The dark volcanic sand was coarse, and closer to the edge, gravely. Boats passed back and forth on the horizon. Fast ferries pulled up to the main pier to pick up passengers going to Amalfi, Sorrento, and Capri. Outboard motorboats whisked tourists off to secret coves. Yachts were moored or lumbering along at a leisurely pace. And since it was Friday, a fleet of colorful wooden boats were making their way out to deeper water to fish. Servers passed by from time to time, bringing espresso, juice, and cocktails to guests.

Patrick tried to get more of a conversation started and said, "So, I am amazed that you have the same photo of Roberto and Stefano that I found a week ago."

"Yes, and even more interesting that you recognized me."

"I recognized the eyes – very alluring."

Zeno blushed. Patrick feared he had crossed a line. Zeno remained silent. Patrick broke the silence, "Who do you think took the photo?"

"No idea. I have wondered that myself," Zeno stated.

"And what's interesting is that at least two copies were made, and our grandfathers kept them over the years."

Zeno nodded.

"So, I can't believe our grandfathers were friends. Do you know any more about their story, their relationship?"

"Only what I shared yesterday – that Stefano was fired because he had shown interest in Roberto's sister and that Roberto stood up for him."

"Roberto and Stefano look like they were very close."

Zeno looked off into the distance. He then turned toward Patrick. "Do you think there was something more?"

Patrick was startled that Zeno had voiced his own suspicions. He timidly replied, "My first reaction was that they seemed very affectionate, close, intimate."

Zeno nodded.

"It was a different time," Patrick noted.

"Times have changed little," Zeno added, continuing to be vague, ambiguous.

"How do you mean?" Patrick pressed Zeno.

Zeno grinned as if embarrassed. Instead of answering the question, he posed another, "*Sei con qualcuno* – are you with someone?"

The blunt question surprised Patrick. He hesitated, looked off in the distance, and then timidly said, "*Ero, ma non ora* – I was, but not now."

"What's her name?"

Patrick hesitated, swallowed, and then said, "Girard."

"*Un uomo*?"

Patrick nodded, "Yes, a man."

"I knew it!" Zeno said triumphantly. "You're gay!"

"How did you know?"

"I can always tell. Servers are experts at reading people. When I serve a table, I look at the eyes. The women are always looking intensely, but when a man stares, I know. Even if he has a ring and his girlfriend or wife is hanging on him, I know. He knows. I caught you looking the other day."

"I was just looking because you looked like Stefano."

"Yeah – sure. And later, on the beach?"

"Well, maybe."

"Do you have pictures of your boyfriend?"

Patrick pulled out his phone and pulled up a picture of Girard. "*Eccolo*. But he was more than a boyfriend, he was my husband."

"Oh," he said in surprise, then continued, "He's handsome – congratulations."

"*Beh!*" Patrick said in typical Italian – an expression that means something like 'well what good is that?' "*È complicato; è finito* – it's complicated; it's ended."

"You know more Italian than you let on."

"It's always good to feign ignorance."

"But – we know!" Zeno said with irony.

"And you?" Patrick pressed with some excitement, Zeno practically admitting he was family.

"I'm engaged – to a woman. It's part of the tradition here. You do the same work as your father, and they pick out a bride for you. It's all very well planned but suffocating!"

"So, how's that working out for you?"

"*È un casino* – it's a mess."

"Is she pretty?"

"She's gorgeous – *una belleza* – but she doesn't have a *cazzo*."

Patrick knew enough Italian to catch the notion – she's missing a dick. He realized Zeno had just come out to him.

"You want to go swimming?"

Zeno stood up abruptly, playfully grabbed Patrick's tee-shirt and pulled it off. "*Andiamo*."

Zeno ran with Patrick in tow to the edge of the water. It was clear, deep, and blue. Large swells crashed on the shore. Zeno dove in, bobbing up a few meters beyond the waves. Patrick walked in, ducked under a wave, and then swam toward Zeno.

The water felt soothing – cool enough to be refreshing but not frigid like New England. It felt like silk on his skin, brine mixing with the oils on his body. Zeno swam up toward him, smiling playfully. "You like to swim?"

"Yes – but we never have water like this. It's incredible."

"Look at the city," Zeno pointed up behind them at the terraced houses of Positano – a curtain of pastel-colored villas carved out of the semi-circular bend in the mountain.

"It's amazing," Patrick affirmed, gazing at the towering town before him. The steepness of the mountainside and the precarious nature of the buildings carved into the rock were majestic and ominous – beauty mixed with danger.

Zeno and Patrick were both treading water - the bottom several meters below. Zeno reached for Patrick's shoulder – a gesture that could have been interpreted as 'I need someone to rest on' or 'I want to touch you.'

Patrick played with the ambiguity, reaching for Zeno's arm.

There was a protracted silence – then Zeno dove deep, picking up a shell from the sand below and gave it to Patrick as he surfaced.

"*Grazie*," Patrick said, smiling.

They remained in the water, treading, smiling. Patrick broke the silence, "How is it being gay here?"

Zeno paused, looked off into the distance, and then turned back toward Patrick. "In one sense, it's easy. No one cares who you fuck. You can play around with men or women – it makes no difference."

"But?"

"But if you love another man, that's a problem."

"I've heard that before," Patrick affirmed.

"Italians are tolerant, but not progressive. In America, you can marry another man. Here it is still against the law."

"Do you have a boyfriend?" Patrick asked.

"I did, but he ended up marrying a woman from a nearby town. *Che cazzo*."

"Do you go out?"

"From time to time a tourist catches my eye, waits for me after dinner, and we go drinking or dancing, but it never leads to anything."

"And your parents?"

"They are supportive, loving, accepting, but they don't know about me. I always think it was Stefano who taught them to make sure people felt like they belonged – that they were loved – no matter their status."

"Roberto was the same with us. I'm sure he would have accepted me had he lived longer."

"*Vuoi un caffè*?" Zeno offered Patrick a coffee.

"That would be nice." They swam to the shore, walked to their chairs, dried themselves with their towels and then Zeno nodded to one of the servers – "*Due caffè, per favore.*"

The server nodded, and a few minutes later, brought two espressos.

Zeno leaned back in the chair, salt crystals forming on his taut skin. Patrick glanced at his swimsuit and felt himself stir as he saw the contours of Zeno's penis, firm and full.

"Why did you break up with your husband?" Zeno began, leaning over with an interrogatory face.

"You want the short or the long answer?"

"Long!" Zeno said.

"My parents didn't come to the wedding. They are very conservative. So, after that, Girard and I didn't go to their house."

"How horrible."

"Yes, and when my father got sick, I couldn't not go. Girard was angry with me, but I'm an only son – what was I going to do?"

"You did right to take care of him."

Patrick smiled, acknowledging Zeno's warmth and thoughtfulness.

"But after my parents died, Girard was distant. Then I found out he was having an affair."

"*Cazzo!*"

"Hmm, hmm," Patrick sighed. "But it is for the best. I think we wanted different things. Family and traditions are important to me but weren't to Girard."

Zeno looked pensive. "He must be English!"

Patrick laughed. "Canadian, French Canadian. I think the English must have messed with his genes at some point.

Zeno chuckled. "For us, family is everything. – as I said before, it can be suffocating – but it's comforting and what makes life worth living."

"I agree." Patrick looked off in the distance, cognizant of how far apart he and Girard had been about what mattered.

"*Sei contento*? Are you happy?" Zeno asked.

"Not entirely."

"That's too bad. Sorry."

"I miss my parents. I miss my grandparents. I miss having a family. Girard doesn't understand that. He kept telling me I had to move on."

"Maybe that's what you have to do," Zeno said tenderly. "Move on."

Patrick realized Zeno had made a profound observation – that Girard had said move on – but what did that really mean – move on from what and toward what? Maybe Zeno was more insightful than he let on – not just a playful flirt. Patrick looked over at Zeno and nodded. Zeno smiled contently, proud of himself.

They sat in the sun and continued to share stories of their families, of their lives, and of awkward boyfriends and girlfriends they'd had in the past. At noon, Zeno suggested they get a little lunch – before the crowd formed later.

They put on shirts and walked up to the terrace. Carlo took good care of them both, keeping their glasses full of wine and bringing them a delicious sea bass that had been grilled whole and served with local vegetables and salad.

"You get the royal treatment here." Patrick noted.

"Not usually. This is very unusual. Servers usually get leftovers. Carlo's being unusually nice – maybe it's taking care of our American cousin."

"Hm," Patrick mumbled. "I'm not sure. Maybe he's trying to set us up."

Zeno looked at Carlo and nodded, as if he recognized something for the first time.

They finished their meal, had a coffee, and then Zeno asked, "You ready for a ride in the boat?"

"That would be fantastic. Where's the boat? Do we need to drive? I have my car."

"I'll call for it."

"Call?"

"Yes. It's anchored offshore. I just need someone to get it and bring it to the pier. We can walk there."

Zeno made a call on his cell phone, and they strolled along the boardwalk toward the pier. A few minutes later, someone began waving to Zeno – a weathered fisherman with a big smile.

"*Zeno – tutto è pronto.*"

"Thanks, Pietro. *Questo è un'amico dall'America – cugino di Paolo e Laura.*"

"*Piacere,*" he said, extending his hand warmly.

Pietro held the boat as Zeno jumped in and then reached his hand up for Patrick's, who then stepped on board. It was a 25-foot outboard motorboat with a small cabin under the bow and a large canvas awning over the main deck. Zeno turned the key. The motor cranked to a start and the propeller sent gurgling sounds into the water, changing pitch as the waves lifted and lowered the boat against the pier. Zeno put the boat in reverse, and they pulled away.

"Where do you want to go?" Zeno inquired loudly over the sound of the motor.

"Wherever you want to take me."

Zeno winked and pushed the lever, sending the boat forward at a fast clip, bouncing in choppy water. They hugged the coast north of Positano – passing a cliff walk, ruins of an old castle, a smaller beach, and then just rugged mountains plunging into the water. The town of Positano receded in the background, the afternoon light beaming off the pastel buildings.

They passed a couple of small islands and could see Capri looming over the hazy horizon. Zeno stood proudly at the helm, spray hitting his face. Patrick ducked behind the windowpane, looking over Zeno's shoulder at the terraced vineyards, lemon groves, and villas clinging to the mountainsides.

It was difficult to talk – the sound of the waves and motor drowning out everything. Patrick glanced at Zeno, smiling approvingly. Zeno seemed content. Zeno slowed the motor and pointed to a small cove. "We can go over there and anchor for a while."

"*Va bene*," Patrick said and nodded.

"Can you go up on the bow and throw the anchor into the water when I give the signal?"

"Certainly." Patrick climbed onto the bow, grabbed the anchor and, as the boat approached the shore, threw it into the water when Zeno nodded. The anchor caught the dense sand on the bottom, and the boat snagged to a stop, hovering over a deep blue inlet of water. The water was calm, protected from the waves by several large rocks that had fallen into the sea many years before.

Zeno stripped off his suit and leaped into the water. He waved Patrick on. "*Dai!*"

Patrick hesitatingly stripped off his suit and plunged in as well, surfacing near Zeno. Patrick looked down to the bottom, several meters deep, the water crystal clear. Zeno swam up toward him. "It's spectacular, isn't it?"

Patrick nodded, treading water, trying to catch a clear glimpse of Zeno's front. He swam away, his light butt bobbing near the surface before he dove. Patrick followed him, swimming under water with his eyes open, the turquoise water and light forming an ethereal display of wavy lines on the rocky bottom. Zeno swam further toward shore, resting on a ledge jutting out in the cove, a few centimeters under the surface of the water. Patrick followed, pulling himself onto the ledge.

They both leaned back on their arms, their torsos dripping with water and their crotches and legs just under the surface. Zeno looked inquisitively toward Patrick – as if to say – *è allora* – 'and what's next?'

Patrick returned the same look, hesitant but curious, reticent but eager. He then leaned toward Zeno and gave him a kiss on the mouth. Zeno reached his hand behind Patrick's head and pulled him closer, opening his mouth to take in Patrick's – tasting the salty contours of his lips.

Zeno ran his hand down Patrick's chest, squeezing his pecs. "*Tu sei bello*."

Patrick felt himself become aroused. He ran his hand down Zeno's side, along his hip and over his legs, brushing the top of Zeno's erection. "Sexy eyes," Patrick whispered, rubbing his fingers over Zeno's dark brown eyes.

"*Oooh*!" Zeno replied in a typical Italian expression.

They kissed again, deeply. They leaned against each other, feeling each other's hardness and the soft water lapping about them. Abruptly, Zeno pushed off into the water, Patrick followed, the boat bobbing in front of them, concealing them from passing boats. Zeno swam up to Patrick and stretched his legs around Patrick, pushing his hardness up against Patrick. Patrick ran his hand under Zeno's buttocks, brushing his own erection between them.

Zeno leaned his head back, "*Madonna*," he cried.

He nuzzled his nose into Patrick's neck, brushing it with his lips. Patrick turned, and they kissed deeply.

Both breathing heavily, they swam back to the ledge and pulled themselves up. Zeno laid on his side, half his torso under water, the rest above, gleaming in the sun. "*Che sorpresa*," he began.

"Yes, quite a surprise," Patrick replied, brushing his hand over Zeno's shoulder and down his hip, sliding his hands up between his legs.

"*Ma fermi*," Zeno exclaimed, "*Mi farai venire*."

Patrick knew enough Italian to know Zeno was worried about coming. He wasn't sure why that was a problem, but pulled back, sitting up on the ledge and looking out nonchalantly over the water.

Zeno sat up, too. His erection bobbing in the water.

Patrick looked at his crotch and said, "*Quanto sei bello*."

Zeno seemed upset.

"Did I say something wrong?" Patrick inquired.

"*No, veramente no*." Zeno nodded.

"What then?"

Zeno paused, "I feel like I've known you before – that there is a connection. *Sono consumato di desiderio – voglio scoparti*."

Patrick understood Zeno's desire to make love to him. He felt it too.

"But it has to be more than a quick *scopata*."

"Wow!" was all Patrick could get out. He didn't disagree with Zeno. He sensed there was more, something to honor, to treasure, to take slowly – but he wanted to reach over and consume this delicious man before him, and it took every ounce of self-restraint to honor Zeno's reticence.

Patrick dove into the water, his arousal dissipating as he swam further away from the ledge and toward the boat. He climbed aboard, toweled himself dry, and slipped on his trunks.

Zeno swam up behind him, climbed aboard and reached for Patrick's towel, breathing in traces of Patrick's smell and rubbing the soft cotton fabric over his chest, down his abdomen and between his legs. He tossed it back to Patrick and slipped on his own trunks.

Patrick sat on the long bench at the back of the boat, and Zeno took a seat in the front. He reached into a compartment and pulled out a cold bottle of white wine and some grapes. He held the bottle up as if to ask if Patrick wanted something, and Patrick nodded yes. Zeno reached into another compartment and pulled out two glasses, unscrewed the top of the bottle, and poured them each a glass.

"*Salute*!" they said in unison.

Patrick swiveled to the side and extended his legs along the bench. He leaned his head back and let the sun warm his face.

"You know these coastlines used to be filled with pirates in the old days," Zeno broke the silence, glancing over at the mountainous ridges plunging into the water nearby.

"Hm," Patrick murmured.

"As kids, we used to play pirates when our parents took us on boat rides and stopped in coves like this."

"It's funny. We played cowboys and Indians and you played pirates," Patrick noted. Then he asked, "Who did the pirates chase?"

"Merchants," Zeno responded without emotion.

"Pirates and merchants don't sound as enchanting as cowboys and Indians."

"I guess not," Zeno mused, "although we had vivid imaginations about what the pirates did to the merchants."

"Like what," Patrick inquired daringly.

"They climbed on their boats, tied them up, and made them agree to serve them."

"This is getting more interesting," Patrick said with a gleam in his eye. "I bet you were quite the pirate!"

Zeno nodded.

"And what if the merchants won? What did they do to the pirates?" Patrick inquired further.

"They won if they kept the pirates out of their boats. The pirates had to swim back to shore."

"I suppose you never lost."

"Never."

Zeno walked toward the bench at the back of the boat, lifted Patrick's legs, and put them on his thighs as he took a seat, taking a long sip of wine. Then he said, "This is nice!"

"I agree," Patrick said, reaching his hand over to touch Zeno's.

"Should we head back?" Zeno asked timidly.

Patrick glanced at the clock on the console near the steering wheel. "Probably so."

Zeno stood up and leaned down to give Patrick a warm kiss. He stood up, approached the controls, and cranked on the motor. He instructed Patrick to pull up the anchor, keeping his gaze on Patrick's rear end as he bent over.

Zeno texted Pietro who, once they arrived in Positano, was waiting on the pier for them. He caught their line and wrapped it around the iron cleats as Zeno and Patrick stepped off.

"*Grazie, Pietro.*"

Pietro nodded, let loose the line, jumped on board, and took off.

"Well," Zeno began. "Do you have time for dinner?"

Patrick looked sad and replied, "I have to leave early for the airport tomorrow. I need to get back to see Paolo and Alberto and pack."

"But you can do that later."

"I have to say goodbye to my cousins."

"I understand, but I don't want this to end," Zeno implored.

"Me either."

"Then stay."

"I can't. I have to go back – to work, to Boston."

"*Resti!*" Zeno repeated, folding his hands in front of him in supplication.

"*Non posso.*"

"Yes, you can."

"I promise I will come back." Patrick added.

"*Quando*?"

"I don't know – soon."

A tear streaked down Zeno's face. Patrick traced his finger over it. He looked up and realized people were watching. "*Andiamo*," he said, dragging Zeno off toward the restaurant.

They saw Carlo as they approached. He looked concerned, noticing how somber they looked. He offered them a drink. "*Volete qualcosa da bere*?"

Patrick looked at his watch and nodded yes. Zeno smiled. They sat at a small table, and Carlo brought them each an Aperol spritzer.

"*Chin chin*," Zeno proffered, raising his glass to Patrick's.

"*Salute*," he replied.

They looked at each other pensively, neither knowing what to say next.

Patrick began, "Thank you for everything. I feel like I accomplished what I came for – to make sense of Roberto and Stefano."

"But did you?"

"What do you mean," Patrick pressed.

"Well, you found out the story – who Stefano was and the circumstances that led to Roberto's departure, but is that all you came for?"

"I still don't know what you mean?" Patrick said with his forehead creased.

"There's a legend in Italy that when someone dies, they see their loved ones just before they pass over. We often hear the dying mention names of those who have passed, they talk to them, they smile in recognition."

"My parents did that in their last days."

"*Appunto*!"

"So – what does that mean?"

"I have a feeling someone guided you here after your parents' deaths – through the photo of Roberto and Stefano."

Patrick wasn't a particularly spiritual or metaphysical person, even though both his grandparents – on both sides – were. All he could do in response to Zeno's statement was moan, "Hm."

"You're here to rectify something."

"You mean Giancarlo's refusal to let Stefano marry Anna?"

"Maybe – or maybe something else."

"Now I don't know what you're talking about," Patrick said emphatically. "You're speaking riddles."

"Let's just say I think there's more to the story."

"I'm not so sure. I wish there were something more – I wish Roberto and Stefano had been in love, that it was impossible in the 1950s, and that Roberto had to leave. Story ended."

"Do you really think that is the case?" Zeno looked intensely into Patrick's eyes.

Patrick looked off in the distance, took a sip of his drink and then turned to Zeno. "Yes. I think that's it."

Zeno leaned back in his chair in exasperation, throwing up his hands, "You're impossible."

"What do you mean?"

"I thought you were a romantic."

"I am. I think Roberto and Stefano were in love."

"But in Italy, unrequited love isn't love unless it is tragic. There's nothing tragic in that story."

"Of course, it's tragic. They loved each other and couldn't consume it given the prejudices."

"Why didn't Stefano leave with Roberto? Why did he stay and get married?"

"I don't know – custom?"

"There's something else there, I feel it."

Patrick looked at his watch. "I'm sorry. I have to go."

Zeno frowned.

"Don't look so sad. I'll come back soon."

"If you don't, I'm going to hunt you down in Boston."

"Do you promise?"

Zeno smiled finally, and Patrick gave him a warm hug and kiss on the cheeks.

"Can walk you to your car?" Zeno asked as Patrick walked up the steps into town.

"*Sì, certo.*"

Zeno walked Patrick up the hill, paid the attendant a tip for taking care of the car, and gave Patrick an enthusiastic embrace and kiss. "Remember – I'll hunt you down."

"I'm counting on it." Patrick said with a twinkle in his eye.

He climbed inside the car, rolled down the window, gave Zeno another kiss, and then drove off toward Praiano and Cava dei Lupi.

7

Chapter Seven

Patrick rose early, his suitcases packed at the foot of his bed. He made a cup of espresso, ate the last piece of fruit in the fridge, and looked around the cottage, making sure it was all in order. He had said his goodbyes to Paolo, Laura, Alberto, and Maria the night before. He had stopped at Nunzia's en route back from Positano in the late afternoon.

As he stepped outside to load the car, Pepe sauntered up the road, his hair tousled and shorts wrinkled, having just gotten out of bed. He smiled at Patrick, cautiously, almost apologetically.

"We will miss you, Patrizio. Hope you come back soon," he said, his hands nervously plunged into his front pockets.

Patrick walked up to him, held his shoulders in his hands, and gave him a kiss on the lips. Pepe closed his eyes, relishing Patrick's affection.

"I'll never understand you," Patrick said to Pepe, who winked at him and stood quietly by as Patrick loaded the car.

Patrick took another look around, the deep blue sea off in the distance, the rows of vines lining the hillside before him, the majestic oak trees along the gravel road, and the deep green vegetation clinging to the rocky ridges surrounding the vineyard. He pulled the wooden door of the cottage closed and made sure it was secure.

He got into the car, turned on the ignition, and headed down the hill, waving at Pepe as he pulled away. He felt a flutter of apprehension, dread at leaving a world that he had grown to appreciate, treasure, and love. He drove through Cava dei Lupi, only a few people wandering about in search of a coffee at the café.

At such an early hour, the coastal road was practically empty, Patrick sailing around the curves with ease, looking out over the sea. He passed through Positano, wondering where Zeno lived, what he was doing, what he might be thinking. He tried to convince himself that it had been the right thing to leave the afternoon before, to say his goodbyes to his cousins instead of a romantic dinner. He had a schedule to keep, obligations to attend to, and a life in Boston. But deep down he could feel his body telling him he was making a terrible mistake, his stomach tightening, his pulse racing, and his legs growing weak – almost as if he was going to faint.

He gripped the wheel tightly and kept driving forward. Just beyond Positano, he stopped at a station for gas. As he stepped out of the air-conditioned car, the aromas of the sea air, the lemon trees, and the soil hit him. They had become familiar and comforting, and he felt anxious thinking about his departure. He got back into the car and kept driving, passing a stretch of the coast filled with small coves, one of them undoubtedly where he and Zeno had spent the afternoon before. He smiled.

He eventually exited the coastal route and took the highway along Mt. Vesuvius and toward the Naples airport. At that point, the logistics of airline travel kicked in. He pulled into the car rental return, delivered his keys, and got a receipt for the two weeks. He walked across the skywalk to the terminal and looked for the check-in counter.

As he stood in the terminal full of frenetic activity, people hastily pulling bags, going through security, hugging loved ones, or grabbing a last coffee or newspaper before heading to their gate, he felt his body halt in protest. It was reflexive rather than thoughtful – as if his body began to act on its own. He felt immobilized, almost out-of-body. He didn't know what to do. He put one foot forward, then another. He walked to the first open check-in agent. An attractive young lady asked for his passport, and he pulled it out of his vest pocket. Almost as if under a spell, he heard the words come out of his mouth, "How much would it cost to change my ticket?"

"Let me check for you," she replied. "When do you want to re-book?"

"In about two weeks," he said mechanically.

"It doesn't look too bad – just a 300 euro change fee."

Patrick handed her his credit card. She processed the change and handed him a printout of his new itinerary. Patrick turned around and rolled his bags toward the car rental, where the man who had helped him two weeks ago stood in the same place. Without recognizing him, he said, "Can I help you, sir?"

"I just returned a car, but I need to keep it longer."

The agent nodded, as if he remembered who Patrick was, checked the computer, identified his return, and processed a continuation of the rental. "That will be a few minutes for us to reposition it – but it should be ready shortly."

"*Grazie.*"

Patrick walked over to a café and ordered a double espresso. After he finished, he retrieved the car keys, loaded his bags, and sped out of the garage back onto the highway.

A text came in from Nunzia on the car phone display: "Patrick, have you left yet?"

He spoke into the car system, "Send text to Nunzia - no, still here."

Nunzia replied: "After you were here last night, I had an epiphany. I'd like to share some information with you. Can you call?"

Patrick pushed a button and spoke into his phone: "Call Nunzia."

The phone dialed and, a few moments later, he heard, "*Pronto, Nunzia.*"

"Nunzia, this is Patrick."

"Patrick, I'm so glad you called." She paused and then continued, "It sounds like you are in the car – did you get delayed?"

"No, I postponed my flight. I'm heading back to the coast."

"Do you need a place to stay? We have some free rooms."

"Actually, that would be quite nice."

"Well, if that's the case, why don't we talk when you get here."

"Perfect. I should be there in an hour."

Patrick continued on the highway until it dumped him into the coastal route, following the same itinerary he had made two weeks before and earlier that morning. Hearing Nunzia's voice helped dissipate the adrenaline in his blood. He calmed down and thought about what he was doing.

The first image that came to him was that of Zeno, sitting on the ledge in the cove, his naked body glistening in the afternoon sun. He thought of Pepe, nervously standing beside the car earlier that morning, almost begging to be held, embraced, kissed. He wondered if he was just horny, his body coming alive after the rough summer of his parents' deaths and his breakup with Girard. Maybe this was nothing more than a need to reclaim his body and emotions and savor the earthy pleasures of the Italian coast. Two weeks had been too short. He needed more time.

The reality of what he had done hit him. "Oh my God," he murmured to himself. "Did I really just decide to blow everything off – my job, home, and life in Boston?" A small parking area on the side of the road appeared in the near distance, and Patrick pulled into it, leaving the car in idle. He looked out over the horizon, the rugged shoreline, the little villages, and the craggy, mountainous peaks. "Maybe I need to turn around, head home, face the practicalities of my life," he said to himself, his hands gripping the steering wheel, ready to make a quick U-turn.

He took a couple of deep breaths and decided to continue, pulling back onto the road and following the route to Praiano. He pulled up to the front of the Belvedere and took one of the parking spots by the front door. Nunzia spotted him from inside and came out to the door, waving.

"*Patrizio, come mai*? What happened?"

"It's a long story – but I decided to extend my stay. There's unfinished business here."

"I agree. I have something to share. Come inside. Why don't you bring your bags? We'll put them in your room."

Patrick pulled a couple of bags out of the back of the car and rolled them to the front door. "*Camera tre*," Nunzia instructed a worker to take the bags to Patrick's room. "*Vuoi un caffè*?"

"Yes, that would be nice."

They sat at a small table on the terrace. The sun filtered through some fronds of the palm tree. Nunzia seemed excited and eager to share something. She began, "Well, Patrick, after you left last night, I had some more thoughts."

"I'm all ears."

"It makes sense that Roberto was angry with his father for not letting Stefano marry Anna. He and Stefano must have been close friends – almost brothers - and he felt it was an injustice to treat an orphan as if he had less value or status."

Patrick nodded.

"What continued to trouble me was the ancestry DNA information. There are the two women nearby I mentioned a few days ago who show up as being closely related to me – very close. They are the daughters of a Nicola and Francesco, Nicola being the daughter of a Rita Marcello and Stefano Voluto. As I mentioned, I can trace Rita's tree, but not Stefano's. Until yesterday, it seemed a dead end but, when you confirmed that Zeno was the son of Giovanni who was the son of Stefano – our Stefano – the pieces fell into place. But the troubling thing is that the only way these two women could match my DNA so closely is if Stefano shared my DNA, too."

"Oh," Patrick reacted, taking a long sip of his coffee as he realized the implication of what Nunzia had just shared. "Wow!" he continued. "That would mean Stefano is related to the Beneventos."

"Exactly. And, if I were to bet, I would guess he was an illegitimate son of Giancarlo senior who brought him to the farm as a teenager but never expected he would fall in love with his daughter who was, in fact, Stefano's stepsister," Nunzia explained, breathing excitedly.

"So that would explain why, despite welcoming an orphan to take such a prominent role on the farm, he prohibited a marriage between him and his daughter – a matter of incest."

"*Appunto!*"

"And he could never disclose the real reason for his objection, so he relied on a lame excuse – that he was an orphan, had no title or inheritance, and therefore not a suitable husband for the daughter of Giancarlo Benevento," Patrick concluded.

"That would appear to be the actual story," Nunzia concluded, sighing.

"Poor Roberto, always thinking his father had been prejudiced and hard hearted. That's why he left for America, in protest and to escape pointless traditions."

"It must have been so hard for him to leave his family and his close friend."

"I'm beginning to imagine it." Patrick said emotionally, thinking about the attachments he had formed already.

Nunzia looked up at Patrick. "So, what are you going to do? Why did you come back?"

Patrick had not disclosed to her what had transpired between him and Zeno, only that he had recognized him and had learned of the connections. Now it was also apparent that Zeno was his cousin – a distant one – but related, nonetheless. Did that change anything? Was there some moral reason that distant cousins needed to avoid intimacy?

"I'm not sure. There are some things I need to sort out."

Nunzia nodded as if she already had an inkling of what Patrick faced. "You can stay here as long as you need. The tourist season is winding down, so we have room."

"That's very generous of you. I appreciate it."

"Do you want lunch?"

"Thank you, but I think I need to visit Positano."

Nunzia smiled and nodded. She got up, went inside the office, and retrieved a key. "Here's a key to your room – come and go as you like."

"*Grazie*."

Patrick went into his room and changed, switching the clothes he had been wearing for the flight with some shorts, a pullover, and some sneakers. He put on a pair of dark glasses and put on a Red Sox baseball cap. He stepped outside, jumped into the car, and made his way to Positano. The ride was becoming more familiar, every curve and irregularity etched in his memory.

As he approached Positano, tourists were already gathering in front of ceramic shops to admire large colorful plates hung on the outside walls. Some tourists were walking toward the beach, dressed in bathing suits, hats, and carrying straw bags filled with towels and snacks.

He arrived at the restaurant parking area, gave his key to Pino, and began walking down to the lower part of the village. Carlo stood at the entryway of the restaurant and noticed him immediately. He smiled. "Patrizio – I thought you were flying back today."

"I was – but change of plans. By any chance is Zeno here?"

"It's his day off. I can call him for you."

"That would be great. Thanks."

Carlo dialed a number. It rang but went straight into voicemail. "*Zeno, è Carlo – mi chiami quando puoi.*"

Carlo looked up. "He's not answering. I left a message for him to call me as soon as he could. Do you want to have lunch?"

Patrick looked at his watch. "I guess so. It's a little early, but I don't have anything else to do. If you hear from Zeno, let him know I am here."

Carlo took him to a nice table near the beach. Patrick looked out over the sand and to the water's edge, where large swells were crashing on the shore. A server approached the table – Carlo standing nearby.

"Patrizio – this is Giovanni, Zeno's father. He's working today. He can take care of you."

The resemblance to Stefano was even more striking than Zeno – a broad chest, lean body, and dark wispy eyes. He was older but in good shape and wore his uniform nicely, handsomely.

"*Grazie. Sono il cugino di Paolo e un amico di Zeno,*" Patrick introduced himself.

"*Piacere,*" Giovanni replied, looking suspiciously at Patrick.

He took his order and then retreated to the kitchen. Patrick opened his phone to check messages. There was another from Girard: "Looking forward to talking when you get in."

Patrick replied to the text: "Taking a little more time here in Italy. Will let you know when I'm back."

There were other texts from friends wanting to see photos and emails from work. He replied to them all and then settled back in his chair, looking out over the water.

Giovanni brought back some wine, bread, and salad. Patrick smiled, but Giovanni only nodded back.

Carlo passed by the table, checking in, "*Tutto va bene*?"

"Yes, thank you."

Carlo wasn't convinced. He looked worried, restless. "I tried Zeno again. No answer. Here's his number if you want to text," he said encouragingly.

Carlo retreated to the front of the restaurant and Patrick ate his salad and sip some of the cold white wine. It felt refreshing in the morning heat. The sea was calm and the air still.

Patrick punched in Zeno's number on his phone and then texted him: "*Dove sei*?" Where are you?

Giovanni brought the rest of Patrick's lunch, a nice plate of spaghetti and clams. The clams were large and tasty, and the pasta had a perfect blend of garlic, oil, and lemon. The terrace of the restaurant filled with people coming off the beach. There were fewer Italians and more Germans and English.

Patrick leaned back in his chair and breathed in the aromas of the salty sea air, the toasty earthiness of the sand, the scent of fresh herbs on pasta, and the fragrances of suntan lotion and cologne on the guests seated nearby. One smell reminded him of Zeno's cologne the day before, and he felt his heart race as it passed under his nose. He looked down at his phone, but there was no response to his text.

He finished his lunch, paid the tab, and decided to take a walk on the beach. He stepped onto the make-shift wooden walkway laid out on the sand and headed toward the town pier. As he approached it, he noticed Zeno holding onto a rope connected to his boat. Pietro was assisting, and a beautiful woman was stepping onto the boat. She wore a yellow one-piece swimsuit that highlighted her tan skin and brown hair with blonde highlights. She looked like she could have been a model – with thin waist, firm curvy hips, and full round breasts. Zeno stepped in behind her, wearing just a swimsuit and cap. Pietro threw him the rope, and the woman put her arms around Zeno's shoulders. He backed the boat away from the pier and headed off to the north along the coastline. Zeno leaned toward the woman and gave her a prolonged kiss.

Patrick felt his heart skip a beat and his legs grow weak. "*Cazzo*!" he said out loud, several nearby people glancing at him, eyebrows raised. "What the fuck? I should have gotten on that plane. At least I would have been home in Boston."

He walked back toward the restaurant along the beach and began the long climb to the garage and his car. He turned on the ignition and put the car in gear and headed down the coast. As he got closer to Praiano, he considered heading up the mountain road and seeing if Pepe was around, but decided that would only make things more complicated. Instead, he drove along the coast toward Amalfi.

The drive was cathartic, shifting gears frequently as he navigated the winding road and snaked through crowded villages along the water. He drove around the Capo di Conca, a picturesque rocky cape surrounded by water, stopping at a small farmer's stand to buy some fruit and take in the views.

When he pulled into Amalfi, he found a parking garage, gave the attendant his keys, and walked toward the center of town. It was larger than Positano – an ancient settlement along the coast that had benefitted over the centuries from coastal trade. The central business district was extensive, a broad flat piece of land wedged between several inclined rocky hillsides and a deep harbor. There were countless shops, cafes, restaurants, and small hotels. The historic cathedral stood at the top of a steep staircase where tourists sat, taking in the sun.

It felt good to walk, to be alone with his thoughts, lost in the teeming crowd of tourists. Patrick felt a warm, dense rush of air brush past him. He looked over his shoulder and there was nobody near him. He pivoted. He felt the warm air again and looked up. Peering across the pavement and between shoppers passing in front of him, he noticed a small café. "Zeno's"

"I'll be fucked!" he said to himself. He slowly approached the café, past a few tables out front, and walked inside. It was a warm space – a large classic Italian bar with liquor bottles stacked along the back wall and an espresso machine and a glass display of pastries and sandwiches up front. A handsome young man welcomed him at the cash register and asked what he wanted.

"A glass of wine and a chocolate croissant," please.

The cashier smiled warmly, "10 Euros."

Patrick handed him a 10 Euro billed, took his *scontrino*, and went to the bar, handing the barista a 2-euro tip. "*Vino e un cornetto con ciocolatto.*"

"*Rosso o bianco,*" the barista asked.

"*Rosso.*"

The barista took a bottle of red wine out from under the counter and poured it into a glass. Patrick looked up and noticed "Benevento" on the bottle. "Oh my god," he said to himself. "Could you be any more direct?" He looked up as if speaking to a ghost or angel.

The barista looked alarmed.

"*Scusi*, It's nothing – just a *coincidenza.*"

The barista said emphatically, "*Non ci sono coincidenze* – there are no coincidences."

Patrick nodded. As skeptical as he was, he was beginning to admit that a bar named Zeno and a bottle of wine from the Benevento vineyard did seem like more than a coincidence – that someone was trying to say something to him. He felt the warm rush of air again.

The barista leaned over the sink and began washing glasses, looking up occasionally at Patrick and finally mumbled nonchalantly, "Where are you from?"

"That's a good question," he said to the barista.

"No philosophy – just a simple answer."

"I'm from Boston."

"But you look like you're from here. You have that middle Italian look."

"My grandfather is from nearby."

"I knew it – you even have a bit of the accent."

"I do?"

"Yes – it's in the way you connect the vowels and consonants – it's distinctive here."

"Hm," Patrick sighed.

"You look deep in thought."

"I am."

"Love?"

"How did you know?"

"What else do we think deeply about?"

"*Appunto*!" Patrick agreed.

"Is she beautiful?" the barista asked.

"Unfortunately, yes."

"What do you mean, unfortunately?"

"*È complicato – ma lei è inamorata con qualcuno che mi piace.*"

"Ahh," the barista replied. "You're in love with a man who is in love with a beautiful woman."

"*Sì.*"

"*È facile* – it's easy – the two of you get together when you want. No obligations, no problems – just good friends having a good time."

He thought of Roberto and Stefano – did they have the same arrangement – were they friends with benefits?

"I want more," Patrick admitted, sharing more than he thought he should with a barista. But – he was a stranger – why not?

"You're American. You always want clear definitions. In Italy, we're comfortable with *ambiguità.*"

"Maybe – but not me."

"*Mi dispiace,*" he said sorrowfully. "It's going to be a hard life, then."

"What about faithfulness?" he asked the barista.

He put down the glass he was washing, looked out over the room and then turned to Patrick saying, "I see you are a romantic. Your heart has been broken, and you are looking for someone who gets you, who will be tender with you."

Patrick nodded for him to continue, realizing the barista understood his dilemma.

"That's going to be a challenge. It has to be something more than attraction – there has to be a deeper connection, destiny – *il destino.*"

"What do you mean?" Patrick inquired; his forehead creased with intensity.

"There are lovers who are meant for each other, who meet in a way that is unexpected, almost impossible. This is the hand of destiny."

"Hm," Patrick murmured, thinking of the magic of the photo of Roberto and Stefano that had brought him and Zeno together. Yesterday he thought it was destiny, but today he was doubtful.

"You don't look convinced," the barista said.

"I thought destiny was involved, but today I'm not sure."

"If it is destiny, it will happen. It will happen no matter what you do. Just watch!" The barista grinned, picked up another glass and began wiping it.

Patrick nodded and said, "*Grazie.*"

"*Niente. Buona fortuna.*"

Patrick finished his glass of wine, shook hands with the barista, and stepped out into the shadowy afternoon air of the piazza. He walked back to the garage, retrieved his car, and drove back to Praiano. He felt the warm rush of air again and felt Roberto and Chiara sitting in the back seat – this time not pointing out landmarks but wagging their fingers at him.

"You're our grandson – and we want you to be happy – like us. There should be no ambiguity – no compromise."

"But what do I do?" he asked his imaginary passengers.

"*Senti il cuore* – what do you feel in your heart?"

Patrick paused, let go of the conflicting thoughts in his mind, and rested his attention and consciousness in his heart. He could feel it beating. He could feel its warmth. The word that kept coming to him – not from his head but from his heart - was Zeno.

Roberto and Chiara nodded from the back seat, smiling warmly.

Patrick felt a calm and peace in his chest, even though his head was tired. He pulled into the parking area of the Belvedere, walked into the pensione, and opened the door to his room. Nunzia had left some cookies for him. He sat down in the easy chair, slipped off his shoes, and checked email and messages.

Later, he brushed his teeth, slipped off his shorts and shirt, and slid under the cool covers. The pillows were soft, and he felt himself dozing off quickly. Suddenly, he heard a chime from his phone and the screen lit up with a message. He reached over to the table. It was from Zeno.

"Sorry I missed your message. Carlo said you were in Positano. Sorry I missed you."

Patrick texted back guardedly, "Me, too."

Zeno replied, "Can we talk?"

Patrick was unsure how to respond. Of course, he wanted to speak with Zeno, but he didn't want to sound too eager. "Sure. I have some things to do tomorrow – maybe later in the week?"

"Call me when you're free," Zeno replied.

Patrick sent back a quick, "OK."

He tried to fall back asleep, but his heart was racing and his mind full of thoughts. He got up and gobbled one of Nunzia's cookies. He felt the soft dough and hazelnuts settle in his stomach and, in a little while, fell asleep.

8

Chapter Eight

Patrick rose the next morning, put on a pair of shorts and a long-sleeve pullover, and strolled down to the terrace for breakfast. Nunzia was serving coffee.

"How are you?"

"*Male.*"

Nunzia frowned. "What's up?"

"Everything. *Sono molto confuso.*"

She smiled like a mother waiting for her son to share.

"I didn't tell you, but I am married. To a man. He's having an affair."

"Wow, that's a lot of information to drop on an old woman."

"You're not old – but yes, it's a lot of information. However, I think you were onto me."

Nunzia smiled sheepishly and said, "I don't know what you're talking about?"

"Oh, I think you do," Patrick said in reply.

"I kind of figured it out. There wasn't chemistry with Sylvia and others – but I saw you looking at the guys in the harbor."

"I thought I saw you notice," he said, chuckling.

"I don't miss a trick," she said proudly. "Were you worried about my reaction?"

"Yes – and Alberto's and Laura's, too."

"*Caro*, things are changing in Italy. We're more open-minded than you think, and we just want you to be happy, to find your path. You've come a long way to reclaim your place in our family, and we will embrace you as you are."

Patrick began to tear up, wiping his eyes with the back of his hand.

"I sense there's more to the story you just told me," she suggested.

Patrick nodded, "I'm in love."

"Ah, I see. Tell me more."

"Zeno."

She looked at him inquisitively.

"Zeno and I had a connection – at least I thought."

"*È gay*?" she inquired, creasing her forehead.

"I thought so – but then yesterday I saw him with a beautiful woman – presumably, his finance. *Peccato*."

"I can see that would be a problem."

"Italians are crazy."

"Yes – we are. You are." She grinned at him.

"I'm beginning to see that. I should just go home and settle back into my life."

"Is that what you want to do?"

"No. That's the problem."

"What do you want to do?"

"I don't know."

"Well, take your time. There's no rush. You're young and you're in Italy – have some fun, relax, enjoy the sunshine."

"Great idea," Patrick said, smiling warmly for the first time.

"You can hang here on the terrace, take a drive, go up to Cava dei Lupi and walk around – just enjoy the day."

Patrick nodded, finished his coffee, and headed back to the room. He took a shower and slipped on a pair of jeans and a light tee-shirt. He decided to drive up to the Benevento farm to see how the wine making was going. Alberto had promised to show him the fermentation process and all the steps it took to produce such a fine wine.

He headed up the mountain road and stopped briefly in Cava dei Lupi to let Paolo and Laura know he was still around. He parked the car and pushed his way through the string of beads in the doorway and, to his surprise, Pepe was sitting at a small table drinking a cup of coffee.

Pepe looked up and he let out a surprised but gleeful, "*Come mai*?" He looked over at Paolo, who looked at Patrick.

"Patrizio – what's up? We thought you had gone back to Boston," Paolo asked.

"I postponed the flight."

Pepe stood up and walked toward him, reaching his strong muscular arms around Patrick's back and giving him an enthusiastic hug and kisses on both cheeks. He leaned his head back slightly, looking intently into Patrick's eyes.

Patrick took a deep breath. He wanted to savor Pepe's body, smell, and warmth, but decided it would be more discreet to extract himself and give his cousin a warm embrace as well. "*Paolo, come stai*?"

"I'm good. Laura will be happy to see you. Do you need a place to stay – the cottage?"

"Nunzia offered me a room at the hotel. I'm good for now. I thought I would go up and see how the wine is made." He looked over at Pepe.

Paolo nodded toward Pepe. "I'm sure Pepe would be happy to take you up to the vineyard and show you the process. Alberto's there, too."

"That would be wonderful."

"*Vuoi un caffé*?"

"Sure, a double."

Patrick and Pepe both sat down while Paolo prepared the coffee. There was an awkward protracted silence as Pepe continued to look into Patrick's eyes.

Patrick felt his legs grow weak sitting across from Pepe. He had a raw intensity to him – a couple of days' stubble lining his chin and circling his full lips. His muscular frame was pressing against a tight-fitting tee-shirt, and his bare legs grazed Patrick's under the table. He felt like he could leap out of his skin and jump on Pepe. It looked like Pepe could do the same.

Paolo brought them each a coffee and sat down with them.

"So – are you back for a while?" Paolo began, looking at Patrick.

"I don't know. I have a flight in two weeks."

"And you're staying with Nunzia?"

"Yes - it seemed like a more convenient place."

"For Positano?" Paolo continued, seemingly alluding to Zeno.

Patrick didn't respond initially, then said, "Yes – and for visiting other places like Pompeii and Naples."

Paolo winked, "Yes, there's lots to see around here."

Patrick glanced furtively at Pepe, who blushed. Laura came to take their cups away and ran her hand over Patrick's shoulder. "We're glad you're extending your stay. It was too short!"

Patrick nodded.

Paolo then added, "Well, men, don't let us hold you back. Pepe, why don't you take Patrizio up to the vineyard and show him the operations."

Pepe smiled and then looked at Patrick as if to ask, "Is that alright?"

Patrick nodded affirmatively and stood up. He thanked Paolo for the coffee and walked out into the piazza. "Pepe – it's so good to see you. What a surprise."

"The surprise is all mine – a pleasant one. Why don't you follow me up to the farm?" Pepe said.

Patrick got into his car and followed Pepe's truck up the gravel road to the main house and the building where the fermentation was taking place. Alberto walked out of the building and looked surprised at seeing Patrick.

"Patrizio – you're back so soon! Are you looking for work? We have some positions open!" Alberto said playfully.

"Yeah, I kind of like it here!"

"Paolo called and said you guys were coming up to look at the wine-making process. Let's go inside."

They walked into a modern complex where stainless-steel tanks were set within a large cement and glass structure. A few employees were moving crates around with forklift machines. The air smelled of fermenting alcohol.

"These are the tanks for the initial fermentation. Once the process is finished, we put the wine into oak barrels in the basement where they age. Let's go take a look."

They walked down a staircase to the basement, a vast cavernous space where row after row of barrels were lined against stone walls. Another section of the space included crates of boxes filled with bottles. Pepe interjected, "This is where the real magic of the production takes place, the careful monitoring of the wine and determination of the exact moment to bottle it."

"How do you know when it's ready?" Patrick asked.

"We have to sample it a lot!" Alberto said gleefully.

"I think that's the job I wanted to apply for," Patrick said with a wink.

"That's mine," Pepe noted. "But I can always use an assistant."

Pepe's friendliness didn't go unnoticed. Patrick began to sweat in embarrassment and looked over to Alberto to make sure he hadn't noticed.

"How much do you produce each year? There seems like a lot of wine here."

"Depending on the yield," Alberto began, "we produce between 100,000 and 200,000 bottles."

"Wow. I didn't realize," Patrick said in amazement. He calculated in his head how much profit that represented for the vineyard, and he realized his family did relatively well. "You must be one of the larger producers in the region."

"Actually, we're not. We are what people call a boutique vineyard," Alberto said, looking over at Pepe, who nodded.

Alberto's cell phone rang. He looked up at Patrick and signaled he had to take the call. He spoke with the person on the other end and then hung up. "I have to attend to something. Pepe, can you continue to show Patrick around?"

Pepe looked inquisitively at Patrick – as if to ask permission. Patrick nodded and Pepe nodded to Alberto.

Pepe showed Patrick the bottling machines and the various labels for the different wines produced. They went into another cellar where older vintages were being held and aged longer. "These are the exceptional years. We hold them back for a while and then release them at higher prices," he said.

"You're quite the expert," Patrick said affirmatively.

"Yes, Alberto puts a lot of trust in me. Over the years, I've learned a lot."

"So, I'm still trying to understand why the young ladies don't see you as a great catch!"

Pepe raised his hands as if to say, "Beats me!" He then said, "Patrick – are you hungry? I have some stuff at the house. I could fix a quick plate of pasta and salad."

Patrick hesitated. He could see the longing in Pepe's eyes and knew more was on the menu than pasta and salad. His body ached with desire, imagining Pepe ripping his clothes off and straddling him with his forceful body. His pulse raced. He looked down at the ground, not able to look Pepe in the eyes. "I'm afraid I need to get back to Praiano. I have an appointment," he lied.

"Come back later if you like," Pepe said longingly.

"*Vediamo*," Patrick replied, looking at his watch. "I need to get going," he tried to convince himself, sensing the crumbling resistance within him.

Pepe nodded and reached over and gave him a warm, moist kiss. Patrick pulled back and smiled warmly. They walked back up to the main level of the building and out into the bright sunlight. Patrick got into his car, turned on the ignition, and began the trek back to Praiano, waving at Pepe out the window as he headed down the road.

"Whew," he said to himself. "That was a close call." He knew that he would have loved to have had sex with Pepe, to have taken up where they left off, but he also knew it wasn't Pepe he was in love with, and that he needed to sort things out with Zeno.

He pulled into the parking area of the Belvedere and walked into the lobby. Nunzia was standing at the counter, tapping her fingers on a notepad, and looking restless. She gave him an alarmed look. "What's up?" Patrick inquired.

"You have a visitor. I let him in."

Patrick didn't need to ask. He knew. He walked down the hallway and slipped the key into the door, pushing it open. Zeno was sitting on a chair on the balcony, his legs shaking nervously. He looked over his shoulder as Patrick came to the sliding door. He stood up and raised his arms in an embrace, but Patrick put his hands out in front of him and stopped him abruptly. Zeno looked frightened.

"*Mi scusi*," Zeno said stoically.

Patrick walked out onto the balcony and took a seat in the other chair. Zeno sat down and looked over at Patrick with sad eyes.

"*Che c'è*? – what's up, what's wrong?" Patrick inquired.

"I don't know where to begin. First of all, it's good to see you. I'm glad you didn't go back to Boston."

"That's not what it seemed like yesterday."

Zeno looked confused and asked, "*Cosa*?"

"Francesca? The boat? A kiss – perhaps more?" Patrick began, angrily.

"It was a mistake," Zeno pleaded.

"In what sense?"

"After our day together, I was frightened. I had never felt what I felt with a man before. It made me realize I could fall in love with a man and that, if I did, I would be ruined."

"How would you be ruined?"

"My work, my family, my community – the shame and rejection." Zeno said, a tear running down his cheek.

"It can't be that bad."

"It is. I would lose everything."

"So, you decided to give it a try with Francesca again, right?"

Zeno nodded.

"How did it go?"

"It was awful."

"I don't believe you." Patrick replied with a scornful look.

"Believe me, it was awful."

"Spare me the details – you couldn't get it up?"

Zeno blanched. "No. Everything functioned okay."

"I can't imagine," Patrick said, trying not to think of Zeno and Francesca together.

Zeno grinned slightly, then continued, "She loves me, she's into me, she's beautiful, but I don't feel anything for her. I feel empty – like I'm faking everything – that it is all a lie."

"But, if you have to do it to survive, could you?"

"I thought I could – that I would - but after yesterday, I realized I couldn't go forward."

"That's a big realization, a big step for you."

"I'm scared. I feel like I'm falling off a cliff," Zeno said with alarm, his legs continuing to shake nervously.

Patrick was feeling some compassion for Zeno, realizing the sense of despair he was describing. He reached his hand over and put it on Zeno's shoulder.

"So, what's next?"

Zeno leaned on his knees, wringing his hands as if in deliberation. "Well," he began timidly, "I've been thinking. I need to come out to my parents – let them know about me – and see how that goes."

"What if it goes bad?"

"It probably will, but at least I will have made a first step. I might have to move to another city, get another job, but at least I will have let them know."

"That's good. You might be surprised. They might be very understanding."

"I don't think so."

"But they love you."

"Yes. But I'm an only child, and they would be devastated if I didn't fulfill their hopes and dreams for me."

"But what about your hopes and dreams?"

"I know. I need to follow them. But in Italy, it is very difficult to break with tradition."

"Things are changing."

"Not fast enough."

"So, do you have a plan?"

"That's what I came to talk with you about. Would you come to my house and be with me when I come out to my parents?"

Patrick looked out over the terrace. Memories of the painful experience coming out to his own parents haunted him, and the idea of repeating it with Zeno's wasn't appealing. "I'm not sure I would be a help."

"Yes, you would. I would feel more secure."

Patrick could feel Zeno's anxiety and hesitantly said, "I guess I could be there with you."

"It would mean a lot – and might prevent a major eruption."

"When are you planning to do this?"

Zeno looked relieved. "*Domani*? My dad doesn't work."

"Tomorrow? That's fast."

"I have to do it before I lose courage," Zeno said nervously.

"Sure, I'll be there with you."

Relieved, Zeno then looked over at Patrick and inquired, "So, why didn't you go back to Boston?"

"Ah, well, I thought there was someone to come back for," Patrick said to Zeno with some chagrin.

Zeno looked at him sadly, as if he had let Patrick down. "*Mi dispiace* – I'm really sorry for fucking up."

"I'm disappointed, too, but it sounds like it wasn't malicious or uncaring. Besides, you thought I was going back to Boston and my life there."

"*Sì*," Zeno said, as if gaining some moral ground. "And? What happened?"

"Well, when I got to the airport, I just couldn't get on the plane."

"*Strano*," Zeno said. "Truly strange."

"I just didn't want to go back. Maybe I'm afraid to confront Girard, who keeps wanting to talk, to reconcile things."

Zeno raised his eyebrows and said, "He's trying to get you back?"

"Yes, he keeps texting and pleading."

"And?" Zeno inquired further.

"*È finito*! I have no intention of reconciling."

Zeno looked relieved. He sighed.

Patrick reached over and held Zeno's hand. "We'll get through all of this."

Zeno nodded.

Patrick was cognizant of other guests on the nearby terrace and stood up, took Zeno's hand, and led him into the bedroom. At the foot of the bed, Patrick reached his hand up under Zeno's tee-shirt and stroked his chest. Zeno moaned and tilted his head back. Patrick kissed his neck, and nibbled his earlobe, whispering as he did, "*Ti voglio bene* – I love you."

"*Cazzo. Tu sei irresistibile* – I can't believe how sexy your eyes are," Zeno groaned.

"Did you say *cazzo*?" Patrick said flirtatiously, stroking the front of Zeno's shorts.

A soft sea breeze blew through the open balcony doors, tossing the linen curtains in the bright sunlight. Zeno lifted Patrick's shirt off. The midday sunlight bounced off the marble floor onto his chest, covered lightly in dark hair. Zeno ran his hands over Patrick's shoulder, down his arms and to his waist. He began to unbutton Patrick's shorts. Patrick could feel himself get hard and reached behind Zeno, squeezing his firm round butt, pulling him close. He reached his hand down inside the back of Zeno's shorts and felt warm, soft skin. Zeno moaned.

Zeno then pushed Patrick down onto the bed and straddled him, unzipping his own shorts, his hard erection protruding out of the undershorts. He laid on top of Patrick, nuzzling his nose into Patrick's neck and kissing him.

Patrick pulled back Zeno's shirt and licked his pecs – moistening the soft dark hair circling his nipples. He tugged playfully on them with his teeth and then kissed his abdomen, moving further down toward the erection that was dangling over him.

Zeno tightened and then rolled over on his side next to Patrick. This was the second time he pulled back, just as they were getting worked up. "Something wrong?" Patrick inquired.

Zeno laid on his back, his hand rubbing his forehead. "*Ho paura* – I'm afraid."

"Of what?" Patrick said tenderly.

"Of AIDS, of other things."

"We can be safe."

"How?"

Patrick realized Zeno was not as experienced as he let on – perhaps he had never had sex with a man before. "The same way you are safe with Francesca."

The look on Zeno's face suggested he hadn't used condoms with her. Patrick looked at him and said, "Oh, I see."

The moment passed, both Patrick and Zeno laying on their backs looking at the ceiling, their erections now relaxed.

"We can take it slow," Patrick assured Zeno, leaning over to kiss him.

Zeno opened his mouth wide and let Patrick plunge his tongue deeply. Patrick stroked Zeno's chest as he kissed him, Zeno becoming erect again. Zeno reciprocated, licking Patrick's face and eyes and then opening his mouth around Patrick's, breathing him in deeply. Patrick reached down for Zeno's penis, hard, warm, and engorged. He stroked it slowly and then stopped. He could feel Zeno's desire rise. Zeno reached over and held Patrick, feeling the hard shaft and the soft sack of balls dangling below.

Patrick looked at Zeno inquisitively. "Are you okay?"

"*Sì – sto bene*," Zeno assured him he was.

Zeno was lying on his back, his erection prominently extended above his abdomen. Patrick leaned toward him and rubbed his hands slowly along the inside of his legs up toward his balls. He squeezed the skin just below his buttock and his perineum. Zeno moaned and spread his dark, hairy legs. Patrick took hold of the glans of Zeno's shaft, massaged it playfully, and then ran his hand down the length of it, the skin supple and warm.

Zeno arched his back and contracted his buttocks, his erection bouncing as he squeezed. Patrick wanted to lean over and swallow it whole but hesitated and, instead, played with his own hardness, looking intensely into Zeno's dark brown eyes. Zeno smiled and reached over, removing Patrick's hand and replacing it with his own.

Zeno's warm hand sent charges of pleasure through Patrick's body. He could feel his pulse speed up and his skin warm and tighten. He leaned over and opened his mouth widely. Zeno leaned toward him and gave him a wet kiss, their tongues exploring the warm moist cavernous space opened between them.

Patrick opened his eyes. Zeno was on his side, his left hand holding Patrick's hardness. He watched Zeno's body move with each stroke, the flex of his shoulder and the rise of his hips. He took his own hand and ran it down the small of Zeno's back, running his fingers deep in Zeno's crack.

He felt Zeno tremble and wanted to climb on top of him, to feel the firmness of his round buttocks. He sensed Zeno wanting to turn over, to let Patrick lie on top of him. He knew it would be too much. Instead, he pressed his hand against Zeno's chest, massaging it tenderly, and pushing him over on his back again.

He pulled himself on Zeno, who now ran his warm hands down Patrick's back, resting them on his buttocks and pulling him tightly against him. Patrick almost came, the end of his penis moist and sensitive. He tried to concentrate on something else, licking Zeno's side. He could feel Zeno's hardness intensify under him, pressing for release.

He raised his head and observed Zeno's face right before him, the wispy dark lashes around his eyes, the dark stubble circling his mouth and lining his chin, the beautiful, sensual nose flared in arousal, and his angular jaws clinched as he moved back and forth under Patrick. He was handsome, cute, and appetizing and, as he became increasingly aroused, his skin smelled of the salty sand and silky ocean outside.

He whispered into Zeno's ear, "I want you to come all over me."

Zeno stirred under him. Patrick held him tight and rolled over, with Zeno now on top of him. Zeno raised himself up, his hardness resting on Patrick's chest. Patrick's erection nuzzled in the folds of Zeno's buttocks. Zeno leaned his head back and stroked himself, his arousal increasing, and his torso flexed. All-of-a-sudden, he erupted in spasms of release, collapsing on top of Patrick's chest.

Patrick reached down under Zeno to find his own engorged penis ready to come. He shifted himself under Zeno and, with a few strokes, felt the end of his hardness explode, the warm wetness filling the space between them.

Zeno laid calmly on Patrick's chest, his ear pressed against the pounding of Patrick's heart below. The rhythmic beat was hypnotic, Zeno feeling relaxed and safe in Patrick's arms. Patrick felt the solidity of Zeno on top of him and smiled as he stared at the ceiling, confident that their stars had crossed and that he was exactly where he was supposed to be – in a little pensione along the Amalfi coast under the shadows of his grandfather's home.

Neither wanted the break the magic, but Zeno finally murmured, "Aren't you glad you didn't go back to Boston?"

"I'm beginning to think it was a good decision." Patrick replied, winking at Zeno. "You know you're gorgeous and irresistible," Patrick continued.

"So are you. What a gift!" Zeno said thoughtfully.

They rose, washed up, and put their clothes back on. "So, what do we do now?" Patrick inquired.

"Are you still upset with me?" Zeno replied.

"How can I be upset with you? I'm proud of the steps you're taking. They aren't easy."

Zeno nodded contently.

"Let's go for a drive."

"Where?"

"What about the Benevento vineyard? I have something to show you – to share with you."

Zeno nodded.

They left the room and walked quietly past Nunzia's office. She heard their footsteps, rose, and said, "Where are you boys headed?"

Both looked guilty. She winked. Patrick began, "I think I'm going to show Zeno the Benevento vineyard."

"Weren't you just up there this morning?"

"Yes – but it's worth another trip," Patrick replied, pulling one of his eyelids down in a playful gesture of "I think you know."

"*Buon divertimento*," Nunzia wished them. "Don't be late."

Zeno and Patrick got into the car and began the ride up the mountain road to Cava dei Lupi. "Zeno, there's something I think you should know."

Zeno looked alarmed.

"Nunzia did a DNA test a few months ago to help her trace some of her ancestors. The first day I went to Positano, when I met you, I was going to visit some distant cousins – some that showed up unexpectedly through the DNA tests."

Zeno didn't look like he understood the concept so Patrick explained, "You can get a test of your DNA and, if you take it with one of the ancestry websites, they can match you with people who share a certain percentage of your DNA."

"So, they let you know who you are related to genetically?"

"Yes," Patrick said. Then he continued, "It seems that Nunzia is closely related to a couple of women who are daughters of a Nicola, one of Stefano's daughters."

"Yes. I know them. I know Aunt Nicola, too."

"Well, the problem is that these cousins are blood relations to Nunzia. They are related to her genetically."

"But how is that possible? She's Giancarlo Benevento's granddaughter. We aren't related."

"It's only possible if Stefano – your grandfather – is related to Giancarlo Benevento, the patriarch."

"Wooow!" Zeno said in disbelief, the implications setting in. "*Impossibile.*"

"No, I'm afraid the DNA doesn't lie. Stefano and the Beneventos share DNA."

"That would mean my grandfather is a Benevento?"

"Well, not exactly. He was an orphan brought to the vineyard as a teenager. Nunzia and I think he was Giancarlo senior's illegitimate son. He brought him to the farm to be part of the family, to work. But he fell in love with Anna, who would actually be his half-sister."

"Oh, shit!"

"Yes – oh shit!"

"So, do you think your grandfather knew this?" Zeno inquired.

"No. Giancarlo prohibited the marriage because he claimed Stefano was an orphan with no title or legitimacy. But the real problem was that he didn't want him to marry Anna but couldn't admit that the real reason was that Stefano and Anna were blood siblings."

"Poor Stefano."

"Yes, indeed."

"So, does that mean we are cousins?"

"I'm afraid so – although very distant – it shouldn't prevent us marrying."

Zeno looked at Patrick in disbelief.

"Kidding," Patrick said to save grace but, deep down, he saw it in the cards.

"So, you're telling me I'm a Benevento?"

"In terms of blood, yes."

Zeno's eyes widened. "Who would have thought?"

Patrick nodded. They pulled up to the vineyard, the rows of vines yellowing in the late September sun. Patrick parked by the cottage and got out of the car. Zeno opened his side of the car and walked over – looking across the vines and down the hillside to the sea in the distance.

"I never knew these kinds of places existed so close to Positano. This is like another world."

Zeno leaned his head back in the sun and breathed in the dry, earthy smell. "It's intoxicating."

Patrick nodded. He took hold of Zeno's hand and walked toward the vines and down one of the rows. A few bunches of grapes, missed during the *vendemmia*, were withering on the branches, clinging to the wires strung between trunks.

"These are old vines," Patrick began. "See how gnarly they are. They draw deeply from the mineral soil, giving the wine a distinctive flavor."

"How do you know so much about this?"

"I picked up a lot in the last couple of weeks helping with the harvest and listening to Alberto talk about the process."

"Do you realize how easy it would have been for either one of us to have grown up here rather than in Boston or Positano?" Zeno added.

Patrick nodded. He held Zeno's hand and walked slowly down the row. "I've begun to think it would be interesting to come back here, perhaps spend more time on the farm. Roberto left his share of the farm to my father, who left it to me. I have a partial title to the place."

"You're kidding!"

"No, it's pretty amazing."

"So, you're an owner of the vineyard?" Zeno pressed further.

"Well, I have a title to part of the land, but there are provisions in the will that limit claims or shares in the profit. It's a more honorary connection, a way of saying I belong."

"So, you will not be a rich vintner?"

"I'm afraid not. I'm going to have to go back to Boston to teach."

Zeno stuck out his lips in a pout.

"I have summers free," Patrick added, smiling warmly at Zeno.

Zeno smiled in return and squeezed Patrick's hand. Patrick looked over at him tenderly.

"Whose house is that?"

"Pepe's – the groundskeeper."

"You mean like my grandfather?"

"Precisely – and he's even an orphan."

"Hopefully not the son of someone in the family again."

"I don't think so – at least there's no sign."

Pepe stepped out of his house and leaned against the doorjamb. He glanced toward Patrick and Zeno and nodded. Patrick walked toward him with Zeno.

"*Sei tornato così presto*?" Pepe inquired why Patrick was back so soon.

Patrick nodded. "Pepe, I want to introduce you to Zeno. Zeno, this is Pepe."

"*Piacere*," they both said to each other. Patrick noticed Pepe scrutinizing Zeno, staring in his eyes, then taking a protracted look at his shoulders, his chest, and his legs.

"I was showing Zeno the vineyard. His grandfather worked here many years ago."

"Hm," Pepe murmured. "And your grandfather now?"

"*È morto – qualche anni fa*."

"I'm sorry," Pepe noted thoughtfully at Zeno's recounting of his grandfather's death. "Did he ever bring you here to the vineyard?"

"No, there was a falling out when Patrick's grandfather left."

"Ah," Pepe noted. "*Roberto e Stefano.*"

"*Appunto,*" Patrick underscored.

A look of recognizing spread across Pepe's face as he spoke Roberto's and Stefano's names – the realization that Patrick and Zeno were perhaps reliving the history of their grandfathers. There was a hint of jealously in Pepe's mouth, a small twitch, a tightening of the jaw. But, to Patrick's surprise, Pepe said, "Do you guys want a glass of wine?"

Patrick looked at Zeno, who looked at Pepe. "That would be nice. Thank you."

Pepe went inside the house and brought out a bottle of Benevento red and three glasses. He set them on the small marble table on the terrace and uncorked the bottle. The cork was moist, and Pepe smelled it as he laid it on the table. He poured each a generous glass and swirled the wine in the goblets. The sun showed through the wine and cast red and purple rays of light on the table. Zeno lifted the glass to his nose, took a sniff, and then a small sip. He let it sit on his tongue and then swallowed.

Zeno looked off into the distance and then said, "Hm, very nice. It has a mineral taste but smells of berries. It's smooth, almost a little velvety."

Pepe's face lit up with a proud smile. "We make an excellent wine here," he noted. "Over the years, it has gotten better."

"I'm surprised we don't serve this in the restaurant in Positano."

"We'll have to talk to Alberto," Patrick added. "I'm surprised with Paolo's relationship there hasn't already been a connection made."

"Alberto is very territorial and strategic where he sells," Pepe noted.

Patrick could see that Pepe was more involved in the business than a simple groundskeeper would be. He could imagine Stefano having developed the same relationship and then being devastated at being cast aside when he wanted to marry Anna. Those must have been terrible times for Roberto, for Stefano, and for the family.

Patrick, Zeno, and Pepe enjoyed their wine, told stories of the vineyard, and laughed at Patrick's discomfort during the *vendemmia.* "You should have seen him after the first day," Pepe noted. "He was in such pain – and he looked a mess – grape juice creating rivulets on the heavy coating of dust and dirt on his chest."

Patrick blushed. Zeno noted Pepe's affectionate smile as he told the story and glanced over at Patrick, who was looking intently at Pepe. There was an awkward, tense silence that followed. Patrick broke it, saying, "Pepe, thanks for the wine. We have to get back to Positano," as he looked at his watch.

"It was nice to meet you, Zeno. I hope we will see you more often."

Zeno extended his hand to Pepe, "Nice to meet you, and finally put a face on the vineyard my grandfather spoke of."

Patrick and Zeno walked back to the car. Before they got in, Patrick said, "Let me show you something else."

They walked up the hill and pushed open the door of the cottage. Patrick opened a shutter to let in light. "Here's where I stayed when I was here."

"It's very cozy. I didn't imagine it would be so nice on the inside," Zeno noted.

Patrick showed him the kitchen, the living area, and the bedroom. When they came back into the living area, Zeno noticed a photo on the mantel of the fireplace. He walked over and picked it up.

"Those are my grandparents – Roberto and Chiara," Patrick noted.

"I can see the resemblance. What's interesting is that I can see the resemblance to my grandfather as well. I don't know if it's my imagination since you told me about his relationship to the Beneventos or if it is obvious."

Patrick scrutinized the photo – looking at Roberto and then at Zeno. "There's definitely something in their eyes – a male Benevento trait. I see it in you most definitely – and certainly saw it in your father."

Zeno nodded affirmatively.

Patrick took the photo with him as he closed the door to the cottage and then said, "Hey, cutie, why don't we head back to the coast. I'd like to take you to dinner."

Zeno beamed happily. "Where? In Positano?"

"Why don't we go to Amalfi. I know a little café called Zeno's. We can have a drink there and get something to eat nearby."

"Zeno's?"

"Yes, Zeno's – it's a long story!"

They got into the car and drove down the mountain road to the coast. En route, Zeno seemed curious about Pepe. "So, is Pepe married?" he began.

"No, in fact, that seems to be a problem for him."

"In what sense?"

"He dates, but women don't seem to want to marry a caretaker, even if it is for a boutique vineyard."

"He's very handsome," Zeno said. "Is he gay?"

"You noticed?" Patrick inquired sarcastically.

"You didn't?" Zeno pressed.

"Well, I might have noticed," Patrick admitted with a wink, but now nervous Zeno might push for more information.

"He seems to be attracted to you," Zeno said pointedly.

"I doubt it," Patrick said evasively.

Zeno looked suspiciously at Patrick. "As I told you before, waiters can spot roving eyes, and Pepe was definitely looking at you."

"So, I won't be able to sneak anything by you?"

"Afraid not," Zeno said proudly.

"Hm," is all Patrick could manage to murmur. There was an awkward silence that followed.

Patrick sped up, shifting gears playfully on the curvy coastal route. Zeno looked out over the horizon, deep in thought. Then he asked, "So this Zeno's place. How did you find it?"

"Destiny."

"You believe that shit?" Zeno said in rebuke.

"No, but when it hits you over the head, yes."

"How so?"

Patrick explained the story of his drive earlier in the week to Amalfi and the experience with the barista. He then said, "It would seem we were meant to meet, to connect."

"I agree," Zeno said contently.

Patrick reached over and took Zeno's hand, holding it firmly. Zeno looked back affectionately. Then he said, "Are you okay with plans to talk to your parents tomorrow? That's a big deal."

"I'm having second thoughts. Maybe I should wait, figure things out."

"What's to figure out. You know who you are."

"Yes, but maybe I'm not ready to publicize it."

"Don't you think they suspect? Parents – particularly mothers – are good at that."

Zeno looked pensive and then said, "No, I don't think they have a clue."

"You have put on a good act," Patrick said with a smile.

Zeno looked preoccupied and not amused. "They're going to be angry and devastated."

"You might be surprised," Patrick said, realizing that his own parents hadn't surprised him, reacting to his coming out with disdain. He wanted to encourage Zeno. "If they love you – which I'm sure they do – they will accept you warmly."

Zeno smiled.

They went to Zeno's to have a drink. The same barista who had served Patrick the other day was there, and he looked inquisitively at Patrick when they came in. They ordered wine and some appetizers. Patrick avoided the bartender's eyes but, at one point when he looked up to ask for a glass of water, the barista held the glass in the air, holding it back, waiting for Patrick to be more forthcoming.

Patrick smiled at the barista and reluctantly introduced Zeno. "Zeno – this is the barista who served me the other day." He looked at the barista and said, "*Questo è Zeno.*"

The barista smiled triumphantly. "*Il destino, no*?" he stated.

"*Sì, il destino,*" Patrick admitted.

Zeno looked perplexed, unable to make sense of their banter.

The barista offered them complimentary *aperitivi* and, when they finished, they went to dinner. Nearby, they found a small trattoria with a few tables. The interior was warm and intimate, with candles on each table. The orange glow on Zeno's face made his dark brown eyes even more alluring. Patrick gazed at him as Zeno opened the menu and began reviewing the options. Zeno looked up, caught Patrick staring and asked, "What – what's up?"

"You have to admit, it's pretty amazing. I find a photograph of my grandfather and a mysterious man. I come to Italy and accidentally meet his grandson with whom I fall in love."

"You have fallen in love?" Zeno asked playfully.

"If it's not obvious by now, then your waiter instincts are failing you."

"They never fail," he said pointedly.

"Then what's the verdict?"

"Well, you're the most handsome man I've waited on."

"What a charmer."

"*Da vero*, really. I didn't tell you before, but when Paolo and you were seated in my section, I almost fainted."

"Tell me more."

"When you were first seated, I lost my composure. I felt something ominous, as if my life were going to be upended."

"Just from seating us?" Patrick inquired, now intrigued.

"Yes, it was quite frightening. It was as if there was some kind of aura that surrounded you and Paolo. I felt it. It made me nervous."

"I thought you didn't believe in that stuff?" Patrick inquired.

"I don't – although I'm Italian. We are superstitious. Your eyes. They were penetrating."

"They are your eyes, you know."

"I know. It was haunting."

"Was it haunting or alluring?" Patrick inquired.

"Both!" Zeno said emphatically. "That's why I almost fainted."

"Love can do that. I can frighten us and compel us."

"I'm beginning to see that," Zeno noted. "That's why I'm certain Francesca isn't for me. She's alluring and beautiful, but she doesn't haunt me – she doesn't compel me. You do."

Patrick smiled. The waiter approached the table and asked if they were ready to order. Zeno made a spur-of-the-moment choice for a seafood risotto and salad. Patrick quickly scanned the menu and opted for veal scallopini, roast potatoes, and a salad. As the waiter left, Patrick leaned over the table and, in a whisper, said, "*Ti voglio bene*" – and then, in English for emphasis, said, "I love you – so much!"

"*Anch'io, ti voglio bene*!"

Zeno said the words with warmth, tenderness, and conviction. Patrick was smitten and couldn't take his eyes off Zeno who, self-conscious of the attention, looked away.

"*Cosa*?" Patrick inquired of his evasiveness.

"It's overwhelming. In just a week, my life has changed completely. I'm still nervous about tomorrow."

"If you can remember tonight, you'll be fine tomorrow. Speak with your heart."

"But I love my parents. I don't want to disappoint them."

"How can they be disappointed if you are happy? Isn't that what they want?"

"Yes, but I don't think this is what they had in mind."

"Did you?" Patrick noted.

Zeno smiled. "No, I didn't expect this or imagine this."

"Love is surprising."

"I'm beginning to see that," Zeno agreed.

The waiter approached with their entrees and placed them on the table. The seafood risotto was steaming, garlic laden vapor rising from the mound of rice mixed with colorful pieces of clams, mussels, shrimp, and scallops. Patrick leaned over and said, "Wow! That looks amazing."

"It's hard to go out to eat at other restaurants. I'm used to our place in Positano. But I have to admit, this looks so fresh. Look at those large clams and mussels! And look at your scallopini."

"Hmm, they smell good. I think the menu mentioned lemon and capers."

"Lemon is common along the coast here. I bet it's a sauce of olive oil, garlic, lemon, capers and sea salt."

Patrick cut a piece and placed it in his mouth. "How did you know? I can taste the garlic and lemon." Patrick pierced one of the roasted potatoes and raised it to his mouth. His Irish mother had perfected the art of crispy flavorful potatoes tossed in olive oil and salt. She used to add fresh herbs from the garden. These had been sprinkled with fresh rosemary, and they brought back memories of home.

A protracted silence ensued as they ate. Patrick interrupted the quiet with a question, "Do you cook?"

Zeno looked up from his plate. "I wish I did. I am around food all day long, and the plates we serve as amazing, but I can't cook for *cazzo*. Do you?"

"I did when I was younger. I used to watch my grandfather and grandmother cook sauce together, fighting about how much salt or oregano or carrots to add to the tomatoes. Grandfather always had a bottle of red wine on the counter, pouring a little in the sauce and taking a long sip himself. *Nonna* would slap him with her wooden spoon, and he'd look at her with pleading eyes to have pity on him. They were fun together."

"It's amazing that our families are so linked – that you are telling stories of my grandfather's best friend," Zeno said thoughtfully.

"I know. It's kind of surreal."

"You mentioned you cooked when you were younger. What happened?"

"I hate to bring it up, but Girard didn't like to cook and didn't like to eat at home. We went out a lot. At first, I liked it. It was exciting meeting friends at small places in our neighborhood. But, at some point, I missed the art of cooking – of combining ingredients and sitting in our cozy apartment sharing a meal – just the two of us."

Zeno smiled. "That sounds so appealing to me. When I'm finished working, I want to be in my own place. Right now, I'm with my parents – and that's not bad. But I've always wanted a place that was mine, that I could retreat to – particularly with someone I love."

Patrick sighed. "Maybe we can arrange that."

Zeno looked alarmed.

"What's the matter?" Patrick inquired.

"Time is passing so quickly. I'm going to hate to see you go back to Boston."

"Maybe I can delay things more."

Zeno smiled.

"Changing the subject, is there anything I can do to help you prepare for tomorrow? Coming out to your parents is always a challenge, and there's no script for it."

"I'm realizing that," Zeno affirmed. "I'm very nervous."

"Your parents will react well. I am certain of it."

"Why are you certain?" Zeno inquired.

"Your father is Stefano's son, and Stefano modeled acceptance and love to your parents."

"That's true. He was incredible in how he accepted people, particularly the black sheep of families."

"Your parents will draw on his example. They will embrace you."

Zeno began to tear up. "I hope so."

"They will," Patrick assured him, placing his hand on top of Zeno's.

They finished their entrees, and the waiter brought them each a salad with bottles of olive oil and vinegar on the side so they could dress their own salads. Patrick poured the last of the bottle of wine into their glasses and took a long sip.

They finished the meal, ordered an espresso each, and then walked to the car. They began their drive back to Positano. Zeno was quiet and nervous. Patrick placed his hands on top of Zeno's and said, "It's going to go well. I'm sure of it."

Zeno nodded but didn't seem convinced. "I have a knot in the pit of my stomach. I'm so afraid."

"What are you so afraid of?"

"I just don't want to lose my parents."

"They don't want to lose you, either. Trust their affection and love for you, and all will be fine."

Zeno seemed more relaxed, laying his head back on the headrest and squeezing Patrick's hand.

Patrick dropped Zeno off at the base of the hill leading up to his home. Patrick then turned around and returned to Praiano, slipping into the hotel as quietly as possible. He undressed and slipped under the covers, sniffing at the sheets, hoping to sense Zeno's lingering scent. He then whispered into the darkness, "Stefano and Roberto. I know you're here. Thanks for helping me find Zeno and help tomorrow go well."

He closed his eyes and fell into a peaceful sleep.

9

Chapter Nine

The next morning, Patrick parked the car at the restaurant lot in Positano and walked across the street, finding a narrow walkway heading up the hill toward Zeno's family's apartment. It was a steep walk between white-washed apartments and through a couple of terraced gardens filled with lemon trees. When Patrick arrived at the front door, he was panting. He rang the bell.

Zeno came to the door, dressed in jeans, a casual shirt, and vest. He looked more mature and serious than in a swimsuit or shorts.

"Come in, good to see you." He kissed Patrick on the cheeks.

Patrick walked into the spacious living area, a long room with large windows looking out over the sea. He walked toward them, drawn by the vast horizon outside.

"Wow, what a view!"

"Yes – it is," Zeno replied, impatient to introduce Patrick to his parents.

Zeno turned toward them, pulling Patrick forward by his shoulder and said, "*Mama – questo è Patrizio. Patrizio, la mia mama, Joanna.*"

Patrick extended his hand, "*Piacere.*"

Joanna was thin, with dark brown hair pulled back and gathered over her elongated neck. She had deep maroon lips, high cheekbones, and lush brows over her brown eyes. She must have been stunning as a teenager, and she had aged well. She bowed slightly to Patrick, looking at him intensely.

Zeno continued, "I believe you have met my father, Giovanni. *Papa, Patrizio.*"

Giovanni extended his hand reticently but forcefully, "*Piacere.*"

Giovanni looked much like Stefano in the photo – lanky frame, handsome, broad chested. He had a narrow angular face, short dark hair, and deep-set alluring eyes.

Joanna then interjected, "*Volete qualcosa da bere – caffé, vino, aqua?*"

"*Un caffé,*" Patrick responded.

"*Anch'io,*" Zeno nodded for a coffee as well.

Giovanni invited them both to take seats on the sofa. He sat in a large straw chair with cushions. Another similar chair was reserved for Joanna, who, a few moments later, came in with coffee and set the tray and cups on a small table with some biscotti.

"*Grazie,*" Patrick said.

Zeno began in earnest. "*Mama, papa, voglio condividere qualcosa con voi.*"

They nodded nervously.

He continued. "I met Patrick at the restaurant the other day - with Paolo. Patrick is the grandson of Roberto – *nonno's* friend from Benevento."

They nodded and gave a little smile to Patrick.

"You remember the photo of Roberto and Stefano?"

They nodded again, still quiet, saying nothing.

"Patrick was trying to explore his grandfather's roots. No one in his family knew who Stefano was – and he was determined to find him. He came to help at the *vendemmia*, and Paolo brought him here to Positano. When they were having lunch at the restaurant, he noticed a resemblance between Stefano and me, showed me the photo, and it was *nonno*."

Giovanni looked at Patrick and smiled again. He seemed to know this was just the prelude to a more significant bit of information. He reached over to Joanna and held her hand.

"I had a pleasant visit with Patrizio on Friday. He told me about his family and the recent passing of his parents."

Giovanni and Joanna nodded reverently, "*Ci dispiace*," they expressed their condolences.

"He also explained to me that he is gay."

Giovanni and Joanna were now expressionless.

Zeno took a deep breath and continued, "For some time, I have felt that I am attracted to men, that I am gay."

"No, no," Giovanni interjected quickly, almost as if he was expecting his son's declaration. "*È una fase*."

"No, papa, it is not a phase. I have felt it since I was 12, and I have tried to change, but it doesn't change."

"But you love Francesca – you're engaged."

"She's beautiful, and we have fun, but I am not in love. I can't marry her. It would be a disaster."

A sadness fell over Giovanni's and Joanna's faces as the full import of what Zeno was saying hit them. No marriage, no grandchildren, no legacy to pass on.

Giovanni began, "It will be a disaster if you don't marry."

"It will be worse if I do. Look at Carlo, Pino, and the others. They are fine, they are happy," Zeno pleaded, acknowledging for the first time that several of his colleagues were gay.

"I know them – I know Carlo – they are not happy. They have no children, no family. How can they be happy?" Giovanni continued.

"That's because they live in a country that shames them. They do the best they can, but it could be better. Things are changing. Look at Spain, Portugal, France, Germany, England, and other countries – gay people can get married, have children, start families. Only in Italy do we continue to shame gay people. Patrick is married in the States. He's able to have a family just like everyone else," Zeno said, looking over at Patrick, who nodded affirmatively.

"*Ma non va bene* – it's not good," Giovanni said with disdain, waving his hand in a gesture of disapproval.

"*Ma dai, papa. Le cose cambiano*," Zeno tried to get his father to recognize things were changing.

Giovanni did not respond. Joanna sat waiting for direction from him.

Zeno looked toward them for some kind of response, some kind of compassion, even a statement – 'we love you,' but nothing, just silence.

"*E allora*?" He asked. "Well?"

"I don't know – it's so sudden, so unexpected." Giovanni continued, shaking his head and rubbing his forehead. "Give your mother and me some time."

Zeno nodded. At least it was a minor breach in their hard shell.

"So – can we speak again, discuss?"

"*Certo*," Giovanni affirmed, "You are our son. We are always here to listen and discuss."

"*Grazie*," Zeno said, a tear running down his face.

Patrick decided to intervene. "*Scusate*, I want to share something."

They all looked in amazement at Patrick, as if his role had been to observe, not participate. They nodded apprehensively for him to continue.

"Joanna and Giovanni, you have a wonderful son who loves you very much. He would never have chosen this for himself or for you. All he wants is your continued love and patience as he tries to make sense of his life. I have seen families ruptured by prejudice and hard-heartedness. Everyone suffers – the parents and the children. All Zeno needs is your continued love and patience as he seeks to make sense of his life. You have a beautiful family, and nothing has to change."

By the time Patrick had finished, everyone had watery eyes. Joanna and Giovanni nodded, as if they understood, but they said nothing – not a "we love you" or anything. They stood up and hugged Zeno and then hugged Patrick. "We will discuss later."

Zeno then looked at Patrick. "Do you want to take a walk?"

He nodded, looking respectfully at Giovanni and Joanna. Giovanni said, "Yes, son, why don't you take a walk. You and Patrick talk. Mama and I will talk."

Zeno led Patrick to the door and let them out. "Thank you for what you said. I think it might have made an impact," Zeno said as they began walking down the steps.

"I realize how much my parents and I suffered, and I don't want it to happen to you."

"How do you think it went," Zeno asked.

"Overall, not great. They seem unhappy."

"They're disappointed – their dreams for me shattered."

"At least they weren't angry."

"They are never overtly angry, but they find a way to make you feel bad later – you'll see."

"Give them a chance. It's a lot of news to process. Maybe they'll come around."

"I'm not so sure," Zeno said, his head tilted down.

They passed the restaurant, and Carlo was in the door. He gave them an inquisitive look. "You two again. What's up? Why so solemn?"

"We just had a conversation with my parents. It didn't go as well as I had hoped."

Carlo seemed to understand. He rubbed his chin, nodded, and then began, "*Ci vogliamo tempo* – it takes time."

Zeno nodded, and a tepid smile crossed his face.

"Why don't you come back for dinner later?" Carlo added.

Zeno and Patrick looked at each other and nodded.

Patrick asked Zeno, "What do you want to do this afternoon?"

"I don't feel well," Zeno began. "My stomach is in knots."

"That's understandable. Let's walk – that always makes me feel better – it clears the head and relaxes the body."

They walked along the beach and took a path beyond the pier, heading toward another smaller beach further up the coastline. The path was shaded by pines clinging to the steep cliffs overlooking the blue water. Waves lapped against the rocky coastline, white foam retreating out over the surface. They stood under a tree and watched the waves.

"So, did you come out to your parents?" Zeno inquired pensively of Patrick.

"Yes. I was in high school. Everyone else was dating, going out with girls, but I was at home, on the computer. My parents got worried and asked if something was the matter. At first, I said no, but they persisted and one night, at dinner, they confronted me."

"You mean they asked you if you were gay?"

"Yes. It was very odd. I was having a hard time accepting it myself and, when I heard them ask me, it clicked. It made sense. It was as if they were naming my truth."

"That must have been shocking, startling."

"Yes," Patrick replied. "But then it got worse. They used the information to shame me. They said I would grow out of it, eventually come around to liking girls."

"But you didn't."

"No, and they were increasingly worried, unhappy, even angry.

When I started going out with Girard, they were hostile. When we got married, they refused to come to the wedding. It was horrible."

"So, what happened?" Zeno inquired, now worried his parents would do the same.

"My father got sick. The topic was no longer brought up. Girard wouldn't come to their house – so I was alone with them. My parents just pretended Girard and my marriage didn't exist."

"That's what I'm afraid of – being alienated from my parents, their only son," Zeno said with alarm.

"We have a lot in common."

"So, after you came out, did you date guys in school?"

"Not at first. Although we lived in Boston, a liberal city, it didn't make it any easier to date. We had 350 people in my high school class. At most, that would mean there were 25 gay and lesbian people in the class. Many of those weren't out. So that only left 8 or so openly gay guys in my class. I remember thinking about it – and identifying them in my head. There was only one of them I had any interest in, and he was already dating someone from another school."

"What did you do?"

"It was very lonely. I think that's why gay people are often depressed. You can be out and accepted, but that doesn't mean you have a lot of opportunities. I went online to see if I might connect with people, but there were a lot of perverts who were just trying to take advantage of young, vulnerable teenagers. It was horrible."

"Then you met Girard?"

"We met later, during college. He was smart, handsome, and seemed very self-assured and confident. I felt good with him – that somehow I would be okay, that someone would take care of me."

"But?"

"Well, as the years progressed, I realized that he was not just self-assured and self-confident, he was also controlling and domineering."

"That's too bad."

"And now, he's having an affair. I don't know if it is because of my parents or that we have simply drifted apart."

"His loss," Zeno said.

Patrick smiled, "You're very kind."

They continued along the path. At a high overlook, they noticed a small restaurant with a thatched pavilion. "*Vuoi un caffé o un bicchiere di vino o una insalata*?" Zeno offered.

"Yes, why don't we get a little something to eat. This looks like a nice place to take a break."

They ordered some wine and salads and enjoyed the shade, the views, and more stories about their childhoods and coming out. Patrick talked more of his life in Boston as a teacher and the acceptance of his colleagues. Zeno noted the fact that he now realized some of his colleagues – particularly Carlo – were gay. None had ever come out to him or approached him, although he always sensed that Carlo had been protective. He recounted how some tourists are abusive, how they touch you, grab you, even use offensive derogatory phrases and language. Some are attractive, and Zeno mentioned he'd gone out for a drink or two with some. But the pushy ones, he noted, were often unattractive. "You can tell they have money. They are used to buying sex – male and female – and they think they can have what they want, what they order."

"That's horrible," Patrick stated. "What do you do?"

"We do our best to be professional. You know being a server in Italy is a profession – it's not a job or a pastime until something better opens up. We go to school. We get certified, and they compensate us well for our work."

"But what happens when a guest doesn't behave?"

"This is when Carlo steps in or, if that doesn't work, the police. Positano is used to tourists who misbehave."

Patrick and Zeno continued their conversation. They enjoyed some wine and an abundant salad of arugula and cherry tomatoes and buffalo mozzarella. Patrick couldn't get over how flavorful the food was – the spicy greens and the soft, slightly salty cheese.

The waiter recognized Zeno and brought them a complimentary piece of cheesecake and coffee. The fluffy ricotta filling was rich and the crust sweet. They finished their lunch and other guests had already left and returned to the beach. Zeno and Patrick remained under the shade of the pavilion, sipping wine, drinking coffee, and getting to know each other. Patrick remarked to himself how easy it was to talk with Zeno and laughed at how anxious he had been a few days before, thinking he would be bored.

In the late afternoon light reflecting off the nearby water, Zeno's face lit up. He rested his chin on the back of his hands, propped up on his elbows. His features – the deep-set brown eyes, his angular face, and the stubble around his mouth and chin were intense but tender, and he smiled warmly as Patrick described his home in Boston and memories of his grandparents.

The sun set over the mountain behind them. Patrick looked at his watch and reminded Zeno that Carlo had invited them for dinner. They paid their tab, walked further along the shore, and then turned around, heading back to Positano proper.

As they came up from the beach to the entrance of the restaurant, Carlo greeted them. "Your table is ready," waving them toward a spot in the upper part of the restaurant, near one of the open windows. As they approached the table, Zeno noticed his parents sitting at it.

"*Ma*?" he looked at Carlo. "But?"

Carlo grinned and sat them, winking at Giovanni.

"*Mama, papa, che c'è*?" What's up, Zeno asked his parents.

"We're here to *discutere* - to discuss," his father said emphatically.

Zeno and Patrick took seats across from Joanna and Giovanni. Everyone looked anxious. Carlo broke the silence. "Some wine and water for everyone?"

"*Sì*," they all said in unison.

Zeno leaned forward in his seat. Patrick put his hands on his lap, maintaining a respectful silence.

"We were thinking, son. We may have conveyed a wrong message to you," Giovanni began, clearing his throat.

Joanna nodded.

"We love you, and we love you the way you are."

Zeno began to tear up.

"Your grandfather was a very loving man. I never saw him speak poorly of anyone. He always said, 'You never know what someone is struggling with. You have to show compassion, understanding, and patience.'"

Zeno nodded for his father to continue.

"He once told me that he was an orphan. I didn't believe it. He and Rita seemed like a normal couple – so in love. Stefano was so much a part of Rita's family that I never noticed he didn't have his own. When he told me that, I realized he was different. He didn't take family or love for granted. Everyone said that if Stefano promised you something, it was a solid promise. He was a man of his word."

"So, you knew *nonno* was an orphan?"

"Only later in life. He didn't elaborate – only that he could understand how hard it is to be rejected by your own family because you don't meet their expectations, their criteria for legitimacy. When you left earlier today, I realized we didn't treat you the way Stefano would have wanted. You are different – but you are our son and our family. We have no idea of the challenges of growing up feeling you are different, not like others, subject to shame and scorn –

easily cast off. That must be horrible, and we are sorry if we made you feel that way."

Patrick now began to tear up, Joanna drying her eyes with a small white lace kerchief.

Giovanni got up and walked toward his son, giving him a warm embrace. "*Ti voglio bene.*"

"*Anch'io – vi voglio bene – tutte e due.*"

Zeno leaned down and gave his mother a kiss.

Giovanni walked around the table and gave Patrick a hug. "You're always welcome in our family."

Patrick became red-eyed, tears streaking down his cheeks.

Carlo had been waiting around the corner, listening in. At the appropriate moment, he brought several bottles of special wine and a plate of appetizers. Giovanni nodded in appreciation. Carlo winked.

They continued to visit, and Zeno inquired, "Papa, did *nonno* ever talk about Roberto? You've seen the photo of them – they seemed so close."

"He did. He said Roberto had been his best friend and tried to defend him. He said the reason he left for America was a misunderstanding with Giancarlo Benevento."

"Did he talk about working at the vineyard?"

"Yes, he mentioned working there, loving the family, but feeling betrayed in the end when he wanted to marry Anna. He couldn't understand it."

"Was he upset that Roberto left?"

"He was sad, but also felt that it confirmed their friendship, that Roberto would do anything for him – even leave his family who was mistreating him."

"Did *nonno* ever go back to the vineyard?"

"No, he never did."

"Why do you think they treated him like that?"

"As I said earlier – people are sometimes cruel, prejudiced, influenced by *stupidaggini* – stupid customs and ideas. People need to change."

Giovanni then turned to Patrick, "So, in America, you can get married?"

"Yes, and we can have a family with children."

"How is that possible?" Giovanni continued.

"Some use a surrogate, but others adopt."

Giovanni looked over at Joanna and smiled.

"Are you married?" Joanna inquired timidly.

"*Sì e no* – yes and no."

"What does that mean?" Giovanni continued.

"Well, my husband and I have been fighting. He's having an affair. It is over, unfortunately."

Giovanni nodded and agreed, "*Sfortunato*," he said, but he didn't look sad. He looked hopeful, the wheels turning in his head about his son and Patrick.

Carlo came to the table to take their orders, visibly content at the atmosphere of the table. Giovanni looked at him proudly and with a new tenderness. "*Caro Carlo*," he began, "dear Carlo – can you see what fish are fresh tonight and prepare us a nice plate of grilled fish and vegetables? And can you make a plate for yourself – and join us when it is ready?"

"*Non posso. Devo lavorare*," he protested – looking at the tables he had to serve.

"It's a small crowd, and it is late – they will be gone soon. It would mean a lot if you would join us."

Carlo nodded. "I'll see what I can do."

Carlo returned later with their food and made a place for himself. He poured himself a generous glass of wine and raised it in a toast, "To family, to love, to friendship!"

"How fitting," Patrick said.

"Indeed," Giovanni added.

Carlo had brought a platter to the table. A large sea bass had been encrusted with sea salt and grilled. It was surrounded by risotto and fresh vegetables. He ceremoniously cut into the fish and deboned it, placing a large piece of the white fish on each person's plate. Giovanni passed around a bowl filled with a bright green sauce. Joanna took it first and ladled some of the sauce on the fish.

When everyone had been served, Carlo raised his glass in a toast. "To family and to new friends!"

"*Salute*!" they all said in unison.

Patrick cut into the tender fish and placed a piece in his mouth. The green sauce was sweet and flavorful – a coarse mixture of oil, garlic, onions, parsley, and lemon. "Hmm," he said, "this is incredible."

Giovanni said, "It's Carlo's recipe."

Zeno looked curiously at Carlo, "I didn't know you cooked. You're always waiting tables and looking over the guests."

Carlo looked embarrassed, hesitant to speak. "Go on, Carlo, tell them," Giovanni encouraged him.

"I might have a little to do with some items on the menu," he said with a grin.

"It's amazing," Patrick said again. "If I'm friends with Zeno, do I get any special consideration for getting recipes?"

Carlo said playfully, "For you, Patrick, anything!"

Giovanni added, "Patrick, I don't know what you've done, but I've been trying to get that recipe for years, and Carlo hasn't budged."

Patrick took a sip of wine, hiding his smile behind the glass. He looked around the table proudly – a table he wouldn't have imagined a few weeks ago – now surrounded by his grandfather's best friend's family. He glanced at Zeno, beaming as he leaned toward his mother, asking her how she was enjoying the fish. She beamed at the touch of her son and the assurance she wouldn't lose him, that there would be many more gatherings like this in the future, even with grandchildren.

Carlo smiled at Patrick, an acknowledgement of his role in forging a new future for him, Zeno, and others like them. They continued to enjoy the meal and shared stories of Stefano, who apparently had been quite the character, a country boy who had to learn the graces of waiting tables in a resort. Giovanni shared stories he had told of his meeting Rita, of their romance, and of their life together.

The group learned more about Carlo, his origins in Naples, and his preference for solitude. He hinted that he had once had a friend from Rome who came each summer, and how they enjoyed swimming and boating – but he eventually married and settled in Milan.

At about 10, people tired and talked about retiring for the night. Patrick looked at Zeno and whispered, "Do you want to come to Praiano tonight?"

Zeno looked inquisitively at Giovanni, who nodded and at Carlo who said, "As long as you're here by 11 in the morning you can go wherever you want."

Zeno smiled, nodded, and squeezed Patrick's hand under the table.

They all rose, gave each other hugs, and then began the long walk up the hill. Giovanni and Joanna continued to their home while Patrick and Zeno got into Patrick's car and began the drive to Praiano. Zeno was relaxed in his seat and said, "Thanks, Patrick, for all you did to make today successful. It exceeded my wildest expectations."

"I give your parents credit! They came around."

"Thanks to you!"

"I didn't do anything. It was your love for your parents and theirs for you that prevailed."

"Maybe Stefano and Roberto had something to do with it, too."

“Are you turning psychic on me?” Patrick said playfully to Zeno.

“You have to admit, their presence was palpable today.”

Patrick nodded and reached over to Zeno, squeezing his hand warmly.

They arrived at Nunzia’s pensione, parked, and slipped inside. They undressed and slipped under the covers today, holding each other tenderly as they fell into a peaceful sleep.

10

Chapter Ten

Patrick had put a do not disturb sign on the door, but he heard knocking and Nunzia's voice outside. "I brought you *prima collazione* – some coffee and pastries."

"*Un attimo, arrivo.*"

Patrick nudged Zeno. "Wake up," and slipped on a pair of shorts and a shirt. He opened the door a crack and saw Nunzia with a tray in her hands.

"I don't want to disturb you but thought you might like some coffee."

"That's very thoughtful." He took the tray. Nunzia peered into the room. Zeno had already ducked into the bathroom. "*Grazie,*" Patrick said, closing the door.

The tray was made up for two people. Either someone had alerted Nunzia or she saw them come in late the night before. Zeno came in from the bathroom, his hair tousled and torso gleaming in the morning light streaming through the balcony window.

"Look what Nunzia brought – for both of us!"

Zeno looked embarrassed. Patrick pushed the door to the balcony open and set the tray on a little table. He walked back in and gave Zeno a warm kiss, stroking his chest with his hands. He felt himself become aroused and noticed Zeno getting hard as well. He playfully rubbed his hand over the front of Zeno's shorts and then grabbed his hand and led him outside.

"*Caffé?*"

"*Sì, grazie.*"

Patrick poured some espresso from the pot into a small cup and handed it to Zeno. He thought to himself how handsome he looked. He loved his broad but gentle shoulders and the thin dark hair covering his chest and running down his abdomen. Zeno was lean, his shorts clinging tenaciously to his hipbone and long legs angled between the chair and table, his feet pressed against Patrick's.

"You okay?" Patrick inquired tenderly.

"*Sì, molto* - very much."

"I'm glad."

"And you?" Zeno inquired in return.

"I'm so happy."

Zeno reached for one of the croissants, and broke a piece off, raising it to Patrick's mouth and feeding him playfully. Patrick smiled and rubbed his hands over Zeno's leg. He looked out over the sea and took a deep breath.

"*Che facciamo oggi?*" Zeno inquired.

"Well, you have to work, and I have some business to take care of."

Zeno looked sad.

"But, if you like, I can pick you up after work tonight."

Zeno grinned and nodded, taking another sip of coffee as he leaned his head back and let the sun caress his face.

They showered and dressed. As they walked out into the lobby, Nunzia winked. He and Zeno drove to Positano, where Patrick left

Zeno off at his parent's. Patrick went back to Praiano and, as he entered the pensione, Nunzia stood at the desk, tapping her fingers.

"Well?" she began.

"Well what?" Patrick replied, lifting his hands up as if he had no idea what she was curious about. "Oh, you mean Zeno?"

Nunzia nodded, "Yes, Zeno."

Patrick recounted the conversation with Zeno's parents, the late dinner, and the overnight. Nunzia was happy for him and then pressed, "Well, what's next?"

"It's complicated," Patrick began. "I'm married. We have property. I have a job. I don't know what to do."

"Oh, I think you do. The question is whether you have the *coglioni* – the balls - to do it."

"Nunzia!" he said, as if offended by her language, and then added, "Who made you a therapist?"

"Dear, if you only knew the number of guests who use me as a sounding board!"

"I love Zeno, but he lives here. I live in Boston, and I have to untangle things there."

"Sounds like you have the start of a plan."

"What do you mean, with Girard?"

"Hm hum."

"What do I do?"

"What do you want to do?"

"I have grown to appreciate how much family and traditions mean to me and how Girard doesn't value that. Part of it is his own background, his abusive and unloving parents, but I don't see any interest on his part to change."

"Do you love him?"

"I did. But I feel that through my parents' deaths, his true colors came out. He likes the idea of us, but he doesn't love me as I am. And he's cheating. I've closed off my heart in defense."

"We all deserve to be loved for who we are."

Patrick nodded.

"Then what? Do you love Zeno?"

"It's early, but I think so."

"Why don't you settle things at home and come back?"

"I have to work."

"We can find work for you here."

"But I don't want to lose my position at the school."

"Why don't you take a temporary leave?"

Patrick nodded in agreement, as if a light came on inside his head. "I think I'm going to make some calls. Can you excuse me?"

"Certainly. If you need anything, just call."

Patrick went to his room and walked out onto the balcony. He felt his heart race as he contemplated calling Girard. He looked out over the calming water, breathed in deeply, then dialed the number.

Girard answered, "Hello, Patrick. Are you back in Boston?"

"No. I'm still in Italy."

"What about school?"

"I'm going to ask for a longer leave."

"When are you coming back?"

"I don't know yet." Patrick cleared his throat nervously and then continued, "I know you want to talk, but there's nothing to talk about."

"I said I'm sorry. I messed up."

"Yes, you did. But that's not the biggest challenge."

There was silence on the other end of the line, so Patrick continued, "I don't think we want the same things. I know my parents were not welcoming, but I have come to appreciate how important family, home, and traditions are. I want to hold on to my parents' home and start a family."

"We've discussed this before, and I thought it was settled. We'd sell it and buy a bigger place in the city."

"The last time I was in the house, I realized I couldn't do that. I'm sorry."

"But we've been through so much. Why throw it all away?"

Patrick was surprised by what Girard said. "You're chastising me for throwing it all away when you were having an affair with Carlos?"

"It was an indiscretion, and I feel bad about it."

"It was more than an indiscretion. You guys were together for months behind my back. I'm not sure you're invested in us."

Girard remained silent. Then he timidly interjected, "So what's next?"

"I think we should get divorced."

"Isn't that a bit hasty?" Girard said with a slight tremble in his voice.

"I don't think so. I've been thinking about it, and I don't see this getting better. You're frustrated with me, and I with you," Patrick elaborated.

"Shouldn't we talk about this? Why don't I meet you in Rome or something?"

"No. I've got things to do here. I think you should talk with Bob about drawing up some preliminary papers for divorce."

"When are you coming back?" Girard inquired desperately.

"I'm not sure. Why don't you send me the documents electronically?"

"This is not really happening, is it?" Girard asked in shock.

"Afraid so," Patrick replied.

"But we can work this out," Girard insisted.

"I'm not confident we can."

"But we could," Girard pressed further.

"Talk to Bob. Send me the documents."

"Wow! You're being pretty hard about this," was all Girard could say.

"I wasn't the one who cheated. Bye," Patrick said as he hung up.

Patrick let out a deep sigh and said to himself, "That wasn't as bad as I had thought."

Next, he called the principal of the school. He explained the challenges of dealing with both parents passing and needing more time to settle their affairs. They discussed a year-long leave and agreed to the terms. He could start up again the following September.

As he hung up, he stepped out of his room into the front lobby. Nunzia wasn't there. He walked downstairs onto the terrace and saw her sweeping. She looked up and raised her eyes curiously.

"*Tutto a posto.*" Patrick stated triumphantly.

"What do you mean, *tutto a posto*? Did you already get things straightened out?"

Patrick nodded, struggling to formulate words as he got emotional. He sobbed. "I . . . ended . . mmmy relationship wi. . with Girard."

"*Caro,*" Nunzia began, a tear streaking down her cheek. "*Corragio!*" She gave him a warm hug.

"It's done. I finally said what needed to be said for some time. It just wasn't the right fit."

"I'm sorry, but proud you were able to say what you needed to say."

"It took the death of my parents and a trip to Italy to recognize it."

"Life is an interesting journey!"

Patrick smiled. "And I don't have to go back to work until next September."

Nunzia looked at him with alarm. "What will you do for money?"

"My parents left money and a house. I'm good for a while."

"You can stay here as long as you like. I can even put you to work."

"Grazie, Nunzia, but I don't want to take advantage of your hospitality."

"*È niente* – it's nothing."

"Can I stay a little while longer? I'll probably go back to Boston but then come back – depending on Zeno. Maybe he and I can find a place together.

She nodded. "Make yourself at home."

"*Grazie*," he said again.

Patrick went back into his room, sorted through some things, and then went out on the balcony to sit, read, and think. He texted Zeno, "*Ciao, caro. Vuoi passare la notte qui*? – do you want to spend the night here?"

Zeno texted back, "Are you sure that's okay with your aunt?"

"Yes – I think she would be happy about it."

"I get off at 10. Can you pick me up?"

"Can you serve me dinner?"

"With pleasure."

Patrick spent the afternoon on the deck reading. He swam, sunned, and napped. The time felt surreal – as if he had been transported to another world and life. A few weeks ago, he was walking through the South End of Boston meeting friends for dinner and now he was overlooking the Mediterranean, speaking Italian, becoming part of his grandfather's family, and falling in love.

The break-up with Girard was disturbing. He never imagined a divorce – gay couples didn't do that. He felt like he had failed but kept reminding himself that Girard was the one who had pursued an affair. If it wasn't for Zeno, he would have felt like he was unlovable, that he hadn't been enough for someone. Zeno's affection was reaffirming – and it didn't hurt that Pepe was in pursuit as well. He chuckled as he thought of him.

He looked around at the coastline, at Positano in the far distance, and realized this could be his home. It felt odd and reassuring at the same time – a sense of time-honored traditions and connection to the earth that grounded him.

At around seven, he put on some slacks and a long-sleeve shirt and drove to Positano. He parked the car in the family lot and walked down the steps, greeting Carlo at the front of the restaurant.

"I presume you want Zeno's section." Carol noted with a warm smile.

"Unless there's someone better," Patrick playfully stated.

"He's the best!"

"Then show me my table."

Carlo took him to the lower terrace where Zeno was waiting tables. They smiled at each other, and Patrick took a seat at a small two-person table near the edge of the deck, just next to the sand. It was a quiet and discrete table, one from which he could observe Zeno as he worked.

Zeno brough him some wine and water and made some suggestions from the menu. Although Positano was known for its seafood, Patrick was craving meat. He ordered veal scallopini with risotto. In Italian fashion, he ordered salad after his main course. The scallopini were tender and succulent – done in a light wine/marsala sauce with capers. The risotto was made with porcini mushrooms, rich and creamy. The flavors were more pronounced than usual. He wondered if the fresh salt air was the reason.

Zeno dashed back and forth between the kitchen and his clients. He was attentive, courteous, and handsome. People responded well to him – smiling, nodding, and chatting with him as he brought dishes to their tables. Patrick had only just met him but got a good vibe – a sense that he was a soulful person.

When he brought Patrick's salad, there was a gentleness in Zeno's gaze. He seemed eager to please and, even more importantly, eager to understand what his clients wanted. Patrick found that so refreshing after years with Girard, who was more interested in making sure his plan was executed and that Patrick had bought into it. For the first time in his adult life, someone seemed genuinely interested in finding out what he felt, what he wanted, what he needed.

11

Chapter Eleven

Patrick took a walk after dinner, waiting for Zeno to finish work. He took off his shoes and walked on the cool sand, swells washing up on the steep shoreline. The moon rose over the horizon, a bright yellow globe beaming across the serene ocean. He glanced back at the bright lights of the restaurant, people clinking wine glasses, telling stories, and enjoying the sensual ocean air. The lights of Positano rose steeply above the restaurant, strings of lights crisscrossing villas, walkways, and terraces.

The silhouette of a figure approached. As it got closer, he realized it was Zeno. He had taken off his waiter's coat, wearing only his black pants and white starched shirt, now open and flapping gently in the breeze.

"Zeno, are you already finished for the night?" Patrick said as Zeno got closer.

"Carlo let me off early."

Zeno walked up to him and gave him a kiss. He grabbed his hand and squeezed it warmly.

"How was work?" Patrick asked.

"Fine except for a troublesome customer."

"What happened?"

"Oh, he was making eyes at me. It was distracting."

"So, did you report him to Carlo?"

"No, I took things in my own hands."

"Oh, did you? And what did you do?"

"That remains to be seen – or should I say – felt!"

Patrick pulled him close and gave him a warm kiss. Zeno kissed him back, but then looked up to make sure no one was looking.

"*Scusi*," I probably shouldn't do that in public.

"It's okay. I'm still a little nervous."

"Do you want to take a walk or go back to Praiano?"

"I'd love to take you for a boat ride," he said with a gleam in his eye.

"Hm," Patrick murmured.

"How about a midnight swim?"

"Here or in Praiano?"

"Praiano – the water is calmer."

Patrick took Zeno's hand and led him toward the boardwalk. They climbed the steps to the main road and retrieved Patrick's car. They drove to Nunzia's inn, parked, and went inside the room, where Patrick quickly pulled Zeno's shirt off.

"Time for our swim," Patrick noted.

"But I don't have a suit here," Zeno protested.

"Who said you need a suit?"

"I'm a good Catholic," Zeno noted.

"By whose definition?" Patrick inquired.

Patrick pulled down Zeno's pants and stroked his growing erection. He turned around, opened a drawer, and pulled out a pair of swim trunks. "*Copriti* – cover yourself."

"*Perché* – why?"

"It's my aunt's inn – we have to behave."

"And you – what are you going to wear?"

"*Questi*," he said as he held up another pair of trunks. "I bought these today."

"They're beautiful – can I see them on you?"

Patrick pulled down his pants, his own hardness obvious. Zeno stroked him and then took the new bathing suit and held it, ready for Patrick to step into. As Patrick stepped into the legs, Zeno pulled them up to just under Patrick's balls.

"*Dai*! – go on," Patrick encouraged him. "Pull them up."

"It's too small," Zeno said.

"What – the suit or my package?"

"The suit, you fool. Your package is *abbondante*!"

"I think the suit can stretch – *così*!" he said as he pulled the spandex suit over his firmness. "*Andiamo*!"

They both left the room, walked down to the lower terrace, and jumped into the dark indigo water. The moon was now higher, and Patrick could make out Zeno's eyes in the glow. "You're so beautiful," he said to Zeno.

"And you, too!" Zeno said, treading closer to Patrick, squeezing his legs around him and giving him an enthusiastic embrace.

Patrick felt nervous about swimming in the dark, imagining the deep water filled with lurking sea monsters ready to bite them. He felt safe wrapped in Zeno's arms. Gentle waves rocked fishing boats tied up to the nearby pier. A few hotel guests were chatting on the upper deck, oblivious to Zeno and Patrick swimming below.

"You ready to get out, dry off, go back to the room?" Patrick asked, eager to leave the dark water.

"*Sì*," Zeno said, nodding. They swam to the ladder, climbed out, and dried themselves with the towels they had brought from the room. They walked upstairs and entered the room. Nunzia had left a bottle of wine and some cookies.

"Your aunt is so thoughtful," Zeno said as he poured a little wine into their glasses.

"She's a meddling matchmaker is what she is," Patrick replied, raising the glass and taking a sip.

"It's cute! I'm glad she's okay with things."

"Me, too. I was worried at first."

Zeno looked intensely into Patrick's eyes and said tenderly, "*Ti voglio bene*. Thanks for making things with my parents go so well."

"It was your courage that made it go well – and their humanity."

Zeno nodded.

"Do you believe in spirits?" Zeno asked of Patrick.

"In what sense?"

"Well, do you believe Roberto and Stefano are here with us?"

Patrick nodded. "It's strange you should mention that. During this trip, I have constantly felt the presence of my grandfather. I feel warm rushes of air and the subtle scent of patchouli oil that he always wore. What about you?"

Zeno hesitated, looked out the window at the moonbeams on the water, and then looked back toward Patrick. "The night before you were going to return to Boston, I was laying in my bed. I was disappointed that an enchanting day had ended, and that you were leaving. I felt sad and disheartened. All-of-a-sudden, I felt as if there was a slight weight on my shoulder, a hand pressed warmly against me. It startled me and, when I looked around to see if someone was there, it dissipated. I calmed myself down, turned over on my back, and looked up at the ceiling. I thought I heard words – whispers. I thought of my grandfather Stefano at that moment and was convinced he was trying to communicate with me."

"Wow, that must have been very cool!" Patrick said.

"It was a bit scary, and I asked out loud, '*Nonno*, what is it?' But there wasn't an answer."

"What did you do next?" Patrick asked curiously.

"It's funny. At that point I thought of you and asked my grandfather, 'what do you think of Patrick?'"

"And?"

"There was silence. However, my grandfather had given me a paper weight made of Murano glass. It was a beautiful piece – a crystal globe filled with specs of blue and turquoise stone. At the moment I asked about you, the piece reflected a beam of moonlight coming in through the window. It was an unmistakable and powerful sign, and I knew then that he was present and was excited that we had met."

"But then the next day you went off with Francesca," Patrick noted.

"I know. I feel terrible about it. I was afraid."

"What have you told her?"

"Nothing yet. It's only been two days. I need to tell her about me. Hopefully, that will help her realize it's not her who is the problem."

"Do you have a plan?"

"Yes. She's coming to the restaurant tomorrow for lunch. I'm going to tell her."

"Can I sit at a nearby table?" Patrick inquired playfully.

"That would be very distracting!"

"Just kidding."

"I've asked Carlo to be there. He knows Francesca and maybe can be of assistance."

"You know she's going to be very upset," Patrick said with concern.

"I'm not so sure. I have a feeling someone else has been pursuing her. She's been a little distant lately."

"Maybe she suspects?"

"No, I think she's just conflicted."

"I wouldn't be," Patrick said with a wink.

Zeno blushed. Patrick reached over, took his hand, and held it warmly. He stood up and pulled Zeno up with him. He pulled him close, held him tightly, and said, "You feel like home to me!"

A tear streaked down Zeno's cheek, and he leaned toward Patrick and gave him a moist kiss. He rubbed his hands over Patrick's shoulder and then down his back, grabbing the top of his suit and pulling it off. Patrick leaned down and pulled Zeno's off, tossing it onto the chair. He then led him over to the bed where they slipped under the covers and fell asleep, Zeno's legs laying over Patrick's hips and his arms resting on his side.

12

Chapter Twelve

The next morning, Patrick dropped Zeno off at his house and continued along the coastal route to Pompeii. He had been wanting to see the large archaeological park and decided, given Zeno's appointment with Francesca, today might be a good one to be out of the way.

It was a warm day, and the parking area of the archaeological park was already crowded with tour buses and private limousines dropping off tourists. Patrick had a timed entry, showed his ticket to the guard, and was waved in past the long line.

The main square of the ancient town of Pompeii spread out before him as he walked into the grounds. Bright yellow and cream pavement stones gleamed in the sunlight. In the main square, there were remnants of temples and public buildings and exhibits of individuals caught in agony as the ash of Vesuvius encased them. Ancient homes and businesses spread out from the center – most only one story tall, upper floors and roofs burned or crushed under the volcanic stone thrown from the eruption.

It was easy to imagine life in the 1st century with ruins of small taverns showcasing cooling basins for drinks and marble bars for food. Luxurious baths with different temperature pools suggested an enviable level of opulence and leisure for the seaside resort. Patrick was amazed at the beauty of intact villas – bedrooms facing garden courtyards and reflecting pools, their walls covered in rich dark red frescos.

He had read in several guidebooks how there had been earthquakes warning of an imminent eruption and how the local population disregarded the signs as they continued their daily life. He remarked to himself how similar modern populations are to the ancient ones – disregarding catastrophic climate change threatening coastal communities around the world.

He continued to wander about the park but, as the heat increased, he decided to have a light lunch and then head back to Praiano. He found his car, snaked his way through traffic outside of Sorrento, and finally got onto the Amalfi coastal route.

As he drove, he texted Zeno: "How did it go?"

"*Ti spiego piu tardi* – I'll explain later."

"When?"

"Now? Where are you?"

"Just outside Positano. Do you want me to pick you up?"

"*Si! Al parcheggio.*"

Patrick pulled up to the restaurant's parking lot and saw Zeno chatting with Pino. He recognized Patrick's car and waved him down. Patrick stopped, opened the door, and Zeno jumped in.

"*Andiamo*!" he said, apparently stressed.

"What happened?"

"She was very upset."

"What did you say to her?"

"I explained that I liked her a lot, but that I had been gradually coming to the realization that I am gay. She laughed."

"Laughed?"

"Yes. She said she didn't believe it – that I was just trying to get out of our relationship."

"And?"

"She cried and said I was her only love and what was she going to do?"

"How did that make you feel?"

"Terrible. I almost backed off. But, when she excused herself to go to the bathroom to recompose herself, she left her phone on the table. A text came in from a Martino."

Patrick's brows raised.

Zeno continued, "I picked up the phone and scrolled through the texts from Martino. It would appear that Francesca and Martino were seeing each other. There were all sorts of romantic exchanges, even a few photos that were rather provocative."

"You're kidding?" Patrick said energetically.

"No. I wish I were. I was dumbfounded!"

"So, what did you do?"

"When she came back to the table, I asked her point blank, 'Who's Martino?' If you could have seen her expression. It looked like she had seen a ghost."

"What did she say?"

"She said it was nothing – that Martino was a good friend. I then recounted the things she and Martino said to each other and suggested these were not things you say to someone who is just a friend. She was embarrassed, stood up, and tossed water from her glass at me."

"That's very grownup of her."

"Yeah. It caused quite a scene at the restaurant. Everyone looked our way. Francesca marched off."

"And what did you do?"

"I sat back down, poured myself a glass of wine, and took a deep breath!"

"Good for you. And now?"

"Now I'm with you. I'm relieved. I don't feel like I'm putting her in a precarious situation by breaking up with her. She's already seeing someone."

"What do you want to do now?"

"I need to take a walk and clear my head," Zeno said. "I have an idea. Have you ever been to Ravello?"

"No, where's that?"

"It's a beautiful town along the coast perched very high on cliffs – just beyond Amalfi. Would you like to go?"

"I don't have any other plans, and spending time with you is marvelous!"

Zeno smiled. He directed Patrick along the coastal route until they reached a small narrow road that wound its way up a steep mountain to Ravello. They parked in a lot near the town square and walked to the Villa Cimbrone, a historic estate with gardens and views of the sea several thousand feet below.

"This is a popular tourist destination and a favorite wedding venue," Zeno began as they entered the grounds.

"It's so serene and beautiful," Patrick noted as he glanced around the sculptured hedges and the majestic cypress trees. The gardens seemed to float in the air with the sea and coastline thousands of feet below. They walked further along and came to a balustrade with unobstructed views of the horizon before them. "Wow!" Patrick exclaimed, feeling a little vertigo from the height.

"It's magnificent. My parents used to bring me here as a little boy."

"I bet you were a cutie!"

Zeno grinned sheepishly.

They continued to walk along the pebble pathway, enjoying the gentle breeze and the sunshine. Patrick paused and turned to Zeno, "Zeno, I have something to share with you."

Zeno looked nervous.

"Don't be anxious – it's all good."

Zeno sighed.

"I have asked for a year's leave-of-absence from my school in Boston and have asked Girard to work up papers for our divorce."

"Wow! That's a lot of news," Zeno said with alarm.

"Sorry. I thought it might be reassuring."

"It is. It's just a little surprising. So, you're not going back to Boston?"

"I'll have to at some point, but I don't have to hurry, and I can go back and forth – at least during the next year."

Zeno grinned, realizing what this meant.

"Nunzia offered me a room and some work off-season. There's someone I would like to get to know better here!"

Zeno let his hand brush Patrick's as they continued walking along the terrace overlooking the sea below.

"And you're officially divorcing Girard?" Zeno asked further.

Patrick nodded, a little emotional. After a paused he said, "Yes, I made it official. He pleaded for time, for a second chance, but I don't think it's a good match."

"Are you sure," Zeno added, sensing that Patrick was making the decision in the light of what had transpired between them.

"Yes, I'm sure," Patrick said, looking warmly into Zeno's eyes.

Zeno was quiet, contemplating the quick development of things.

"What's wrong?" Patrick asked.

"It's just a lot of change."

"I know. Do you need more time?"

Zeno nodded an unconvincing no.

Patrick interjected, "We can take our time, get to know each other. No pressure."

Zeno's face brightened slightly. There was an awkward silence, and Patrick said, "I know this is a lot but, for some reason, I feel like I have known you for a lot longer."

Zeno nodded.

Patrick looked directly at Zeno and said, "But I want to know more. Like what you enjoy doing during free time? What dreams do you have for the future?"

Zeno was at a loss for words, then he said, "Well, I am not sure I could ever dream. The script was handed to me – marry, have children, be a waiter."

"So, if you could do what you want, what would you do?" Patrick asked.

"That's a good question," Zeno noted. "I think I would like to have a family, to have kids someday."

Patrick smiled warmly.

"And for the most part I like my job."

"You're good at it," Patrick said. "It seems like a pleasant life here."

Zeno nodded again. Then he said, "I guess what's different is that I want to be with a man, not a woman. I'd like to have a relationship with a man, have children, and live in a place where people accept me and my family."

"Don't you think that's possible?"

"Until recently, no. But my parents surprised me. Your aunt surprised me. It seems like things are changing, and I have to have the courage to embark on a path that is genuine."

Patrick smiled proudly.

"I would love to do that with you," Patrick said thoughtfully. "I've always wanted a family, and Girard didn't. I would love to recreate the traditions that Roberto and Chiara carried to Boston from here – the food, the family, the holidays."

"But how is a family possible? That is what made my parents most sad – the prospects of no grandchildren."

"We can adopt or hire a surrogate."

"In America, will they let gay people adopt?" Zeno inquired incredulously.

"Yes, and we can get married, too," Patrick said.

Zeno's eyes widened, and Patrick realized what he had just said.

"Oh, *scusi*!" Patrick said, holding his hand up to his mouth. "Did I just say that?"

Zeno nodded.

"Is that a problem?"

Zeno nodded no, and Patrick looked relieved.

"*Senti*, Zeno. I may be way ahead of myself, or of ourselves, but I get a good vibe – a good feeling about this. But we can take our time."

"It's all new to me, and it has all happened in a matter of days. Just be patient with me."

"I will. However, I have an idea."

"Oh no," Zeno said playfully, "another one of your ideas?"

"Hear me out. How would you like to go to Boston?"

"What?" Zeno said excitedly.

"Yes. I need to go back to Boston to take care of things. It's the end of the season here. Why don't you come with me? We can spend some time together, get to know each other, and you can see where I'm from."

"When were you planning to go back?"

"I was thinking sooner than later. When would Carlo let you off work?"

"I don't know. I'd have to talk with him."

"I have a feeling he would encourage you," Patrick said with a gleam in his eyes.

Zeno nodded.

Patrick turned excitedly toward Zeno and held his hands. "This could be so exciting! I would love to show you Boston and the house Roberto and Chiara built so many years ago."

"That would be nice. I've always wanted to go to America. Could we go to New York?"

"Of course. It's only a few hours from Boston."

"Oh my God. I can't believe this," Zeno said, jumping up and down.

"You're like a little kid," Patrick said, smiling widely.

They walked back to the car and returned to Praiano. They parked in front of the inn and walked into the lobby, Nunzia working at her desk.

"What's up with you two? Looks like you're guilty of something," she said, pointing her finger at them.

Zeno blurted out excitedly, "Patrick's invited me to Boston!"

"Oh, has he?"

Zeno nodded.

"Don't you have a job?" she pressed.

"It's the end of the season, and Carlo is bound to let me go."

"Well, that's fine and good, but I think Patrick just accepted a position here," she winked.

"I'm negotiating for more pay," Patrick said with a stern but sarcastic face.

"Come here," she said warmly. "I need a hug!" Nunzia hugged Zeno and Patrick warmly. "You're both so cute!"

Zeno grabbed Patrick's hand and dragged him to Patrick's room, "Sorry, Nunzia, we have some things to research on the internet – like flights!"

"By the way, Patrick, I got a message from Alberto. Pepe is looking for you." She handed him a note.

Patrick opened it and read, "Patrick, can you come up for dinner? I have something to show you."

Patrick looked up at Zeno and said, "Would you like to go up to the Benevento vineyard for dinner, with Pepe?"

Zeno looked worried. "What does he want?"

"I don't know. He says he wants to show me something."

Zeno looked over at Nunzia, who nodded. "Well, I guess so. Tonight?"

Patrick nodded, then turned to Nunzia. "Can you let Alberto know we'll meet Pepe at his place for dinner this evening?"

She nodded.

"Let's go, Zeno. We have some flights to book."

Zeno relaxed, smiled, and followed Patrick down the hall.

Patrick booked Zeno on the same flight of his return to Boston. They made a list of things Zeno would need to pack and sketched out an itinerary of things to see and do while in the States. Around 6, they drove up to the Benevento vineyard and knocked on Pepe's door.

The sun had set over the ridges behind Pepe's cottage, and a gentle breeze blew up from the water across the vines. A small grill was glowing near the porch, and Zeno and Patrick both smelled fresh herbs and garlic through the screen door.

Pepe appeared and smiled warmly. "Come in," he waved to them, pushing the door open.

Patrick gave him an embrace and kissed him on both cheeks. Zeno shook Pepe's hands, and Pepe reached over and gave him a kiss on one cheek. Pepe was wearing a pair of jeans and a tight-fitting polo shirt that showed off his muscular chest and broad shoulders. His hair was still moist from a shower, and he rubbed his fingers nervously over several errant strands.

"It smells incredible," Patrick began. "I didn't know you cooked!"

"I have a lot of hidden talents," Pepe said with a wink, looking awkwardly at Zeno, who seemed ill at ease.

Zeno surveyed the space, walking up close to a painting on the wall. "*Bello*!" he said.

"*Grazie*," Pepe replied.

Patrick interjected, "Pepe paints. It must be one of his."

Pepe nodded.

It was a landscape painting of a vineyard with hints of the ocean in the distance. The sun was shining through the leaves, creating a beautiful contrast between the yellow translucent vines and the darker green heavier growth closer to the trunks.

"Something to drink?" Pepe offered.

"*Un po' di vino*?" Patrick answered in a question.

"*E per te, Zeno*?"

"*Vino, grazie*," he replied similarly.

Pepe opened a Benevento bottle of red and poured them all a glass. "*Salute*!" he said, raising his glass.

Patrick and Zeno raised their glasses and took seats around a coffee table where cold cuts and cheese had been artfully arranged. Patrick looked scrutinizingly at Pepe, who was picking up a piece of prosciutto and glancing over at Zeno. "He has to be gay," he said to himself. "There's no doubt!"

Zeno felt self-conscious. He cut a slice of cheese and took a long sip of the wine.

"Well, Patrick, I'm sure you're wondering why I asked you to come up."

Patrick nodded.

"When you told me about finding out who Stefano was, I realized he must have lived here, in this house."

"I thought so, too," Patrick admitted, looking over at Zeno to draw him into the conversation.

"Well, as I shared with you before, there was a small library and study when I moved in. The other day I decided to look through some of the older books to see if there might be anything of interest."

Patrick leaned forward on the edge of his chair.

"There were some old schoolbooks with the name Stefano Voluto written inside the front cover."

"That's my grandfather's name," Zeno interjected.

Pepe nodded. "There's more," he added, taking another sip of wine. He reached for an envelope on a small table near his chair, opened the flap, and pulled out some yellowed pieces of paper. "I found these in one of them. I had never noticed them before since I had no interest in the schoolbooks and had simply placed them together on the case."

"What are they?" Patrick inquired.

"Love letters."

Now Zeno was curious. "Between whom?"

"It would appear between your two grandfathers," Pepe said with a gleam in his eye.

Patrick reached for the papers and opened them up, his hand trembling. They were in old Italian script, and he couldn't decipher them. Zeno reached over, took them, and began to read them slowly.

"*Caro, Stefano*," Zeno read in Italian. He slowly translated in English, "You are my heart. You are my soul. With you the days are bright and the evenings warm."

"Should I go on?" Zeno asked.

Patrick nodded nervously.

"When I look into your eyes, I see the ocean. When you speak, I hear the gentle breeze." Zeno read further along silently. He shuffled the papers. "Here's one from Stefano to Roberto." He read, "I can't wait for the harvest. Your father will let you stay with me to get an early start with the workers. We can make dinner together and enjoy the night together."

Pepe blushed, and Patrick stirred. Zeno's hand shook as he continued to shuffle through the letters. "Should I read more?"

Patrick didn't reply. He was looking off into the distance. Zeno began quietly, "Stefano, when the harvest is over and the wine ready, I'll ask my father to send us to Naples to meet with the distributors. It will be a wonderful getaway – just the two of us."

"Here's a small note. 'Meet me at our place in an hour. I need to see you.'"

Patrick reached over and took the letters from Zeno's hands, shuffling them, glancing at the signatures – affectionately, Stefano; with love, Roberto; with all my heart, Roberto; devotedly, Stefano.

"But these could just be the letters of good friends, no?" Patrick suggested. "Italians are more expressive, right?"

Pepe and Zeno looked at each other and nodded no. "These are beyond that," Pepe interjected. "If you look at these as a whole – and there are more – it would appear your grandfathers loved each other – a lot."

"But they married," Zeno said, confused.

"It was a different time," Pepe noted. Patrick thought Pepe's words ironic. Pepe continued, "They did what they had to do but were true to their hearts."

"Do any of the letters mention their marrying?" Patrick inquired.

Pepe nodded and handed him two more envelopes. "These appear to have been written at the time of Roberto's marriage with Chiara."

"*Carissimo Stefano*. I'm sorry you will not be at the wedding. I have been lost since you left, and I hope your marriage to Rita brings you half as much love and as we have had together. I am sorry I could not persuade my father to let you marry Anna. It is unfair, and I will never forgive him. He has forced us to separate, one of the most painful things of my life. Chiara and I have decided to go to America. It is too painful to remain here and feel your absence

- in the breezes, on the horizon, and amongst the vines. I hope you understand, and I hope one day we can be reunited. Love forever, Roberto."

"Oh my God," Patrick began. "This makes Robert's departure even more tragic. How horrible to have to leave the person you loved most."

"*Veramente*," Pepe stated thoughtfully.

"Roberto must have felt it would be easier to make a definitive break," Zeno suggested.

Patrick and Pepe both nodded.

"Wow. This really changes things," Patrick said.

"How so?" Pepe inquired.

"I had concluded that Roberto and Stefano were friends, but nothing more. Roberto was happily married to Chiara and Stefano to Rita."

"But they were," Zeno said.

"Yes, I guess you could say that," Patrick conceded. "They were happy. But it's sad that their real passion and love was unlived."

"Are you sure?" Pepe interjected. "Did your grandfather seem sad, Patrick?"

"No. He was a happy man. He cherished Chiara and was devoted to his family."

"*Appunto*," Pepe underscored.

"But even if he was happy, there had to be part of his heart that was broken, wounded. In fact, he died of heart disease."

"Stefano died of the same," Zeno added.

Pepe leaned back in his chair, a look of alarm on his face. He looked restless and stood up, going to the stove to check on the sauce he was making and to season the steak he had prepared to grill. Patrick looked over at him compassionately, sensing the story of Stefano and Roberto hit too close to home.

There was a solemn silence in the room. Zeno broke it, saying, "Pepe, do you need some help?"

Pepe, his eyes watering, nodded yes.

Zeno went to the kitchen and helped Pepe carry the steaks out to the grill. Patrick remained inside, holding the letters in his hands, and trying to decipher the script. Later, Pepe and Zeno returned with the steaks, placed them on plates with roasted potatoes, marinated asparagus, and peppers, and set them on the dining table.

"*Buon appetito*," Pepe said. "Thanks for coming."

"It's our pleasure," Patrick replied. "Thanks for sharing the letters so respectfully. What an unexpected discovery."

"Indeed," Pepe underscored. "I hope you both realize what a legacy you inherit from your grandfathers."

"How so?" Zeno asked, looking up from his plate.

"I can see it in you – you both share the same love Roberto and Stefano had. It's almost as if they were reincarnated in you."

Zeno and Patrick looked at each other.

"It's as if their love continued to search for a way forward, and it finally did, after seventy years."

Patrick looked down at his plate, afraid to look up again at Zeno or Pepe. He felt it – he felt the heart of Roberto pounding within him, but he was embarrassed to admit it, to recognize it, for fear he would experience the same painful loss. He sensed that Zeno had the same apprehension, two souls destined for each other, carrying traces of heartache and remorse deep within their DNA.

Pepe, sensing their anxiousness, raised his glass. "I want to propose a toast."

Zeno and Patrick raised theirs.

"To courageous love!"

"To courageous love," they all repeated.

"And to fortitude," he proposed again.

Zeno and Patrick nodded, raising their glasses again.

Patrick placed his glass down on the table and glanced over at Pepe, cutting a piece of the pink-red meat on his plate. "What a wise and loving man," he thought to himself. He took a deep breath and sighed, a faint but perceptible scent of patchouli oil floating over the table.

13

Chapter Thirteen

Zeno followed the path for non-US citizens in the customs area at Logan airport. Patrick took the one for citizens. A few minutes later, they reunited at the baggage claim, waiting for their suitcases.

"I can't believe I'm here," Zeno began excitedly, looking around the claim area as if beginning his tour of America. Other passengers on the flight stood nearby, mostly Brits and Americans who had flown in from London.

"Me, too! I can't wait to show you Boston," Patrick said warmly, holding Zeno's hand as they waited for their luggage. Zeno looked nervously at him. "It's okay. This is Boston – it's very liberal."

Zeno sighed and let his shoulders relax as he squeezed Patrick's hand.

"Oh, there's mine," Zeno said enthusiastically as a blue suitcase circled the carousel. He grabbed it and checked the label. Patrick's followed soon after, and they wheeled the cases outside into the main part of the terminal and picked up the shuttle to the car rental building. After they got their car, Patrick began driving them to his parent's home in West Roxbury.

Zeno pressed his face against the window, looking at the illuminated skyline as they came out of the tunnel and began heading on the turnpike. "It's bigger than I anticipated," Zeno remarked. "I thought you said Boston was a small city."

"Well, compared to New York and Chicago, it is. But it's still a major center, and there's been a boom in recent years with all the pharmaceutical companies expanding here."

Patrick reached over and held his hand. They exited the turnpike and made their way through the well-established neighborhoods of Newton. As they passed Boston College, Patrick remarked, "Here's where I went to college."

"It's beautiful," Zeno began. "It looks like a typical New England campus with the old-style traditional buildings and tower."

"I have a lot of fond memories of my time here."

"How fond?" Zeno asked, casting an accusatory glance toward him.

"Hm," Patrick murmured, looking off into the distance. He looked back at Zeno and said, "Actually, in terms of dating, the memories weren't good. I still harbored a lot of shame and reticence when I was young, and the student body was rather conservative."

"I thought you said Boston was liberal."

"It is, and a lot of my friends at BC were liberal. But there was also a significant population that was politically and religiously conservative."

"When did you meet Girard?"

"After college, through some mutual friends."

"Are you going to see him while we're here?"

"I might have to, although I would like to avoid it."

"I'd like to meet him," Zeno said with confidence.

"Why?"

"I don't know. Maybe to put a face with a name. See the competition."

"But you've seen pictures."

"I know, but there's something about the vibes you pick up in person that is revealing."

Patrick nodded. "We'll see. I don't want to create problems for you."

"I can handle myself. Remember, I'm a waiter in a town that sees a lot of people who think they are entitled."

"I wouldn't want to mess with you," Patrick said playfully.

They continued driving toward the house. They crossed a busy boulevard into another neighborhood and then down a side street. Zeno's pressed his face against the window, observing a world that was very different from his own.

They pulled into Patrick's driveway. "It's so big!" Zeno said as he looked through the front window of the car. "And you have a yard."

"It's very different from Positano, where homes are terraced and jammed into every space possible. Here there is room to spread. We have yards – you have the ocean."

Patrick opened his car door, lifted the trunk hatch, and unloaded their suitcases. Zeno followed him to the front door. Patrick unlocked the door, turned on the lights, and breathed in the familiar smell of his home.

Patrick realized he and Girard had emptied the house before selling it, so a week before he and Zeno left Italy, he ordered some basic furniture online – a bed and some bedside tables for the main bedroom, a sofa and some easy chairs for the living room, a dining table that was placed in a sunny nook next to the kitchen, and a few appliances and essentials for the kitchen. He had his agent and friend, Bill, accept them in advance of their arrival. "I got a few things, but I'm afraid we're going to have to go shopping. There's a lot to replace."

"It looks wonderful already. It's so spacious and homey," Zeno said, his mouth agape as he walked through the house.

"As you can see, this is the main room – the living room," he pointed to the space they were in. The bare hardwood floors, little furniture, and no lamps or art made the space feel cold, empty. "Here's the kitchen," he said to Zeno as they walked around the corner. "My father was a plumber, so he remolded it just a few years before his death."

"It's beautiful. I love the tile floor and the marble countertops. It reminds me of home." He ran his hand along the gleaming center island.

"We'll have to get some stools to put under here," Patrick said as he pointed to the overhang. He opened a cabinet, "And we'll have to go get plates, glasses, and food!"

"I can't wait to do that with you," Zeno said excitedly.

Patrick took his hand and led him upstairs. "There are three bedrooms and two baths up here." He poked his head into the two smaller rooms and then led Zeno into the master bedroom. "*Ecco, nostra camera* – here's our room." He turned toward Zeno and gave him a kiss.

Both stood quietly in the doorway, an unspoken tension floating in the air. The word "our" made them both nervous. Things were progressing rapidly, but both were reluctant to put on the brakes. It was Zeno's first male relationship and Patrick was on the rebound. Both realized the risks they were facing.

Linens for the bed and towels for the bathroom were laid out on the bed. Patrick walked over to the closet and opened the door. "Will this be large enough for your wardrobe?" he asked Zeno playfully.

"Well, for the summer, yes. But I have no idea what it's like to dress for winters here. I might need more space! By the way, where are your clothes?"

"Unfortunately, they are still at Girard's. I'm going to have to get them, eventually."

"I can go get them for you," Zeno offered.

"You're really ready for a confrontation, aren't you?"

Zeno grinned.

"Let's go get our suitcases and unpack," Patrick suggested.

Zeno nodded and followed him downstairs. They retrieved their bags, carried them upstairs, and placed things in the closet and in the bathroom. A half-hour later, they went downstairs and took a seat in the living room. "What would you like to do for dinner?" Patrick began.

"What are your favorite places?"

"Well, most are in the city, and I'm not sure I want to drive in. My dad and mom used to love a place in Dedham, nearby. It's a nice bistro – American food. We could go there and then stop at a grocery story on the way back and get some essentials."

"*Andiamo*," Zeno said enthusiastically. "*Ho fame.*"

"I'm hungry, too."

They slipped on light jackets and headed out the door. The drive was short and the restaurant able to accommodate them right away. Zeno kept looking around him, absorbing the idiosyncrasies of American life. The first thing he noticed was how informally the waiters were dressed. It was a late September evening – so people were still in summer attire – shorts, pullovers, sandals.

"Are you sure you're from here?" Zeno asked.

"What do you mean?"

"Well, compared to these people, you look like a model."

"I've been incognito for the last couple of weeks. People thought I was a schoolteacher, but I was really in Italy for a photo shoot."

"Seriously, you hit the jackpot."

Patrick looked around the room and realized that compared with the local population on the Amalfi coast, the local population looked weathered and frumpy. He began defensively, "It's the cold weather. People are putting on weight now to insulate them for the harsh winter to come."

"*Ma dai* – come on, that can't be true."

Patrick nodded, then added, "This part of Boston is known for being frugal. People don't splurge on clothing or makeup. They have a lot of money, but they don't show it off."

"It's very different in Italy. Even if you don't have money, it's important to look like you do!"

"There are parts of the States like that, but not here. You'll see the difference in the center of Boston or in New York."

At the mention of New York, Zeno smiled. Patrick realized he needed to sell him more on Boston and added, "Wait till we go into the city tomorrow – you'll see the difference."

Zeno continued to look around in observation. They ordered their dinners – braised short ribs, mashed potatoes, and roasted vegetables. They began with a salad and ended with carrot cake. Patrick kept filling Zeno's glass liberally with wine – a nice cabernet from California.

After dinner, they stopped at a grocery store to get essentials for the kitchen. As they entered the doors of the market, Zeno said, "Oh my God. Unbelievable. It's huge."

"Yes, quite different from a local market or small grocer in Positano."

Zeno began eyeing the produce, mounds of colorful peppers, fruit, greens, potatoes, tomatoes, avocados, and other assorted things. Patrick picked out some bananas and blueberries. They continued to other areas of the store, picking up cereal, sugar, salt and pepper, milk, yogurt, coffee, butter, bread, and paper products.

"Is this normal – this kind of store?"

"Yes, this is a typical American supermarket."

"But it's gigantic. We only have these places on the periphery of the cities."

"I know. It would be hard to open something like this in old Italian cities. You still have markets, though, and I miss that here. This is like a large market – but it is too organized and clean compared to Italian ones. I love the markets in Italy where you smell the greens and the tomatoes and the fish and the meat. It's fresh and earthy. Here the food has been in cold storage for weeks, traveling from California or Mexico."

"I still like it," Zeno said in amazement. They wheeled their cart through the cashier and loaded up the car for the return home.

Once home, they unpacked groceries and placed them in the refrigerator, in the cabinets, and in the pantry. Patrick had a preference for where things should go, but asked Zeno from time to time, "Where do you think we should put this?"

Zeno seemed hesitant to weigh in, throwing up his hands to express indifference.

They headed upstairs. Patrick made the bed, and Zeno went into the bathroom. He began sorting through toiletries, placing them in drawers and in the cabinet behind the mirror. He seemed anxious. Patrick approached Zeno and reached his arms around him from behind to give a warm hug. Zeno jumped. "*Caro*, are you okay?" Patrick said, noticing his reaction.

"I'm just a little edgy. Maybe it's the jet lag or the long flight – I don't know."

Patrick kissed the back of his neck and Zeno stiffened. "What's up?" Patrick asked again, realizing Zeno wasn't okay.

"I don't know." He paused and then began timidly, "There's a word in Italian – *domesticare*. I don't know if there's a similar word in English."

"You mean, domesticate?"

Zeno nodded.

"Are you afraid this is too domesticated?"

Zeno nodded again and then said, "It's not that I don't like it or want it. It just feels very all-of-a-sudden. Two weeks ago, I was serving you lunch on the beach and now we're sorting toiletries in a shared bathroom and planning to go shopping tomorrow for plates and glassware."

"Is it too much?" Patrick asked thoughtfully.

"*Sì e non,*" Zeno said ambivalently.

"I have a proposal. Why don't we think about this differently?" Patrick began thoughtfully.

Patrick took his hand and led him into the bedroom, where they sat on the edge of the bed.

"What if we think of this as a vacation – a trip for two new lovers? You're here visiting the States. I've invited you to my home and, next week, we'll go to New York. The plates and glassware and furniture are for me – you're helping me reclaim my house – as a friend, as a lover, but not as my husband."

Zeno fell back on the mattress and sighed, the tail of his shirt having popped out of his pants and his taut, hairy abdomen showing. Patrick wanted to reach over and caress it but held back.

"But I want to be your husband," Zeno responded.

"I get it – it's too fast. I'm glad you're being honest. We're both in vulnerable situations, and we don't need to put pressure on ourselves to adapt to roles that are premature." Patrick fell back next to Zeno and turned on his side, resting his head on his arm and looking deeply into Zeno's eyes. They were mesmerizing, and it took every bit of self-control to keep from leaping on top of him. "Let's enjoy being lovers. We can settle into something else later – when it feels more natural."

Zeno nodded.

Patrick then added, "Besides, if you're my lover, you can try to seduce me."

Patrick noticed Zeno become aroused at the suggestion, and he said, "And you me."

Zeno rolled over toward Patrick and gave him a warm, moist kiss. Patrick reciprocated, plunging his tongue deep within Zeno's mouth. Zeno moaned and ran his hand along Patrick's side, tugging at his pullover until it became untucked. He reached under the shirt and explored Patrick's chest, squeezing his pecs tenderly.

Patrick laid back and unzipped his pants. Zeno ran his hand down Patrick's abdomen and under his shorts, feeling the warm hardness underneath. He massaged Patrick, who arched his back in pleasure.

"*Un attimo*," Patrick said as he pulled himself up, rolled off the edge of the bed and walked to the windows where he closed the blinds and, on his way back to the bed, dimmed the lights. He walked into the bathroom and brought back a couple of condoms. At the sight of them, Zeno looked alarmed.

"Well, you said we're lovers, right?"

Zeno gulped and nodded.

"I want you to be inside of me," Patrick whispered.

Zeno seemed relieved about roles but still anxious. Patrick sat on the edge of the bed and ran his hand up under Zeno's shirt. He leaned over, raised the shirt higher, and licked the sides of Zeno's pecs. He ran his tongue down along Zeno's side and then unbuttoned Zeno's jeans. He spread the fly open and rubbed Zeno's hardness, pressing against the fabric of his undershorts. Zeno moaned.

Patrick slid the shorts off over Zeno's erection and leaned over and sucked him. Zeno closed his eyes and flexed his buttocks, savoring Patrick's warm, wet mouth around him.

Patrick slid his own undershorts off and laid on his back. Zeno straddled him and took Patrick's engorged cock in his hands and massaged it. Patrick spread his legs and Zeno pressed himself against the inside of Patrick's legs.

Patrick reached up and handed Zeno a condom. Zeno looked perplexed, as if he didn't know how to use it. Patrick took the condom back, opened it, and placed it on Zeno's erect penis, rolling the condom down the shaft. He massaged it, and it became more engorged and harder.

"*Dai*," Patrick said. "Go ahead."

Zeno held his cock and guided it into Patrick, who grimaced slightly, then relaxed as he felt Zeno inside of him. Zeno closed his eyes and thrust himself slowly and tenderly inside Patrick. He opened his eyes and rubbed his hands on Patrick's chest, then grabbed his cock and began to massage it.

"*Ti voglio bene*," Zeno murmured.

"I love you, too," Patrick said, looking at Zeno's dark brown eyes hovering over him. "I want you to come inside of me."

"*Madonna*," Zeno said with more abandon. "*Quanto sei bello - i tuoi occhi – cazzo*!"

Patrick could feel charges of pleasure rise within him and noticed Zeno becoming flush, his skin taking on a sweaty sheen and his erection becoming harder, pulsating within him. He rubbed his hands on Zeno's dark, hairy thighs.

Zeno spit into his palms and took hold of Patrick's cock, giving it long, wet strokes. Zeno's thrusts quickened, and he took hold of Patrick more firmly and quickly. Suddenly, he arched his back and writhed as he felt spasms of intense pleasure gush forth. Patrick came at the same time, tightening around Zeno within him.

Zeno collapsed on top of Patrick, who placed his hands on his back. They both laid together, listening to their hearts pounding in unison. Zeno nuzzled his nose in the nape of Patrick's neck, breathing in his scent.

"How was it?" Patrick whispered to Zeno.

"Everything I imagined, and more," he whispered. "And to think, I get to spend the night with you, too."

Patrick smiled contently. They laid there quietly for a while until Zeno said, "*Andiamo*, I need a shower." He got up and walked into the bathroom. Patrick followed him, handing him a towel, and looking for some soap. Patrick turned on the water and, in a few minutes, steam floated out of the glass enclosed space. Zeno went in first while Patrick wrapped himself in a towel and checked emails on the side of the bed. When Patrick finished his shower later, they made the bed and slid under the covers. Jet lag began to hit them, and they fell quickly asleep.

The next morning, Zeno woke to the smell of coffee. He slipped on some shorts and walked downstairs where Patrick was brewing coffee.

"How are you making coffee? I thought we had to go get some things for the kitchen," Zeno inquired as he scratched his tousled hair and approached Patrick, giving him a kiss.

"Hey cutie," Patrick said. "I ordered a few appliances with the furniture – like a coffee maker. Have a seat," he said, pointing to the table in the sunny window nook. "Do you want some cereal or yogurt or perhaps a pastry we picked up last night?"

"Just coffee, now," Zeno mumbled groggily. "What's on the agenda for today?"

"Well," Patrick began, "does my boyfriend want to help me pick out plates and glassware and other things for my house?"

Zeno looked sad. "*Mi dispiace* – I'm sorry for what I said last night. I think it was the jet lag."

"No. I think you were right on target. We need to enjoy being lovers before we settled into other roles. Let's just have fun."

Zeno smiled. "You mean, like last night?"

Patrick blushed and nodded yes.

They finished their coffee and pastry and went upstairs to shower. It was a warm late September day, so they put on shorts, pullovers, baseball caps, and dark sunglasses. "You ready?" Patrick asked as they checked their pants for wallets, phones, and keys.

Zeno nodded. They walked out the door into the sunshine, got into the car, and drove to the city center. After parking, they walked along Boylston Street to visit a large home goods store. Both were surprised how similar their tastes were regarding plates, silverware, glasses, and place settings. They loaded the car and returned to several furniture stores to look for rugs, bedding, and lamps.

"Is this all going to fit in the car?" Zeno inquired.

"You'll see. It will fit. That's why I got an SUV."

Zeno looked skeptical. "Remember, I need room for some clothes, too."

They placed the larger items in the car and then returned to the shopping area to look for clothing. Patrick was amazed how everything Zeno tried on fit him like a model. The slim jeans and colorful shirts looked good on his lean body and dark complexion.

"We need to get you a light coat for when the weather changes."

"Already?" Zeno asked.

"It changes quickly and dramatically here. It's better to be prepared."

They found a nice selection of fall clothing at one of the large department stores, filled several shopping bags, and then took a break for lunch. They selected a small restaurant on Newbury Street, the outdoor section filled with people enjoying a nice sunny afternoon. Zeno was eager to enjoy an authentic American burger.

After lunch, they returned to West Roxbury, unloaded the car, and arranged things in the house. The process felt surreal to Patrick, who had just dismantled the home a month ago. He opened the cabinets that had been filled with his mother's Irish plates and crystal and replaced them with things he and Zeno had purchased. He had saved the platters his grandparents had brought back from the Amalfi coast, but they were at Girard's. He wondered when he would finally go there to pick up clothes and personal things.

It felt good to make the place his own, arranging silverware, utensils, pots, and pans. Zeno had a good eye for decorating, finding the perfect locations for the rugs, lamps, and other decorative items. He went upstairs and arranged clothes, towels, and accessories they had purchased. Whatever reticence he had felt the day before seemed dissipated as Zeno went through the house and made it his own.

That evening they had plans to see Dale and Craig, two of Patrick's closest friends and, as the afternoon progressed, he felt his stomach tighten, thinking about introducing Zeno to them. It would mark a more definitive end to his and Girard's relationship and the beginning of a new chapter. Around 5, he and Zeno took showers and dressed for the evening.

"So, who are these guys again?" Zeno inquired.

"Dale and Craig. They are my best friends. I've known them since college."

"What do they do?"

"Dale is in finance and Craig is a dentist. You'll like them. Dale is the troublemaker. Craig is more thoughtful and sensitive. They can't wait to meet you."

Zeno blushed and stiffened.

"Don't be nervous. They'll love you. What's not to love?"

"Does this look okay," Zeno asked of the shirt he had pulled on.

Patrick unbuttoned the front of it and said, "It looks better like this," as he rubbed his hands over Zeno's chest. "It reminds me of the first day we were together. You were wearing a thin linen shirt open in the front – just like this. You were so sexy – that is – you are so sexy!"

Zeno re-buttoned the shirt. "For your eyes only."

"I hope so. You know the guys in the South End are going to be salivating when they see you."

Zeno looked anxious, and Patrick asked, "You okay?"

Zeno nodded unconvincingly then said, "I've never been to a gay restaurant or a gay club before. This is all new to me."

"Oh," Patrick said, forgetting Zeno lived in a small town and had just come out. "You'll be surprised at how natural it will feel once you're in the situation. And you'll be with me."

They drove to the South End, found a parking space, and began walking along Tremont Street toward the bistro where they were to meet Dale and Craig. They rounded a corner and saw the yellow light filtering through the large windows onto the pavement. Dale and Craig were sitting at a table in the window and waved at Patrick as he approached the front door.

Once inside, Patrick gave kisses on the cheek to the hostess. "Where have you been, dear? I haven't seen you in ages."

"Long story – for another time. But, let me introduce you to Zeno. Zeno, this is Michaela. Michaela, Zeno."

"It's a pleasure," she said.

"Mine," he replied.

She detected his accent and asked, "Where are you from?"

"Italy."

She pulled down the bottom of her eye and stared at Patrick as if to ask – "And what's the story here?" She showed them to Dale and Craig's table. They were both standing, ready to embrace Patrick and meet Zeno.

"Dale, Craig – this is Zeno. Zeno, these are trouble!"

Everyone chuckled. Dale and Craig kissed Patrick on his cheeks and shook Zeno's hand. They all sat. A buff waiter approached. "Drinks?" he asked Patrick and Zeno.

They both ordered some red wine and turned to Dale and Craig. Dale began, "So spill!"

"Where do I begin?" Patrick murmured. "As you know, I discovered Girard was having an affair."

"I told you to look out for those moralistic types," Craig said with irony.

"I know. I should have listened."

Dale interjected, "So, you went to Italy. I think last time we spoke you wanted to find out more about your grandfather and his friend – in the photo you had shown us."

Patrick pointed to Zeno. "This is my grandfather's friend's grandson."

"Amazing," Craig commented. "Tell us how that happened."

Patrick recounted the details of his trip to Italy, the *vendemmia*, and the excursion to Positano, where he met Zeno and finally made the connection with Stefano's family.

"That is so sweet," Craig said. "What an incredible story."

Zeno and Patrick each nodded and looked at each other warmly. The waiter came and took orders. The intimate restaurant filled, and the bar where locals came to meet each other was now full. As men entered to sit at the bar, they glanced toward Dale, Craig, Patrick, and Zeno. Zeno was getting a lot of attention, and Patrick became more vigilant, recognizing some of the characters, aware of their dating histories and proclivities. He also realized there was a remote change Girard would come in, and he hoped that wouldn't happen.

"So, you're back now?" Dale asked of Patrick.

"Well, I've taken a leave this year from the school. Zeno and I are here for a while. We're going to go to New York, and I think we might need to make a trip to Provincetown to pick up some art."

"Good idea," Craig said. "If you want to use our place, you can."

"That would be generous of you. We'll see."

"My aunt offered me some work in Italy, and Zeno is quite busy there in the summers. Our plans are open at the moment, but we definitely plan to return before the summer."

"What about this vineyard you mentioned?"

"Well, I have a title to some of it, but it's not like I own a lot of land or have any involvement in it."

"It must have been beautiful," Craig noted.

"It was – it is. It's incredible. I fell in love with the coast, with the people, and with my family."

The four of them finished dinner. Patrick then said, "You guys up for a visit to Club Café? I haven't been there in a while, and I thought I would show Zeno."

"Thanks, but I think we'll head home," Dale said.

"Oh, you have to come. It will be like old times. You don't have to stay late."

Dale looked at Craig, who nodded. Dale then said, "Ok, why not?"

They paid their tab and walked the few blocks to the club. People were lining up to get their ID's checked, and the inside was packed. They walked inside. The front of the club was a restaurant. In the back of the front section was a piano with a player and a vocalist. In the back of the club was a large bar area and a music-video room, filling with young patrons.

Zeno's eyes widened as he walked into the venue. He had never seen so many handsome men in one place. As an Italian, he was used to the *lo sguardo* – the glance or look – and as a waiter, he had learned to spot diners who were cruising him. But the intensity of the club was more than he expected with multiple pairs of eyes following him as he, Patrick, Dale and Craig made their way deeper into the room.

"Something to drink?" Patrick asked Zeno, Dale and Craig.

Craig said, "I'll come with you. Dale, what do you want?"

"I'll have a bourbon on the rocks," Craig said.

"Do they have Campari here?" Zeno asked.

Patrick nodded. Zeno continued, "Then I'll have a Campari and soda."

Craig and Patrick went to the bar, squeezing their way into a small opening to get the bartender's attention.

"He's really cute," Craig began. "And is in love with you – you can see it."

"I'm crazy about him," Patrick added. "I don't want to screw this one up."

"You won't. You both play off each other well."

Patrick smiled. They ordered their drinks and made their way back to Zeno and Dale, who were talking with some friends of Dale's and Craig's.

"Patrick, did you ever meet Ian? Ian, this is Patrick."

"Maybe we met at one of Dale's and Craig's parties. Nice to see you again," Ian said to Patrick. "And I just met your boyfriend, Zeno."

Ian's head was in constant motion, surveying the room. Each time he circled back, he took a long look at Zeno. Patrick noticed and felt territorial. As he looked around the room, he noticed a number of eyes fixated on Zeno. Although Boston was a big city, the gay community was close-knit and Zeno was new to the scene, foreign, handsome, and people noticed.

Patrick inched up closer to Zeno and put his arm around the small of Zeno's back, squeezing him tightly. Zeno looked over at Patrick affectionately.

"You okay?" Patrick inquired.

"Hmm, hum," Zeno affirmed. "I'm a little intimidated, but okay."

"What do you think?" Patrick inquired further.

"It's really different – all these people – all gay. It's overwhelming in one sense and like I'm home, maybe part of a clan."

"Yes, it's very tribal," Craig interjected. "You'll find the same thing when you go to Ptown."

"You mentioned Ptown earlier. What is it?" Zeno inquired.

"It's a village at the end of Cape Cod – on the shore. It also happens to be a large art colony and very gay," Patrick explained. "Imagine the entire beach in Positano filled with gay men."

"*Cazzo*!" Zeno exclaimed.

Patrick chuckled. "*Mille di cazzi.*

Zeno looked apprehensive. Craig noticed, grabbed his and Patrick's hands, and led them into the video dance area. Zeno instantly relaxed and moved in rhythm with the music. Dale followed shortly, and the four stood in place, nursing their drinks, dancing, and looking around the room.

Patrick leaned over and gave Zeno a warm, moist kiss. "*Quanto sei bello*," he whispered into his ear. Zeno reached his arm around the back of Patrick and massaged his buttocks.

Suddenly, Dale looked like he had seen a ghost. He leaned over and whispered something in Craig's ear. Craig looked alarmed, too. They tried to act as if nothing was wrong, but Patrick noticed they kept looking over his shoulder. Patrick turned around. All he could see were lots of handsome men moving to the music.

Craig leaned into him and said, "There's Carlos – Girard's boyfriend."

"What!" Patrick said in alarm.

Craig nodded.

Patrick surveyed the room for Girard. Zeno continued to dance, oblivious to the consternation of his companions.

Craig said, "It's strange. Carlos is hanging onto some cutie over there. They look like more than friends. I'm glad to go over."

"No. Don't," Patrick said anxiously.

Craig walked toward Carlos, approached him, and gave him a kiss. "Carlos, what a surprise to see you."

"Yes. How are you? How's Dale?"

"We're fine. And you? And Girard?"

Carlos leaned closer to Craig and whispered, "We broke up last week."

"Sorry to hear."

"It was for the best. He didn't seem over Patrick. Isn't that him over there? Who's he with? He's a cutie."

"Oh, just a friend," Craig said evasively.

"This is Ethan," Carlos said, introducing his partner to Craig.

Craig shook his hand and excused himself, returning to the others. Craig whispered to Dale, "Carlos and Girard broke up."

"That's a problem."

Patrick leaned over. "What's up?"

"Carlos and Girard broke up."

Blood rushed to Patrick's head. He realized this would be trouble. He put on a brave face to Zeno, who was clearly enjoying his time in the bar. He seemed increasingly comfortable with the attention. After a few more songs, Patrick suggested they return home. Zeno nodded. The four of them exited the club into the cool night air.

"That was fun," Dale said.

"What did you think, Zeno?" Craig added.

"Loved it. Everyone is so friendly."

"Hm," Dale sighed, thinking to himself that it was more than people being friendly. Zeno was new and had garnered a lot of attention.

"Where's your car," Craig asked Patrick.

"Just down here," he nodded. They all kissed, and Patrick and Zeno walked to their car.

On the way home, Patrick asked Zeno, "So, how was your first gay bar?"

"I loved it once I got over the initial shock."

Patrick seemed alarmed. Zeno noticed and said, "*Senti, caro* – listen – I realized as I looked around the room that you would have been the person I would have spotted and hoped to have met. Your alluring eyes were dazzling tonight. I would have been hooked immediately." He rubbed his hands on Patrick's thighs.

"That's kind of you to say. But I wouldn't have dared approach the person everyone had their eyes on."

"I would have approached you," Zeno said, looking intensely over at Patrick.

Patrick felt his heart skip a beat in delight.

They soon arrived home, undressed, and slipped into bed, holding each other warmly as they fell asleep.

14

Chapter Fourteen

Several days later, Patrick and Zeno arrived at the crest in Truro overlooking Provincetown harbor. The iconic cottages lining the shore reflected the bright sunlight beaming off the placid blue water. Majestic yellow sand dunes lined the Atlantic Ocean on the opposite side of the bay, and the Pilgrim monument towered in the far distance.

"Here we are," Patrick said excitedly to Zeno, who was peering out the front window at the unique Cape Cod landscape.

"It's beautiful," Zeno said. "I can't believe the sand dunes. They're huge. I've never seen anything like it. Where's the beach?"

"The town is surrounded by beaches on all sides. There's one on the ocean side, several on the bay side and then several smaller beaches along the harbor side."

"Where do all the gay people go?" Zeno inquired.

"Everywhere, but there is one section that attracts the younger gay boys and clothing is optional."

Zeno's eyes widened.

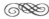

They continued their drive toward the center of town. Patrick took Commercial Street so that Zeno could get a feel for the place. Dale's and Craig's condo was on the far end of town. As they got closer to the center, there were more pedestrians walking in the street and bicyclers darting in both directions. They passed the gallery district and came into the center where the street was filled with pedestrians, and cars snaked slowly forward.

Zeno rolled down his window and took in the scene. It was a warm day, so many of the men were shirtless, walking down the street in tight shorts, flip-flops, and holding hands with each other.

"*Madonna*!" he exclaimed. "*Tanti bei uomini* – so many handsome men!"

"Look, but don't touch!" Patrick admonished him.

"You, too!" Zeno replied, staring at Patrick and pointing his fingers at his eyes, "I'm watching you."

"Agreed," Patrick said.

They continued to drive through town and made a few turns toward the end of Commercial Street, where it turned into Tremont. Dale and Craig had a modern condo with views of the water. Patrick parked the car, and they both carried their suitcases into the unit.

"This is incredible," Zeno remarked. "Look at the views!"

"It's not Positano, but it's not bad."

"I like it. It is different – less dramatic - more soothing, peaceful, serene. I love the sandbar out there with the lighthouse at the end."

"That's Long Point – the end of the Cape. The Cape makes a long broad hook."

"It's beautiful. I love the way the light reflects off the sand and contrasts with the blues of the water."

"Let's unpack and walk into town. I want to take you to Tea Dance and then do the gallery stroll before dinner."

"What should I wear?"

"I want as much of this covered as possible," as he waved his hand over Zeno.

"*Ma dai* – come on – that's no fun."

"It won't be fun or pretty if the boys begin to salivate over you."

"Why not?" Zeno asked teasingly.

"The Beneventos will come after you," Patrick said, winking at him.

Patrick slipped out of his jeans and rummaged through his suitcase, looking for some shorts. Zeno walked up behind him and began to play with the back of his undershorts, stroking the backs of his legs. Patrick got aroused, turned around, and pressed himself up against Zeno.

Zeno took off his shirt. "It looked like this was the uniform on the street."

Patrick stroked his chest and leaned into him, giving him a warm kiss. "Not for you or for me," Patrick said emphatically.

"But you're very handsome and well-built," Zeno lamented, tugging at Patrick's pullover. "I want to show you off."

"Honey, they won't be looking at me. It's you who will turn heads, and I want to keep that at a minimum, too. Here," he said, picking out a cotton pullover and some slim cut shorts. "These will be perfect. They show off your eyes!"

Zeno slipped off his jeans and undershorts, his erection in full view. "What are you doing?" Patrick asked, stroking the top of Zeno's hardness.

"Getting dressed."

"Looks like you're getting undressed."

"I want you to remember what's yours later."

Patrick smiled and threw the shorts and shirt at him. "Get dressed. Let's go."

They dressed and headed out the door, joining others making their way down the street to Tea Dance. At the Boat Slip, they passed through the entrance and out onto the deck. Zeno's mouth was agape as he surveyed the large space where over a thousand tanned and buff men were standing, drinking, chatting, and dancing.

"A drink?" Patrick asked.

"Campari and soda, *grazie*."

"Let's go over here and order," Patrick took his hand and led him across the deck.

They went under a shade tent and approached the bar and ordered drinks. They walked to the edge of the deck overlooking the water. Countless boats moored just offshore reflected the late afternoon vermillion and gold light. "It's magical," Zeno remarked.

Patrick nodded, taking a sip of his drink. He looked back at the crowd packed into the dance area. The DJ was playing a great set of tunes, and Zeno was moving his head to the beat. "Let's walk this way. You can get a sense of the crowd," Patrick suggested as they made their way through the densely packed space. They had to turn sideways from time to time to squeeze between people, brushing up against shirtless chests. Zeno had an exotic allure – darker complexion, deep-set brown eyes, and dark stubble circling his mouth and lining this chin. As they passed groups of men standing together, eyes followed Zeno, and an occasional hand stroked his buttocks. He was enjoying the attention, and Patrick kept a close eye on him.

"And this happens every day during the summer?" Zeno asked, looking out over the crowd.

Patrick nodded. "Some days are more crowded than others but yes, throughout most of the summer it's a nice gathering."

"I had no idea," Zeno added.

They nursed their drinks, listened to the music, and surveyed the handsome crowd. Around 6:30, Patrick led Zeno out onto Commercial Street to begin the gallery stroll.

"So, what's a gallery stroll?"

"There are a lot of galleries in Ptown – maybe 40. On Friday nights, they host openings where artists meet patrons and enjoy some wine and cheese while looking at art."

"There are 40 galleries in town?" Zeno inquired in disbelief.

"At least. It's an art colony going back to the late 1800s and early 1900s."

Zeno shook his head in disbelief. They approached a nice two-level gallery just near the town library. There was a show of the gallery's local artists and a large crowd of people had gathered inside. Patrick and Zeno walked in. Patrick knew the owners who spotted him across the room. Jill walked up to Patrick and gave him a kiss on both cheeks and Scot waved from the upper level.

"Jill, this is Zeno. Zeno, Jill."

"A pleasure. Are you visiting?"

Patrick interjected, "Zeno is from Italy. I met him when I was there recently on some family business."

"Well, welcome! Enjoy," she said as she pointed to the walls and moved on to another group of patrons.

A large painting of the dunes caught Patrick's eye. The colors were brilliant, and the detail of the dune grass waving in the breeze was striking. "What do you think?" Patrick asked Zeno.

"I like it a lot. It's warm and meditative. Is this what the beaches look like?"

"Yes – it's suggestive – the light and shadows along the sand and the water in the background."

"It's very calming."

"Let's get it for the house," Patrick asked Zeno.

Zeno looked down at the price under the painting and looked back at Patrick, alarmed.

"Don't worry about the price, dear. My parents left me money, and we need to decorate our – I mean – my house."

Zeno smiled. Patrick walked over to Jill to let her know he

wanted the painting. Zeno was standing in front of another set of images – abstract depictions of men on the beach. Patrick walked up behind him. "You like these?"

Zeno nodded. "They're sensual and draw you in."

"Let's get them, too. Remember the wall that separates the living room from the dining area? These would go great there."

They paid for the paintings, and Jill invited them to return the next day to pick them up. Patrick and Zeno wandered deeper into the East End to explore other galleries. They bought a few more pieces and then decided it was time for dinner. Patrick had made reservations at one of his favorite places, an upscale restaurant right on the edge of the beach, looking out over the water and the wharf.

The maître d' showed them to their table, one right on the edge overlooking the sand. Zeno looked out over the beach and smiled. "This is magnificent. It reminds me of our place in Positano."

"That will always be special to me – the place where we met and where I finally tracked down Stefano!"

A tall, blonde waiter approached the table. He was lanky but had beautiful tan legs covered in dark blonde hair. He appeared to have been cognizant of the asset since he was wearing tight fitting shorts. He smiled at Zeno when he offered to take their orders. Patrick cleared his throat, garnering his attention, and ordered a bottle of wine. Patrick and Zeno opened the menus and considered what to eat. "If you like lobster, they're great here. They also have wonderful local striped bass and other seafood specials."

"What are you going to have?" Zeno asked Patrick whose face was aglow in the late afternoon light that had turned a deep red and pink as the sun began to drop behind the horizon and cast beams of light on wispy clouds hovering over the bay. "By the way, your face is so luminescent in the light."

Patrick sighed. He reached over and held Zeno's hand. He looked back at the menu and said, "I think I'm going to have the haddock. It's done nicely here."

"I think I'll get the lobster. I've never had an American lobster before. And should we get salads?"

"What about a caprese – in honor of the Amalfi coast?"

"Perfect," Zeno said.

Just as the waiter had walked away from the table, Patrick looked across the room and saw Girard. "Oh my God," he whispered to Zeno. "It's Girard."

Zeno turned around and looked in the direction Patrick was staring. Girard was looking up across the room and had spotted Patrick.

"What do I do?" Patrick whispered in alarm.

"Let's go say hello to him. We have nothing to be afraid or ashamed of."

Patrick nodded nervously and stood up. Zeno joined him, and they walked across the deck to Girard. Girard was with a slightly older man, and they were sipping martinis.

"Girard, what a surprise," Patrick began.

Girard didn't seem happy to see Patrick. He rose and said with little emotion, "Patrick. Glad to see you."

"Girard, this is Zeno. Zeno, Girard."

They shook hands, both looking intensely at each other.

Girard then looked toward his dinner companion and said, "Patrick and Zeno, this is Samuel." They all shook hands.

"We must talk," Girard said to Patrick.

"I know. And I need to pick up some things at the place."

Girard nodded. "Should we set a date?"

Patrick looked at Zeno and said, "Zeno and I are traveling. Let me check our schedules and text you with some options."

"Sounds good," Girard replied. "Have a nice dinner."

"You, too," Patrick said. He leaned over and gave Girard a hug. He and Zeno walked back to their table.

"That was awkward," Patrick began, taking a long sip of his wine.

"He's not as handsome as the pictures you showed me, and he doesn't look happy."

"He's not happy in general," Patrick noted. "And he doesn't look good. It's probably because he just broke up with Carlos."

"So, he has an affair and screws things up with you, only to be dumped by his lover. Priceless," Zeno remarked.

"I feel sorry for him, but I don't feel sorry for the divorce. We were not good together."

"So, what are you going to do? Are you going to meet with him?"

"I want you to be comfortable with whatever I do. If I meet with him and picked up my things, would you be upset? I probably need to bring things to a closure sooner than later."

"I think you should do it. Now it is something hanging over your head. If you finally talk to him, you can finally cut the cords."

"You're so wise," Patrick said thoughtfully.

Zeno blushed. They ordered and began to eat. Zeno began, "What do you think Girard wants to discuss with you?"

"Some of it has to do with the practicalities of the divorce and the sharing of property and assets. But, and I hesitate to mention this, I imagine he's not over me and wants to see if there is a way to reconcile."

Zeno placed his hand deliberately on top of Patrick's and said, "I trust you, and I encourage you to take care of this."

"It's unfair to you."

"How is it unfair? If you are finalizing things with Girard, it is a sign that you are moving on. If you don't, then it is unresolved. That's more of a problem."

"Should we go together?" Patrick asked.

"Absolutely not. This is between you and Girard. I'll wait at home sipping wine and fretting until you return."

"See. That's what I thought."

"*Scerzo* – I'm joking. You need to do this – sooner than later."

"We're going to New York on Tuesday."

"Then why don't you do it on Monday after we're back from Ptown?"

Patrick nodded. He pulled out his phone and typed in a text to Girard. Zeno said excitedly, "What are you doing?"

"Proposing a time for Girard."

"Absolutely not! Let him stew and worry. You can text him tomorrow."

"For someone who just came out of the closet, you're awfully wise to things."

"I'm Italian. We're used to drama."

Patrick didn't seem reassured by Zeno's declaration, wondering if their future relationship would have its share of the same. "Okay," he said.

The next day, Patrick texted Girard and proposed they meet in the South End to pick up his clothes and have a conversation. They agreed to lunch in the neighborhood. In the meantime, Patrick took Zeno to Herring Cove. It was a sunny day, and the beach was crowded. They walked from the parking lot down the length of the shore to the predominantly gay area of the beach.

"It's very different – no organized beach establishment that rents chairs or brings drinks. It's rather primitive."

Patrick said, "Agreed. I like the set up in Positano better – although I feel like I'm with my tribe here, and it's fun to see so many gay boys splashing in the water."

Zeno nodded. They found an open place on the sand, spread their blankets, planted their umbrellas, and unpacked snacks and drinks they had brought. Zeno laid out in the sun while Patrick rested under the shade. He looked over at Zeno – his lean abdomen gleaming in the bright light and his sensual neck elongated as he laid his head back on the towel. He wanted to lean over and kiss Zeno's pecs but held back. Zeno looked over at him, and they smiled at each other.

The waves were gentle and soothing. The tide had gone out, so people were walking in the shallow water, picking up colorful pebbles and shells. Patrick rolled over close to Zeno, his shoulder pressed against Zeno's. "Do you realize we were laying on the beach only a few weeks ago in Italy?"

"I know. It's kind of surreal how one day you're home and the next you're in a totally different world."

"I hope you like it here."

Zeno nodded. "I love it. Thanks for making it happen."

Patrick felt himself get hard and reached over, stroking Zeno's chest. He could see the firmness of Zeno fill his dark spandex trunks and smile sheepishly. "Careful," Zeno admonished him.

"Of what?"

Zeno looked around to make sure no one was looking and then leaned over and kissed Patrick. Patrick rolled over on his back, his erection obvious. "Do you have no shame?" Zeno asked.

"I can't help myself when you kiss me."

"Looks like you might be helping yourself," he said, as Patrick adjusted himself.

"*Andiamo*," Patrick began. "Let's swim."

They stood up and ran to the water's edge. When Zeno put his foot in the water, he yelled. "It's freezing."

"Actually, it's warm today," Patrick noted.

"This is not warm. This is artic!"

"It's New England," Patrick asserted. "It's part of the reason the Cape is so enjoyable in the summer. The air is cooled by the Atlantic."

"Okay, but I'm not going in."

Patrick splashed Zeno, who splashed Patrick back. Zeno ran up to Patrick and held his hands, "*Fermi* – stop!" he said.

Patrick struggled to break free of Zeno's grasp and, instead, pulled him into the water with him. Zeno yelled, leaped out of the water, and ran toward the towels. He grabbed one and wrapped himself snuggly with it. Patrick kept waving him in, and Zeno nodded no.

They spent the rest of the afternoon at the beach, repeated tea dance later, and had dinner along Commercial Street. The next day, they headed back to Boston.

The day after they were back in Boston, Patrick drove to the South End to meet Girard. Patrick planned to go to the condo, get the rest of his things while Girard was at work, and then meet for lunch. He unlocked the door of what had been his home for the past years. It felt oddly comforting – as if he belonged. He glanced at the art they had bought, the arrangement of the furniture they disagreed over but compromised on, and the views of the city from the living room windows.

He walked into the bedroom, breathing in Girard's scent and the aroma of the verbena soap in the adjoining bathroom. He opened the closet and instantly began to sob as the impact of their joined lives in the mingling of clothes became overwhelmingly apparent. He realized the process of getting his clothes was going to be more difficult than he had imagined. He rummaged through the shirts, pulling out his and leaving Girard's. He grabbed a couple of jackets, several pairs of pants, and then opened drawers, pulling out underwear and socks. Eventually, he decided just to take a few things and leave the rest. It would be easier to get new clothes than having to sort and divide what belonged to whom.

He left the condo as quickly as possible, putting the clothes into the car, and walking to the restaurant for lunch. He was early, grabbed a table, and ordered a big glass of wine. 20 minutes later, Girard walked in the front door. He was dressed in a business suit. He looked older and weary.

Patrick stood and gave him a kiss. Girard said with little emotion, "Patrick, you look good. I'm glad we could finally do this."

Patrick nodded without saying anything.

They sat. Girard ordered a drink.

"I'm so sorry," Girard began. "I fucked this up."

Patrick hadn't expected so much contrition. He just stared at Girard, insinuating he should continue.

"I broke up with Carlos. I realize that I love you and want to do what I can to make things right."

Patrick's stomach began to knot. He then said, "I think it's too late for that."

Girard shook his head no. "It's never too late. I love you. We have a good history. It can work. I realize I wasn't understanding of what you were going through with your parents. I was cold and controlling. I saw a counselor, and I'm ready to do the work."

Patrick had always longed to hear those words from Girard. As he looked over into his hazel eyes and his handsome dark head of hair, his heart raced. The feelings of attraction were still there, despite the infidelity. He looked down at Girard's hand wrapped around his wineglass, the delicate fingers that had held his and had caressed him so passionately.

Mustering all the self-control and fortitude he could, he said, "I can't."

Girard bristled, his demeanor changing from contrite to confrontational. "You owe it to us to give it another chance."

"I don't owe you or us anything. For the past couple of years, while my dad was ill, you never once expressed compassion to him or me. I realize he wasn't welcoming, but I needed you, and you weren't there. Instead, you were having an affair."

Girard turned red in embarrassment.

Patrick continued, "I love you. I loved you. But I have come to realize we aren't a good match. There are things I want that aren't important to you – family, children, traditions. You want to sell my family home for a bigger condo. I want to reclaim my home and establish new traditions there. I realize that's not you. We need to set each other free."

Girard began to speak, hesitated, and then said, "I'm willing to move into your family home. God, I'll even have a kid with you."

Patrick looked at Girard in disbelief. "Where did all of this come from?"

"I'm lost without you. You're a compass for me. I am sorry I couldn't admit that earlier or express it to you. At least think about it."

Patrick nodded timidly. They ordered lunch, caught up on Girard's work, and Patrick talked about the Beneventos, avoiding references to Zeno. They finished lunch, paid their tab, and walked out onto the sidewalk, where they embraced and walked away in opposite directions.

Patrick drove home. He walked in the front door, his arms laden with shirts, jeans, and bags of underwear, socks, and shoes. Zeno had been reading and looked up.

"How did it go?"

"Fine," Patrick said evasively. He approached Zeno and gave him a kiss. Zeno looked up, a worried look on his face.

"*Cazzo*! It didn't go well," he said declaratively, yet hoped Patrick would persuade him otherwise.

"It did," Patrick assured him as he walked upstairs to hang his clothes. Zeno followed him.

"What happened?"

"We talked. He was apologetic. As I anticipated, he wanted to get back together. But, as we talked, I was more and more convinced we want different things."

Zeno seemed reassured and helped Patrick hang and organize his clothes.

"So, where did you leave off?"

"We sign the divorce papers in a week," Patrick lied.

"And your property?"

"Since technically this house is his, too, he'll take the condo, and I get the house and my parents' estate."

"That's all good, right?"

Patrick nodded without looking at Zeno.

The next morning, Patrick rose early and made a cup of coffee in the kitchen, looking out over the garden at the back of the house. He imagined Girard sitting next to him, their son swinging on a gym set in the yard. He imagined them preparing for a dinner party for friends, marinating streaks, and prepping veggies and appetizers.

He tried to imagine Zeno in the same picture but couldn't. He asked himself why.

He heard Zeno come down the stairs. He was only wearing a pair of boxer shorts. He scratched his tousled hair, leaning over to give Patrick a kiss.

"Coffee?"

Zeno nodded. "What are we doing today?"

"We have to pack for New York. We have a train tomorrow morning. We can see a few things in Boston, too."

Zeno's eyes lit up. "What's the schedule in New York?"

"We get there around noon. We'll check into the hotel, grab lunch, and begin seeing the sights – perhaps those in mid-town first – Times Square, Central Park, Bryant Park – things like that. We also have tickets to a Broadway play in the evening."

"It all sounds incredible."

Patrick smiled at Zeno's excitement. He got up and fixed Zeno a bowl of granola with yogurt and honey. Zeno opened his iPad to begin reading Italian news. Patrick went back upstairs to take a shower and dress for the day. He continued to muse over Girard's offer to move into the house. He pondered moving their furniture, rugs, and art into the house – perhaps creating an office out of one of the bedrooms so Girard could work remotely, and he could prepare for classes. He heard Zeno laugh downstairs – probably over a social media posting made by a friend. He felt guilty over his thoughts but found it impossible to shake what Girard had said.

After packing for New York, he and Zeno went into Boston to visit the North End and the Waterfront. They visited some of the historic sites along the Freedom Trail – the Paul Revere House, the State House, and the USS Constitution. They had dinner in the North End at one of Patrick's favorite Italian restaurants. Zeno was surprised the food was as authentic as home.

When they returned home, Patrick received a text from one of his cousins on his mother's side of the family. "Patrick. I hope you are okay. I have some sad news. My mom just passed this morning."

Patrick picked up the phone and called Lisa. She answered. He began, "Lisa, I'm so sorry to hear about your mom. Was this sudden or had she been ill?"

"It was rather sudden. She had been having some heart problems, but nothing serious. She didn't wake up this morning."

"Was anyone with her?"

"No. She's in an assisted living facility. I was headed there just after breakfast. They greeted me at the door with the news."

"Is there anything I can do?"

"My dad has Alzheimer's and doesn't know us anymore. Maria is in Chicago and flying here tomorrow. Paula is driving in from Maine. Is there any way you might talk with the people at the funeral home you used for your parents? I don't know anything about all of that, and I'm just trying to manage with the kids and all."

"Sure. Did someone already pick up the body?"

"Yes, the funeral home did – the same one. We just need to make arrangements for a funeral and visitation."

"I'll take care of it," Patrick assured her. "Let me know if there's anything else you need. Otherwise, I'll be in touch." He hung up.

He looked over at Zeno and said, "Caro, bad news. My aunt Jennifer just passed this morning. I think I'm going to have to stay here and take care of things for my cousins."

"How horrible. I'm sorry. Were you close?"

"Yes and no. My uncle had developed Alzheimer's and my aunt was in assisted living. The last couple of years were not the same. I was preoccupied with my parents' illnesses, too. But we used to be close, and my cousins need me to help set up the funeral."

"I'll stay with you and help."

"No, I want you to go to New York. We're heading back to Italy next week, and you've always wanted to see the city. Go. If I get through with this sooner than later, I'll join you."

"But I can't leave you," Zeno implored.

"I'll be fine. It will be boring for you with all family you don't know."

"But that's what we are good at," Zeno pressed.

"I insist you go to New York and proceed as we planned. I have a friend there. I'll call him and he can show you around and go to the play with you."

Zeno stared at Patrick, realizing Patrick wasn't going to change his mind, and nodded. "Okay. But come when you can."

"I will," Patrick said, leaning into Zeno and giving him a kiss.

The next day, Patrick dropped Zeno off at the train station and then drove to the funeral home to make arrangements for his aunt's services. The visitation would be the next evening and the funeral the day after that. If all went well, he could join Zeno for a day or two in New York.

He drove back home. He exchanged some texts with Zeno and then sat in one of the living room chairs with a glass of wine. "Wow – I can't believe Jennifer is gone," he mused to himself. He felt restless, vulnerable, unsettled. The house felt empty, and the sad memories of his parents' last months overwhelmed the happier ones of earlier years. He longed for someone to hold him, to comfort him.

During the past months, he had always wished Girard could have risen to the occasion and understood his pain. In talking with him yesterday, it seemed like he had come around. Maybe he had changed. He picked up his phone and texted him: "Girard. Are you free this evening?"

Girard texted back: "I am. Why?"

"Dinner?"

"Sure. Where?"

"The bistro?"

"7 PM? I'll call for reservations."

"See you then."

At 7, Patrick strolled up to the front door of the restaurant, walked in the door, and gave Michaela, the maître d', kisses on her cheeks. "Patrick – twice in one week!"

"I know. Kind of interesting."

She pointed to Girard, already seated in one of the cozy booths. Patrick walked over. Girard stood, gave him a kiss, and they both slid into their seats.

"What a pleasant surprise," Girard began.

"I'm afraid it's not under ideal circumstances."

Girard looked worried.

"My aunt Jennifer passed this morning. I'm in the middle of arranging things for her funeral."

"And Zeno?" Girard asked.

"He's in New York. We had planned to go there today, and I sent him off."

"And you called me?"

Patrick nodded.

Girard smiled. "I meant what I said the other day. I'm sorry for what happened, and I wish we could start over, make it work."

"Do you really mean that?" Patrick asked.

"I do."

"What does that mean, exactly?"

"Whatever it takes."

Patrick smiled. He looked down at the menu as if studying what to order, but he was deep in thought. They ordered drinks and entrees and continued their talk.

"Would you move into the house in West Roxbury? I know you didn't like the idea before, but it makes sense. It has more space. We can make it our own. There are lots of gay couples moving to that area."

Girard looked up from his drink, "Yes. I would move there in a heartbeat if we could make this work."

"But what happens when you get resentful for moving out of the city?"

"I won't. If I'm with you, that's all I need."

Those were all the words Patrick ever wanted to hear from Girard. He felt a warmth fill his chest and his shoulders relax.

The waiter brought their salads and, before they could begin, Girard excused himself. "I have to go to the john quickly. Go ahead, start without me."

Girard got up. As he went into the restroom, his phone vibrated with a call. Patrick looked over, and the name Samuel appeared on the screen.

Girard returned, glanced at his phone, and then began to eat his salad.

"I'm sorry to hear about you and Carlos," Patrick said, tentatively hoping to explore more of Girard's recent exploits.

He looked embarrassed and said, "I was an asshole. It was a fling. Nothing more. He saw right through me."

"Have there been others?"

"What do you mean?" Girard asked with concern.

"You know – other indiscretions?"

Girard hesitated. "I want to be honest so we can start on a good footing. Yes, there was one other – a long time ago."

"Anyone I know?"

"No, it was someone I knew through work – in another city."

Patrick looked disappointed. He pushed the salad around on the plate and took a big sip of wine.

"Patrick. I'm sorry. I'm not proud of myself. I realize I fucked up, and I want to change – for us – for me."

Patrick nodded but then said, "And Samuel?"

"You probably saw the phone call, right?"

"Hmm, hum."

"It's complicated," Girard began.

"I'm all ears. Let's get it out in the open."

"When you said it was too late the other day, I panicked. Samuel had broken up with his partner a few months ago. When Carlos dumped me, Sam and I got together for solace. At first it was just dinners and drinks, but then it got more serious."

"How serious?"

"Serious."

"So, when you were asking to get back together with me, were you still with him?"

"Yes, and no."

"Either you were, or you weren't."

"When he saw you and Zeno in Ptown the other day, he realized you were back from Italy and began to make more demands that I finalize the divorce. He realized I wasn't moving very aggressively on things, so he got upset and moved out. He had been staying with me.

"So, it would seem it had ended."

"Well, I called him after our last conversation. I felt restless. I didn't think you were going to even consider working on things. I told him we met, and we signed the papers."

"You didn't?"

Girard nodded.

"So where does he think you are now?"

"I told him I had a business dinner with some clients. He's waiting for me back at the apartment."

Patrick realized Girard was at least a borderline pathological liar – that he had been unfaithful not once but at least twice during their relationship - and that he was now being dishonest with his new boyfriend.

"Girard. This isn't good."

"I know. I'm sorry. I want to make this work."

"I'm not feeling very secure right now. In fact, I feel like I'm an accomplice for an indiscretion – oddly with my legal husband."

"What about you and Zeno?" Girard asked pointedly.

"Yes. You're right. This isn't fair to him, either. I should never have called you."

Girard looked alarmed. Patrick folded his napkin and tossed $100 on the table. "I have to go."

"But Patrick. We can work this out."

"I don't think so. I'll sign the papers tomorrow and give them to Bob. I expect you to do the same. Give my regards to Samuel. You'll make a good couple."

Patrick walked past Michaela, who smiled as if relieved he was leaving Girard. She had undoubtedly seen a lot in the last few months. He walked out into the cool September evening, found his car, and drove home.

15

Chapter Fifteen

The next day, Patrick attended the visitation for his aunt. It was a typical Irish wake – with lots of tears and stories. He hugged and kissed his cousins, recounted earlier years when his mom and their mom would organize family reunions, and shared news about his trip to Italy. After the visitation, he took a taxi to Logan airport and caught the last flight to New York.

He texted Zeno: "I'm on my way. I'll see you in a couple of hours."

"I can't wait," Zeno texted back. "Arthur was very hospitable, and I enjoyed the play, but I need to be with you."

"And I with you."

Once in New York, Patrick took a taxi from the airport. Thankfully, traffic was light, and he was knocking on Zeno's hotel room 40 minutes later. Zeno came to the door and threw his arms around Patrick, giving him an enthusiastic kiss. "I've missed you. You realize this is the first time we've been apart since Nunzia's?"

"Absence creates fondness, right?"

"I didn't need absence to feel fondness," Zeno assured him. He grabbed Patrick's hand and led him into the room. He took him to the window and said, "*Guarda* – how beautiful!"

"How did you get this room," Patrick asked as he looked around, realizing he was in a mini suite.

"I don't know. There was a cute guy checking me in. He asked if I minded going to a higher floor and a larger room."

"I hope he didn't think he was going to get an invitation."

"He probably did, and he's probably in mourning now that he saw you heading to the elevator."

"He doesn't know who I am."

"Actually, he does. I had to explain why I was checking in and not you. I showed him your picture on the phone. He was impressed and wished us a pleasant stay in the city."

"And Arthur?"

"He was very attentive. He has nothing but good things to say about you. He must have been in love with you."

"Maybe," Patrick grinned.

"Anyway. He's not my type."

"What is your type?"

"A little Italian mixed with a dash of Irish. I love the dark brown mysterious eyes and this," he said, as he traced his fingers over Patrick's dark stubble of a beard.

"And?"

"Well, there's also this," he said as he rubbed his hands over Patrick's crotch. He leaned toward Patrick and opened his mouth wide to give him a large, wet kiss.

"Let me drop my bag and get undressed," Patrick suggested.

"*Ma dai* – come on – we have to go out to a club. It's only 11 PM. It's New York – the city never sleeps."

"What, did you become a bar queen overnight?"

"No, but it's part of the tour, right?"

"Well, maybe one. Then we're off to bed. We have a busy agenda tomorrow. And I bought tickets to another play."

Zeno's face lit up. They dressed for a night out and headed out the door, winking at the front desk guy who waved at Zeno.

They walked around the corner to a neighborhood gay club. It was dark inside, with reverberating techno music filling the space. There was a bar just inside the door with people squeezed together along the length of it, and there were low sitting sofas lining irregular walls, forming little sittings here and there. Patrick spotted two seats on the far side of the room and led Zeno there. They sat down. A classy waiter approached. He was wearing dark pants, a white shirt, and a vest. He was from some South American country, with dark hair, deep brown eyes, and a heavy accent. "What would you like to drink?" he began.

Zeno, in Spanish, ordered two brandies. Two guys sitting nearby cocked their heads on hearing Zeno speak to the waiter and asked, "*De donde eres* – where are you from?"

"*Italia, y ustedes*?"

"*De Mexico y Texas. Soy Jon Paul y mi campañero es Juan Pablo*," they introduced themselves and where they were from.

"*Soy Zeno y esto es Patrick*," Zeno said, introducing him and Patrick to their table companions.

"*Encantado*," Juan Pablo said. Then shifting to English. "What part of Italy?"

"The Amalfi coast," Zeno said.

"Oh my God," Jon Paul interjected. "We were just there last summer. We loved it."

"Where did you go?" Juan Pablo pressed further.

"All over. We loved the beaches, the coves, the historic sites, and the food. Are you visiting?"

Zeno explained the story of his and Patrick's meeting and their journey back to Boston and now New York.

"What a cute story," Jon Paul said.

"And you guys? Are you visiting?" Patrick inquired.

"No. We live here. We were just at a play."

"What did you see?"

"Moulin Rouge. Have you seen it? It's incredible."

"No, but I got tickets for tomorrow night."

Jon Paul talked about the history of the show and its reception in the city. He was friendly and effusive about the stars. Juan Pablo nursed his martini, batting his cute eyes at Zeno, whose head continued to turn right and left as handsome men passed their table. Zeno then paused and turned to Juan Pablo. "How is it that you two have the same name – an uncommon one at that?"

Juan Pablo recounted the story of their meeting and their own surprise at learning each other's names. They told stories of their travels in Italy, and Zeno recounted more about Patrick's search for Stefano and the chance encounter at the restaurant in Positano.

Zeno leaned to Patrick and whispered, "People are so friendly here. I feel like I'm in a neighborhood café in Italy chatting with old friends."

"I know. Even with the size of New York, things are intimate, familiar, neighborly."

"I love it here," Zeno said with emotion. "I'm so glad you're here with me," he said as he put his arms around Patrick's shoulder and gave him a kiss.

Patrick rubbed his hands along the inside of Zeno's legs. They stared at each other intensely.

"It's a nice bar," Patrick noted, looking around the room.

"Yes, a lot of handsome men – but I'm sitting with the handsomest."

"Ahh, you're so generous."

"No, it's true. I would pick you out in an instant."

"You keep saying that."

"It's true. I'm totally hooked!"

Patrick sighed. He took a sip of his brandy and continued to chat with Jon Paul. The four of them ordered another round of drinks and talked about favorite things to do in New York. The Jon Pauls talked about their love for Provincetown and plans to visit in the summer. Around 1, they finished their drinks, paid their tabs, and walked out onto the street. The Jon Pauls hailed a taxi, and Zeno and Patrick walked back to the hotel where they undressed and slipped into bed.

The next morning, Patrick rose early and went out to get coffee and pastries. He returned to the room and woke Zeno, handing him a steaming cup of coffee. Zeno pulled the sheets up over his abdomen, putting his hands around the warm cup and putting a few pieces of croissant into his mouth. He opened his phone to check for messages. Patrick slid up next to him, taking sips of the coffee and checking his own email.

"I'm thrilled we have tickets for the play tonight! Jon Paul seemed very excited about it."

"Both of them did. They were cute together. We should stay in touch with them."

Patrick nodded. "So, what should we see today?"

"The Museum of Fine Arts?" Zeno inquired.

"Perfect. And we can take a walk in Central Park. I imagine some trees are beginning to put on fall colors."

Zeno's eyes lit up. He then leaned over and unbuttoned Patrick's shirt. He continued to look at his phone, checking messages, but Zeno was persistent, slipping his hand inside the folds of the shirt and rubbing Patrick's chest tenderly.

Patrick began to get aroused and adjusted himself. Zeno reached down, unzipped his shorts, and reached in to feel Patrick's hardness. Patrick leaned his head back and moaned. Zeno then climbed out from under the sheets, placed his coffee on the bedside table, and straddled Patrick, giving him a long warm moist kiss, his own erection dangling over Patrick. Patrick reached up to hold it, and Zeno sighed.

Zeno laid on top of Patrick, his erection nestled between Patrick's legs, and his bare butt in the air behind him. He looked up from Patrick's chest into his eyes. Patrick looked back at Zeno, his ruffled hair hanging over his forehead and his shoulders gleaming in the sunlight filtering through the window shades. He closed his eyes, recalling the failed attempt just two days ago to picture Zeno in his home, working in the garden, playing with their son on a gym set, getting ready for a party with friends. He opened his eyes, and for the first time, Zeno's eyes felt like home. They were still alluring, mysterious, and sexy. But now they had taken on the glimmer of belonging – eyes that mirrored home, companionship, and refuge.

He reached down and pulled Zeno up higher on his chest, feeling Zeno's erection rubbing against his own. He rubbed his hands over Zeno's shoulders and down the small of his back, pressing his fingers into Zeno's crack, feeling the moistness of Zeno's desire. Just before Zeno opened his mouth and spread his wet lips over Patrick's, Patrick made a decision – one that would forever change his life.

They made love, Patrick enjoying Zeno's emerging comfort and imagination with sex. They showered, dressed, and explored more of New York. They returned to the hotel, took a nap, and then went for an early dinner before the eight o'clock play on Broadway.

Patrick had chosen a small French bistro on the edge of the theater district. The maître d' showed them a nice booth toward the back of the classic space. They ordered a bottle of Italian red, Patrick lamenting the absence of wines from the Amalfi coast. For a first course, they ordered *moules frites*. The server brought them a mound of mussels steaming in a bowl with a basket of crusty French bread they used to soak up the juice. They both ordered a filet for the main course – one *au poivre* and one classic. The velvety *au poivre* sauce had an abundance of crushed green peppercorns and the classic steak had a red wine reduction drizzled on top.

Patrick looked at his watch and realized they had time for coffee and dessert before they had to make their way to the theater. They ordered profiteroles and two espressos. The profiteroles came with a generous pour of dark chocolate dripping over the small balls of pastry filled with cream.

Zeno looked up warmly at Patrick, savoring the last morsel of pastry and looking content and happy. Patrick reached into his jacket pocket and pulled out a small box. Zeno's eyes widened.

"Zeno Voluto, you have made me so happy. I can't imagine spending the rest of my life without you. I know this may be premature – and if it is – I can give you time and space. However, I am certain we were destined to meet and meant to bring full circle what began many years ago with our grandfathers. Will you marry me?"

"Patrick Benevento, my heart belongs to you. It races when you approach. Yes, I will marry you!"

Patrick asked, "It's not too fast?"

Zeno shook his head no. "I'm ready."

Patrick leaned over and placed the ring he had secretly bought in Ptown on Zeno's finger. He gave him a kiss. A few people at nearby tables had witnessed the proposal and clapped enthusiastically. Zeno and Patrick both blushed and smiled affectionately at each other.

16

Chapter Sixteen

A Year Later

The square in Cava dei Lupi was set up for the *vendemmia* feast. Lights were strung between trees, a stage was set up for music, and long tables lined up outside Laura and Paolo's restaurant. It was a warm sunny late-September day.

At the small Benevento cottage, Patrick laid out the dark suit he had picked out in Rome on the bed. He slipped on a pair of undershorts and walked into the living room to double check that his small leather bag contained his vows and Zeno's ring. The cottage felt unusually quiet, Zeno having spent the night in Positano with his parents. They were probably driving up the coastal route now.

The picture of Roberto's and Chiara's wedding 71 years before was framed and hanging over the mantel. The photo of Roberto and Stefano had been restored and enlarged and paired with a similar photo of Patrick and Zeno at the vineyard hanging over the dining table.

Someone knocked on the door. Patrick inched the door open.

"Pepe, what a surprise," he blurted out as he saw him on the terrace.

"I wanted to see if you needed anything and wish you a wonderful day!"

"Come in," Patrick said, giving Pepe a warm hug. "Thank you."

Patrick felt self-conscious standing in front of Pepe in just a pair of boxer shorts. He caught Pepe's eyes glancing up and down his torso.

"Excuse me. I don't want to interrupt you. I just wanted to wish you well." There was an awkward silence, and then Pepe continued, "I'm happy for you. Zeno seems like a great guy, and it will be nice to have you around in the summer."

"Yes, I couldn't believe it when Alberto offered us the cottage."

"Well, you both deserve it – both descendants of old Giancarlo."

"Kind of ironic, isn't it?"

Pepe nodded.

"Are you bringing Daniela to the *festa*?"

"We fought earlier in the week. She doesn't want to come."

"Sorry to hear. She is a wonderful person. I like her a lot."

"Me, too," Pepe added.

"So, what's the problem?"

"It's the same as usual. They want me to move to the city and get a proper job."

Patrick sighed, "Hm. Is that all?"

"What do you mean?"

"Are you hesitant? Do they detect that?"

"Hesitant about what?"

"About women, about men?"

Pepe grinned sheepishly. He knew Patrick was onto him, had unveiled his proclivities, but he replied assertively, "I know what you think, but it's not true. I prefer women. I always have and always will."

"So, we have to find a woman who wants to be a vintner?"

"Yes, that would be great. I like it here. This is my home. This is where I want to raise a family."

As much as Patrick would like to have believed Pepe was gay, he realized that he really did want to marry a woman and settle here, raising kids, being part of the Benevento clan. "I can see that. Zeno and I will have to recruit for you."

"I have a feeling you guys might not be too good at sniffing out a good partner for me."

"You'd be surprised!"

"Well, at any rate, it is nice that you are here, and I wish you many blessings!"

Patrick reached over to him to give him a big hug. Pepe stroked Patrick's bare back, grazing the top of his shorts with his index finger. Patrick pulled back. He felt himself get slightly hard as the firmness of Pepe's chest had pressed against his. Pepe looked embarrassed and said, "Sorry, I should let you get ready."

"Yes, I should."

Pepe reached for the door, and Patrick grabbed his upper arm, pulling him back around. "You know, Pepe, you are a very thoughtful and sensitive and incredibly sexy guy. You would make a great partner for someone. Trust yourself and trust others. You will find someone special."

"*Grazie*," he replied, smiling warmly. He walked out the door and down the road to his house.

Patrick closed the door and went back to the bedroom to dress. As he slipped on his shirt, he looked in the mirror. He rubbed a little cream on his face to sooth the redness from the intense sun. As he leaned closer to check for any errant hairs, he had an odd sensation – as if he were looking into Roberto's eyes and Stefano's and Zeno's all at the same time. He didn't believe in reincarnation, but he had a strange feeling of déjà vu – as if he were no longer Patrick, but now Roberto. He sniffed for the familiar scent of patchouli oil but smelled nothing. Perhaps that was the point – the circle had been closed.

An hour later, Patrick pulled into the square, parked his car, and joined the crowd gathering under the shade of the trees, savoring the gentle afternoon breezes blowing up from the sea. Nunzia spotted him and waved. She walked over and gave him a warm embrace. "*Auguri!*" she expressed warmly. "Congratulations and cheers. What a wonderful day. Where's Zeno and his parents?"

"They're on their way. They'll be here shortly."

The provincial magistrate walked over from the stage and extended his hand warmly. "*Patrizio, sei pronto?*"

"Yes, I'm ready. Are you? Do you think everyone will be okay?"

"I'm certain of it. People here are eager to show they are welcoming and embracing change. We are traditional but also fiercely loyal to our families and to their well-being and happiness. If that means doing something novel, so be it."

"I'm grateful for your willingness to witness our ceremony. Officially, in Boston, our marriage is recognized and, someday, it will be official here, too. It's nice to know it has some legitimacy with your presence."

"The legitimacy is about your family's and community's love and acceptance. That's obvious in how you've been welcomed here. I understand you are adopting a little boy."

"Yes, an orphan from a nearby town. We're excited to start a family."

"So, I understand you will spend summers here and winters in Boston?"

"Yes. I'll teach during the school year, and Zeno will stay with Massimo. In the summer, Zeno will work in Positano, and I'll watch Massimo here. Next month we are adding to the cottage. We'll need more room."

The Magistrate smiled and as he turned to walk away, Zeno arrived with his parents and Carlo. Zeno's mother, Joanna, was stunning. She wore a long turquoise dress that showed off her dark olive complexion. Giovanni walked proudly beside her, sporting a dark suit and blue tie.

Zeno walked behind them, chatting with Carlo. He also wore a dark suit that had been impeccably tailored to accommodate his tall frame, broad shoulders, and thin waist. He was beaming as he looked around the crowd, noticing friends, colleagues, and relatives. Carlo had a commanding air to him – undoubtedly something he learned to carry as maître d'. He spotted Patrick and waved.

The magistrate welcomed Zeno and his family and answered questions they had about the ceremony. Alberto walked up and reviewed the agenda and timing of things with Patrick.

At 4 PM, the bell of the local parish rang loudly, signaling the commencement of the festivities. Everyone gathered around the stage where a couple of chairs - for Zeno, Patrick, Nunzia, and Carlo - stood near a podium.

"*Attenzione, prego*," the magistrate began. "*Benvenuti a tutti*."

People pressed in closer to hear him speak. "In a few moments, we will begin. If you can create an aisle here," as he pointed in front of him, "the music will begin, and our guests will make their way to the stage."

The band began to play a beautiful, classic piece. Nunzia and Carlo walked arm in arm to the stage and then separated, each standing near their chairs. Then Patrick marched forward, shaking hands with Alberto, Laura, Maria, and other family members. Once he was standing on the stage, Zeno walked forward. He stopped to greet his mother and father and then proceeded to the stage.

Patrick and Zeno looked at each other with intense smiles, undoubtedly processing the novelty of their ceremony and the love they shared. They stood holding hands for a moment and then let them fall to their sides as the magistrate invited them to sit.

"Today is a historic occasion in our community. It is not often that we witness the power of love to overcome obstacles and prejudices. Zeno's and Patrick's love is strong, deep, and inclusive. Many decades ago – in this very place – Patrick's grandparents married. His grandfather was committed to justice, to making sure people were cared for, loved, and welcomed. He left for America to forge a new life and to work for a better world. I wonder if he imagined a day like this – a day when people who were told they couldn't love were able to join their lives and be affirmed by their family, friends, and the larger community?"

Zeno and Patrick, we are indebted to your courage and your pioneering spirit. We will be a better place because of your love, because of your generosity, because of the family you form.

"As the magistrate of this region, I am honored to witness your vows before your family and friends."

Nunzia read a scripture passage, and Carlo read a passage from an Italian poet. The magistrate asked Zeno and Patrick to stand. They both were handsome – dressed in form-fitting suits, their dark hair slicked back in place, and their dark brown wispy eyes gazing at each other.

Patrick took Zeno's hands and began to recite the vows he had written. "Zeno, I came to Italy searching for my grandfather's friend and, instead, found my life companion. You have helped me connect with my heritage, and I long to follow the footsteps of my ancestors in forming a strong family with love, affection, and generosity. I promise to love and support you all the days of my life."

"Patrick, you were an angel from heaven that landed at my table, stirring an awareness of my grandfather's legacy and shedding light on who I am. I am forever indebted to you – to your encouragement and support and love. I love you so much, and I promise to love and care for you all the days of my life."

The magistrate then interjected, "The rings."

Patrick placed Zeno's ring on his finger and said, "*Con quest'anello, ti prendo come il mio sposo.*"

Zeno placed Patrick's ring on his finger and said, "*Con quest'anello, ti prendo come il mio sposo.*"

"To all of you gathered, I would like to invite you to celebrate Zeno's and Patrick's union!"

Everyone applauded and whistled enthusiastically. Zeno and Patrick kissed and raised their hands together over their heads in celebration. The band struck up a celebratory tune, and Nunzia, Carlo, the magistrate, Zeno, and Patrick, left the stage and walked into the center of the throng gathered in the town square.

Alberto rose to the podium and offered a toast. The band stopped playing. "To my cousin Patrick and my cousin Zeno – may you both have a long, happy life together. We are delighted that you have made this your home – at least part of the year – and help us make great wine! We know that your love will give the land more sweetness and our wine more complexity." He raised his glass – "*Auguri – et ad multos annos*!"

"*Salute*!" everyone said in unison, clinking their glasses and kissing each other in joy. The band played again, now a local dance tune, and Patrick and Zeno danced. Others joined, and soon the entire piazza was in movement as people celebrated the wedding.

Laura and Paolo had set out a large table with appetizers – roasted peppers, slices of salami and prosciutto, stuffed mushrooms, fried calamari, and olives.

Everyone went up to Zeno and Patrick and gave them warm kisses and congratulations. Everyone was curious about their son, Massimo, a newborn they were adopting in Salerno. Patrick had a picture of him on this phone and shared it with everyone proudly.

Later, Paolo and Laura and their staff brought large platters of grilled chicken, pork, and beef garnished with roast potatoes. They brought out bowls filled with cheese-stuffed ravioli covered in a light, creamy mushroom sauce. People served from the buffet, and then took seats around the piazza, music playing in the background.

Zeno and Patrick sat with Zeno's parents and Nunzia and Davide. Nunzia was dressed in a stunning dark gown with white pearls around her tanned neck. "You look fabulous, Nunzia," Patrick said as they sat and began to eat.

"It's a beautiful day! I think we can finally complete the ancestry tree now," she noted.

"Well, we'll have to create a new line - from Massimo on."

She smiled. "Have you chosen a godmother?"

"There's no choice to make," Patrick said with a wink. "You're it if you're willing."

Nunzia sighed and squeezed Davide's hand under the table. "I'd be delighted."

Zeno looked over at Joanna and Giovanni, both sipping wine and looking out over the crowd. They beamed with joy and warmth, looking over at their son with admiration.

As the dinner concluded, late in the evening, Zeno and Patrick said their goodbyes. Patrick had bought a new Alfa Romeo SUV and had it parked near the band stage. They got into the car and drove off down the hill, a string of cans bouncing behind. They drove to Rome, where they would spend their honeymoon.

A week later, they had an appointment in Salerno to pick up Massimo. A local official waved some regulations about single adoption, allowing Zeno to adopt Massimo officially. Once they returned to the States, they were going to register the adoption under both of their names.

Massimo was now three weeks old. They brought the car seat into the residence, met with the nurse and director, and signed papers.

A few minutes later, a young woman brought Massimo out to Zeno and Patrick, their faces aglow with excitement. They peered down into the folds of the blanket. A little bundle of chubby cheeks, arms, and legs looked up at them. Zeno reached down and touched his nose with his finger. Patrick brushed the top of his head. Massimo smiled; his dark brown eyes opened wide.

They went out to the car, locked the car seat in place, and began the drive back to Benevento. They rode up the winding road to the little cottage and parked out front. The sun had already sunk below the highest ridges, casting long shadows over the vineyard in front of them. Off in the distance, rays of light reflected off boats sailing back and forth along the sea.

Alberto had given Patrick and Zeno title to the cottage and had added another bedroom, bath, and office. In the summer, Patrick planted a garden on the side, and expanded the front deck, placing some large terra-cotta pots with geraniums out front.

Patrick parked the car, and Zeno unhooked Massimo's car seat, bringing him inside. Patrick brought in packages of formula, diapers, and body lotion for the baby. In the new bedroom, they had arranged a crib, a baby monitor, and a little dresser to hold his diapers and clothes.

They planned to spend a month in Italy and then head to Boston. Patrick would begin the school year late. He and Zeno agreed that it would be better to spend the first month in Italy to make sure Massimo was healthy and could travel.

Pepe had left a note. "There's some lasagna in the fridge. You can heat it up in the oven or in the microwave. There's a caprese salad in there as well. Congratulations!"

Patrick's heart pounded in warmth. He could feel Pepe's affection and care. He closed his eyes and imagined Pepe joining them for dinner with his new wife. Patrick could visualize her – caramel skin, dark brown hair, a tall frame, and long legs. She spoke English and Italian - and Patrick got the notion that she taught in a local school. He smiled, eager for Pepe to meet her.

Zeno and Patrick fed Massimo and put him to sleep. They heated the lasagna, divided the salad, and poured generous glasses of the local red wine. They sat at the dining table, under framed photos of Stefano and Roberto and their own wedding picture. Patrick raised his glass and said, "*Ti voglio bene.*"

Zeno raised his glass and said, "And I love you, too. Welcome home."

Patrick nodded and sighed, "Yes – welcome home!"

The End

Michael Hartwig is a Boston and Provincetown based author specializing in LGBTQ stories set in historic settings around the world. The narratives are remarkable for fast-paced plots, passionate love stories, exploration of sexual identity, and evocative settings. Hartwig's books draw on his having lived in Europe, his professional work in international travel, and his college-level teaching in sexual ethics and religion. Plots push boundaries around gender and family and introduce new paradigms of spirituality and magic. His novels are sensual – celebrating sexual desire, food, art, and geography.

For other titles and information visit: www.michaelhartwig.com

CPSIA information can be obtained
at www.ICGtesting.com
Printed in the USA
BVHW041858091221
623674BV00014B/794

9 780578 934457